A loose cannon...

In the event he fell into police custody, Skass was told two things: either cooperate fully while looking for the most likely means of escape, or, if possible, create a diversion and leave the area quickly. Unlike Germany, the U.S. did not have an integrated crime reporting system. Nor did it have a national police. Each municipality operated independently, and this was to his advantage, his Gestapo handlers said. Should he get away from the local authorities and put more than fifty miles between himself and the point of his arrest in a few hours time, the chances the local authorities would find him were almost nil.

So be amiable, be low-key, be observant, know the local constabulary, and don't commit even the smallest of crimes. These were the points his instructors had repeated to him over and over again.

Still, Skass chose to ignore them all....

IRON STAR

BRIAN KELLEHER

JOVE BOOKS, NEW YORK

IRON STAR

A Jove Book / published by arrangement with
the author

PRINTING HISTORY
Jove edition / April 2001

The Penguin Putnam Inc. World Wide Web site address is
http://www.penguinputnam.com

ISBN: 0-515-13040-0

A JOVE BOOK®
Jove Books are published by The Berkley Publishing Group,
a division of Penguin Putnam Inc.,
375 Hudson Street, New York, New York 10014.
JOVE and the "J" design
are trademarks belonging to Penguin Putnam Inc.

PRINTED IN THE UNITED STATES OF AMERICA

10 9 8 7 6 5 4 3 2 1

PART ONE

1

BERLIN
JANUARY, 1945

THE PRISON WAS ON WECHT STREET.

It was a cold gray structure, five blocks long by two
blocks wide, surrounded by a high concrete wall. The
streets around the prison were nearly impassable. Three
years of Allied bombing had cratered many beyond repair,
leaving piles of rubble everywhere. Yet the prison seemed
unaffected. It stood untouched; for the most part its ram-
parts undamaged. In the heart of the dying capital, it was
an oddity amidst the devastation.

The battered Benz sedan pulled off Wecht Street and
rolled through the entrance to the prison. A single guard
was manning the movable barricade. He saluted lazily as
the car passed by, unchallenged. Beyond was a ribbon of
barbed wire, a row of sharpened steel spikes and a third
barrier of concertina. The Benz slowly made its way
around the S-curves cut through the obstacles and came
to a halt in front of the prison's main door.

A graying, wrinkled man emerged from the backseat,
carrying a bulging briefcase. He was Dr. Heinrich
Meinke, psychiatrist. A colleague of Jung, an acquain-
tance of Freud, he was stooped with age. He climbed the
ten stairs leading up to the prison entrance, nodded curtly
to the pair of SS guards watching the door, and disappeared within.

The prison was as dank and gloomy inside as it was
out. Standing in the receiving hall, studying the long,

damp corridors ahead of him, Meinke sniffed in dark amusement. The walls seemed so sturdy, the floors hardly bore a crack. He knew the city's military leaders would have liked nothing better than to see the prison bombed into rubble, thus relieving them of the 113 prisoners remaining inside, many awaiting execution. But the place was simply too thick, too solid.

Meinke exchanged papers with the officer manning the entry office, and after picking up a sullen SS guard, began a long walk down musty hallways and interminable metal staircases. Slowly descending into the basement of the place, a foul moisture filled the psychiatrist's nostrils, making the trek even more uncomfortable.

It took ten minutes for Meinke and his guard to reach their subterranean destination: a corridor containing five cells, each with a heavy metal door, latched twice and chained shut.

The guard stopped at the third door and went through a ritual of jangling keys and clicking locks. When the door finally sprung open, he stepped back and looked to Meinke.

"After you, Doctor . . ."

Inside the cell was a bunk, a chair, a small toilet and two trays of uneaten food.

There was no sign of its occupant.

"He is not here?" Meinke asked the guard.

The SS man was unaffected. "He's here," he replied with a snap.

Meinke studied the small room again. He even looked under the bunk. It seemed impossible that anyone could be inside the cell.

He threw up his hands. "I've suddenly lost my mind then," he said.

The SS man pushed him aside, walked over to the bunk and lifted its very slender mattress. Curled beneath the spring below was the prisoner. He had somehow contorted himself into a state so small, he could fit under the rickety metal frame, an area just two foot square.

"*This* is how he sleeps," the guard hissed.

"How he sleeps?" Meinke repeated the words.

He thought the man was more probably dead. No living being could arrange himself so. But the guard promptly kicked the metal railing and the figure twitched.

"Out!" the guard bellowed.

The figure dropped to the floor, quickly untangled himself, slithered out from under the bunk and stood up, all in one long, fluid movement. He was six foot tall at least, and not exactly lanky, making his contortions even more astounding. Blond, balding slightly, with an angular handsome face, he was about thirty, Meinke guessed. He looked German, or maybe even Russian, though the psychiatrist knew he was neither.

"Sit down," Meinke told him.

The man sat on the edge of his bunk while Meinke eased himself into the chair. He waved the guard away.

"You are my minister?" the prisoner asked him.

"I'm a doctor," Meinke replied, ruffling through his briefcase. "A psychiatrist. Do you know what that means?"

The prisoner's eyes looked dull and tired. His fingernails were filthy. He seemed healthy though, considering his surroundings.

"They sent a brain doctor?" he asked, putting on a pair of wire-rim eyeglasses. "You are here to read my mind?"

Meinke shrugged. The man's glasses made him look at least ten years younger.

"That's not a bad assessment," he told him.

The prisoner leaned back a little. "That's odd," he half whispered.

Meinke found the file he was looking for and flipped it open to the first page. "Do you know the date of your execution?" he asked the prisoner.

The man nodded. "A week from tomorrow."

Meinke checked his file. "Correct. And how do you feel about knowing the day you're going to die?"

The prisoner tugged at his very dirty sleeve. "It might

happen even sooner. Even way down here, we hear the bombs falling."

He was speaking German but with a British accent. Yet Meinke knew this man was not English either. He was South African.

"Your name is Willy Skass. But Skass is your mother's maiden name, correct?"

"Yes. I took her name the day I turned twenty-one."

"Why?"

"Because I had a dream on my tenth birthday that I should."

Meinke checked his file again.

"Your mother . . . she was a prostitute?"

"Yes."

"And your father . . . a politician?"

Skass nodded. "Quite true. He was deputy mayor of Johannesburg. Twelve years."

Meinke looked up from his file. "Did your father know what your mother did for work?"

Skass smiled amiably. "Of course."

"And they both abused you? Physically? Sexually?"

The smile remained. "Yes, they did. I suppose you could say I got it from both ends of the stick."

Meinke thought about this for a moment, then moved on. "You were educated at university?" he asked.

"Just two years. Business. Languages. Some engineering. Some third-class medical training," Skass replied with a wink.

"It says here you speak Russian fluently?"

"*Da . . . bieglo.*"

"And English?"

"Yeah . . . it's cool aping those American dialects . . ."

Meinke made the note: ". . . language skills exceptional," and moved on.

"While in school, you worked in the university's hospital morgue?"

Skass's eyes brightened a bit.

"For eighteen months. Again, I was feeding my ambitions towards the medical arts."

Meinke leaned forward slightly.

"Willy—do you know how many murders you've been convicted of?"

Skass wiped his eyes nonchalantly. "Nineteen."

"And are you guilty of these crimes?"

The prisoner shrugged. "Most of them."

Meinke turned the page; here was a black-and-white photo of one of Skass's victims. A young girl. Blond, leggy. She had been trussed up, hung upside down from a tree and butchered. Her stomach, liver, lungs, heart and ovaries had been removed and lined up neatly beneath her body. Parts of her skin had been torn away and teeth marks were evident on her breasts, neck, and thighs. Two carving knives and a pair of scissors rested on a perfectly-folded white towel lying nearby.

Meinke showed Skass the picture. He didn't blink.

"You remember this I take it?" Meinke asked him.

Skass yawned. "She was French. About three years ago."

Meinke presented another photo, this of a teenage boy. He was lying on a bed of bloody leaves, his eyes open, his body naked except for his shoes and socks. He had been rendered from his groin up to his clavicle, his organs placed next to him. Long strips of skin were missing from his stomach and buttocks. Two butchering knives, meticulously cleaned, lay nearby.

"And this one?"

"Dutch. Traveling alone to visit his aunt near Rotterdam. Two years, three months ago."

A third photo revealed another young female hanging by her feet from a tree, disgorged, and strips of skin missing. Her hair had been cut off and piled next to her organs.

"This one. From one year ago. You cut off the hair. Why?"

Skass studied the photo for a moment.

"She was my first Jew. I heard their hair was valuable. I left it for the police. As a gift."

The next photo showed a woman in her thirties, lying on a small kitchen table. She had been stabbed so many times, her housedress was completely soaked through with blood. Her stomach was a wide maw. Her eyes and tongue were missing, with large chunks of skin obviously bitten away from the face and neck.

"This one looks a bit . . . untidy."

Skass wet his dry lips. "Well, there was a struggle."

"Meaning . . . she was alive for some of this?"

"For some of it, yes."

Meinke made a shaky note. "She was number fourteen. Why did you concentrate on her face?"

"Fifteen actually, from February, last year," Skass politely corrected him. "Her face reminded me of my mother. I wanted her to become a part of me. So I ate part of her features."

Meinke made another note. "And you masturbated over the corpses when done?"

"Yes."

"Some more than once?"

"All of them more than once."

"Did you ever have intercourse with any of them?"

"Most of them."

"You killed a dog, a pet of your thirteenth victim. This too you had sexual relations with?"

"Well, I'm pansexual, Doctor—isn't that what you'd call it?"

Meinke looked up at him over his thick glasses.

"That's accurate."

Skass smiled. "Well, then my answer is yes."

Meinke pressed on. "You were employed here in Berlin at the time of your arrest, true?"

But Skass did not reply. He just smiled. "This *is* somewhat interesting, isn't it, doctor? That you're here, I mean."

Meinke looked up at him. "Interesting, in what way?"

Skass took off his glasses and began cleaning them. "Well, that my jailers think it's important a psychiatrist be my final visitor—and not a priest."

He paused a moment.

"Why do you think they sent you here, Doctor? What could the real motive be?"

Meinke waved his questions away.

"I'm just following orders," he said. "As we all should. Now, we must continue. You held a job at the time you were arrested, correct?"

Skass put his glasses back on. "I held two positions," he replied. "One at Berlin Military Hospital, that was during the day, and then at Metro Hospital at night."

"You worked in the morgue at both?"

"Of course . . ."

"Did you ever mutilate bodies at either place?"

Skass frowned. "Certainly not, Doctor. *That* would have been against the rules."

Meinke stared at him queerly. Was he joking?

"It says here you fancy yourself a magician?"

Skass nodded. "I have my moments."

"Could you demonstrate for me?"

Skass smiled. "If you insist, Doctor."

He reached behind Meinke's ear and produced a lit cigarette. He took a deep puff of the Linet Gold, blew the smoke in six concentric rings, then crushed it out, lit end first, on his tongue, before swallowing the thing whole. He completed the stunt by squinting and somehow forcing a few wisps of smoke from his ears.

Meinke was astonished.

"My God, where did you ever get a Linet Gold?" The premium British cigarette had been a rarity in Berlin even before the war.

Skass smiled again; he was being almost bashful. "An illusionist never tells."

Meinke just stared back at the man, wiping his brow with his handkerchief. It was getting hot inside the cell.

"You ran track at university?" he asked, returning to the questionnaire.

"Long distance, actually. Five-kilometer races were my specialty. My coach said I had the lungs for it. Thought I'd qualify for the 1936 games, but . . ."

His voice trailed off as the guard looked into the cell, checking all was well. Skass nodded in a friendly manner toward him.

"This is standard procedure, is it?" he then asked Meinke. "Each prisoner gets a session with a mind reader before his execution?"

Meinke hesitated a moment. "Not exactly. Yours is a special case."

Skass smirked, betraying a hint of smugness. "Really? I find that so very intriguing. Of all the minds that need mending in this city, in this country—in the entire world. They send someone so obviously eminent as you to salve a lost soul such as I. It's a bit curious, don't you think, Doctor?"

"Dealing with curious things is my profession," Meinke replied. He dispensed with the rest of the murder photos and went directly to Skass's biographical summary.

"All this killing, Willy. How did it start?"

Skass stared down at his very dirty fingernails.

"At a carnival. When I was eight. It was the same day I became interested in magic. I attended a sideshow where I saw a live rat fed to a cobra. It was so fascinating! Even as a child, I wondered if the rat was still alive inside the cobra's stomach, which of course, it was, at least for a while. That was the beginning. That enchantment.

"After that, I began catching small animals in the bush. Mice. Gophers. Rats. Then cats. Then dogs."

"And you tortured them?"

"I *experimented* with them," Skass declared calmly. "I got to know the inner workings of these creatures."

"But you tore them open while they were still alive . . . and began to eat them . . ."

Skass hesitated a moment. "Well, yes. But I just wanted

to see how their insides ran. And, by digesting them, I became stronger. I really did."

"And you did the same to your human victims as well?"

Skass began examining the crud beneath his fingernails.

"It helped in my medical studies."

Meinke almost laughed. "Willy, you've never done anything in the medical profession other than work in morgues. No state would recognize that as medical studies."

Skass just shrugged. Meinke's little lecture did not make the slightest dent in him. "We should move on," he suggested.

Meinke went through the last of his notes. "You set fires as a boy too?"

Skass nodded. "I was a little terror," he said.

"And you wet the bed?"

Skass smiled. "Still do . . ."

"It says here you describe yourself as a methodical person, true?"

"Accurate."

"Your flat was spotless when the police arrested you, even though it is located in one of the most bombed sections of the city. Why?"

Skass shrugged. "Is your flat not spotless at all times, good Doctor?"

Meinke did not reply.

"You would travel some distances to commit your crimes?" he asked instead.

"In the beginning, yes," Skass replied. "I felt it was better that way. I knew every German would be needed one day. So . . ."

"So you killed foreigners."

"Yes, until February 1943. After that, I confined my activities to within the fatherland."

"And killing Jewish girls?"

"Yes. Exclusively."

"And where did you find them?"

"Train stations. Soup halls. The city relief centers.

Many still work at those places. The prettiest ones, I came to find out."

"And your lure?"

Skass shrugged.

"Most of them came to me," he replied. "Most were foolish that way. A smile, some friendly conversation. That's all it took. But really, they should have known better."

"But you stalked some of them, correct?"

"Yes, that's a good term. I followed some of them, sometimes all day. It allowed me the time to plan out exactly how I should take them. Not unlike the lioness, stalking a prey."

"And you kept copious notes on each incident, did you not?"

"I did. Again, for the educational end of it. I learned from those writings. Perfected the art of it, I suppose you could say."

"Well, you did elude the authorities for a very long time, even after they discovered a pattern to your crimes," Meinke told him. "Yet when the police finally searched your apartment, they found a coat belonging to one of your victims. That does not seem wise now, does it? It was the turning piece of evidence against you."

Skass rolled his eyes. "But it was such a beautiful coat! I loved it from the moment I saw it. When my flat lost its utilities, which was often, I might add, I would use the coat for warmth."

"But it was a woman's garment . . ."

Skass seemed annoyed.

"My good doctor, if it was the only article of clothing to keep you warm, would you not curl up in your wife's best fur?"

Meinke felt the hair go up on the back of his neck. He turned to the last page of the file.

"Willy, why do you think you killed these people?"

Skass ran a hand through his hair.

"Out of loneliness, I guess," he said. "If you want the simplest explanation."

Meinke made a quick note, put the files back into his briefcase, and then leaned forward for one last question.

"You were born in South Africa," he began. "Lived there, in some comfort, were educated there. First worked there."

"All true."

"Then why did you come to Germany of all places? Especially in 1939? It's a strange choice for someone like you to make."

Skass crossed his arms. "Not really. I read everything I could about the *Reich* before coming here. I followed the fuehrer's exploits through the South African *Nationalist*. I listened to the English version of Radio Berlin every night. I read between the lines and had a notion that people were being disposed of here every day, on a rather methodical basis. And certainly the ensuing years have borne me out. I really didn't think anyone would even mind my activities, or pay me much notice. Getting rid of Jews and other riffraff—I actually thought I'd be appreciated, as a specialist of a sorts."

Meinke's jaw drooped slightly.

"But Willy, surely you should have known we would have laws and rules against outright murder."

Skass went back to examining his fingernails. The blood of most of his victims was preserved beneath them.

"Well, good doctor, I guess that's where I miscalculated," he finally said, almost sadly.

At that moment, a faint yet familiar sound began to fill the prison. The city's air-raid sirens were beginning to wail again.

The guard walked into the cell. "Doctor, we must go."

Skass quickly had his ear up against the wall, contorting his body again as he did so.

"What time is it, Doctor?"

"Noon," Meinke replied, hastily packing the last of his things. "It's the Americans, I should think."

"And this is Wednesday, no? That means they'll be hitting the rail yards then."

"A good guess," Meinke said as the sirens grew louder and the guard more anxious.

"Yes, the Americans, they are very good," Skass said in a half whisper. "At the hospitals, the casualties brought in from American bombing are different than those from the British. Almost always the victims are killed instantly in an American bombing. With the British—well, let's just say they are messier about this sort of thing."

Meinke had his hat on and his coat slung over his shoulder.

"So, you'll be there, Doctor?" Skass asked him slyly.

"Where?"

"At my execution. A week from tomorrow. Remember?"

Meinke studied him for one last moment. Skass was one of those Nordic types who seemed perpetually young, especially with his glasses on. His face was as appealing as a college student, his mannerisms normal, with a touch of sophistication. He'd stalked his victims so well, many had come to him at the end. And then he slaughtered them, like a butcher would a calf, and ate them. Even in these mad times, it was a chilling image.

"If it happens," Meinke told him, "I'll be there."

DR. MEINKE SPENT THE DURATION OF THE AIR raid inside the shelter beneath the prison commandant's office.

There were worse places to be. The shelter was solid concrete and heavily reinforced, and it was smack in the middle of the luckiest four walls in the *Reich*. Even the guards—and they were all there—seemed at ease.

"The Americans refuse to bomb us on purpose," one told Meinke. "They want us to continue to suffer here, and not put us out of our misery. The British—they just plain miss."

And sure enough, after a long noisy half hour went by, Meinke and the others emerged, barely ruffled, to the sight of Berlin burning once again.

Meinke's driver had spent the raid hiding under the Benz. He was sweeping pieces of debris from the hood when Meinke came out of the prison. The psychiatrist climbed into the back of the car; they turned around and headed for the main gate. Meinke was hoping to return quickly to his office, write his report, messenger it to army headquarters and then get to his suburban home before dark and the beginning of the British bombardment.

But just as the Benz reached the main gate, the driver found his path blocked by another car. As he braked to a halt, four men got out of the second sedan. They were wearing dark trench coats, black hats and muddy shoes.

Gestapo . . .

They ran to Meinke's car and sternly pulled the psychiatrist from the backseat. Meinke lost his briefcase in the momentary tussle; it was snagged by one of the Gestapo men. Lifted off his feet, he was put into the back of the blocking car, his hat and briefcase thrown in behind him. Then his captors climbed in, the driver hit the accelerator and the car squealed out onto the street, across a great puddle of water, and disappeared down the *Reichstaffer.*

Meinke's driver was so frightened he could not move for five long minutes.

Only then did he very slowly drive away.

MEINKE ENDURED A SCREECHING, TEN-MINUTE ride through the rubble-strewn streets, winding up at 28 *Prinzalbrechstrasse.* This was the secret location of the Gestapo's foreign intelligence office.

The psychiatrist was not as terrified as his driver had been—"concerned" was a better word. The special order he'd received purportedly from the German High Military

Command to do an analysis on Willy Skass *had* been unusual. True, Skass was known as the *"Peinlich genauer Kindermöder,"* roughly "meticulous child murderer." As such he was a fascination to some in the German government. But as one who was but a week away from death, in a country that was beginning to drown in death, Skass's pedigree did seem trivial. Meinke had suspected all along there might be even darker elements at work here. Now he knew he'd been right.

He was pulled from the car and carried up the stairs of the Gestapo building, all without his feet touching the ground. He was put in an elevator, the doors closing with a resounding thud. The lift creaked its way up to the third floor, where it opened to reveal a drab ugly hallway. Meinke was ushered into a room whose door numbers had been crudely scraped away.

Inside, he was left with another quartet of men. He recognized only one of them: tall, gray hair, scar under his left eye, late fifties. It was Carl Heintz, provisional chief of the Gestapo for Berlin proper, a man with close ties to Goebbels himself.

Heintz indicated Meinke should sit down. As the doctor did so, the three other men, faceless individuals in dark, bulky suits, circled around in back of him. Meinke found himself looking at Heintz across the vast expanse of his desk.

The Gestapo chief began going through Meinke's briefcase. "You've talked to this freak Skass then? What did you learn?"

The psychiatrist knew he would have to speak with great caution.

"My report will be detailed and lengthy," he replied.

Heintz frowned. "Well, is he totally mad? A raving lunatic?"

Meinke relaxed a little. "He's extremely psychotic. Lacks any kind of remorse. He butchers people, but without conscience. But raving? No . . ."

Heintz read over Meinke's less than copious notes.

"This man was very hard to track down, very hard to finally capture. Is he as organized as they say? As meticulous?"

"As a result of his psychosis, yes, he can be. Very much so."

"And yet he had a talent for blending in. Is that not true, Doctor?"

Meinke nodded. "He certainly does not seem to be who he really is. On the surface, he's actually quite charming, if a bit quirky. But below, he's like a blank canvas. Besides these horrible things that he's done, he has no real personality traits to hook on to. This too helped him in avoiding the authorities. He doesn't just blend in—he fades away. So, to answer your question, could you pick him out of a crowd? Probably not."

Heintz put Meinke's papers aside and now stared back at him.

"So, what are your recommendations then, Doctor?"

Meinke froze. He knew Heintz was a ruthless man, even though he had the face of a wounded pastor. Again, his reply had to be very carefully said . . . or perhaps not said at all.

"It is usually procedure for me to file a written report, Herr Heintz," he answered at last. "One must collect his thoughts and so on."

Heintz leaned back and smiled. "I understand, Doctor. But, unofficially, you can tell me. I am making a verbal report to General Schuller this afternoon on this very matter. I would like a little of your wisdom to pass on to him."

Meinke felt a great relief lift from his shoulders. Speaking the name Schuller was like a code. The general was one of the most powerful men left in Berlin; in many ways, he was running the city. His name would never be taken in vain, even by a Gestapo chief. Meinke now believed Heintz was simply functioning as a messenger boy for Schuller, and that his main concern was to make the correct impression.

Meinke took off his hat and leaned forward in a familiar manner.

"For our mutual friend, General Schuller then, it will be my pleasure."

Meinke went on to explain in detail each of the crimes Skass had committed, and how he had methodically stalked his victims, slaughtered them, had sex with their remains, then ate them—all with little thought of being apprehended. He reviewed the man's dark childhood and his fascination with morgues and such. He discussed his trait of murdering foreigners, switching only to Jews in the last two years of his spree. Meinke spoke with great animation while describing Skass's uncanny ability to elude authorities. Heintz seemed most interested in this.

"My recommendation is that Skass be executed even sooner than scheduled," Meinke concluded. "Then his brain should be excavated and studied by our top neuro-surgeons. I think from some kind of clue—perhaps in the fluids that encase a brain like his—we might learn very much about what causes his extremely aberrant behavior."

Heintz leaned back, as if he was making sure he'd taken it all in. Then he clapped his hands once and bellowed, "Excellent!"

He stood up and extended a handshake to Meinke.

"Thank you, Doctor, I appreciate your help and your time."

Meinke put his hat back on and reached to take pos-session of his notes. But Heintz collected them instead.

"That won't be necessary," he told Meinke. "I'll have them sent to you tomorrow. Will that be fine?"

"Yes, certainly."

Heintz gave him a quick bow, then gestured toward his three colleagues. "Escort the doctor out, please?"

With much courtesy now, the three men led Meinke from the room and back into the elevator. Yet when the lift reached the first floor, the doors did not open. One of the men was holding the lever tight, keeping them shut. The elevator continued downward. Meinke felt no small panic rising inside him. His escorts remained mute, silently staring ahead. One seemed to be fighting a smirk.

The doors finally opened in the subbasement. A room was located directly across from the lift. Shoved inside, Meinke was stunned to find the body of a man lying on the floor. The pasty white features staring up at him were terrifyingly familiar. It was General Schuller. He'd been shot, twice, in the side of the head.

Meinke turned back to his escorts, paralyzed by the knowledge of what was to come. He saw the gun flash before he could say a word. The first bullet entered his head in front of the right eye, knocking off his glasses. His last conscious thought was that they could never be replaced . . .

The next shot fractured his skull. His body dropped to the floor with a thump. His executioner nudged him to better position the gaping head wound over the drain in the center of the concrete room.

Then he and his two companions left, locking the door tightly behind them.

2

IT HAD BEEN RAINING FOR THREE DAYS.

The Princeton campus was almost deserted, typical for a Sunday morning, even more so today. Small groups of umbrellas hurried by in the driving rain. The white brick classroom buildings had turned a sullen shade of gray. Young flowers everywhere were drowning in the early spring downpour.

One man walked alone. He was carrying a red umbrella in one hand, a copy of the February 9, 1944 edition of *LIFE* magazine in the other. His name was Donald Peter Whitemeyer. He was an associate chancellor at the university, an overseer of Princeton's school of history. He was married with two children: a daughter in high school and a young son. In addition to holding a powerful position within the school's administration, Whitemeyer and his wife were fixtures on the campus social circuit. They entertained at their house frequently, giving parties every other Friday night for selected members of the faculty and staff.

Whitemeyer and his wife were also Nazi agents. They'd been working with German Intelligence since March 1939, after a chance meeting with an *Abwehr* recruiter during a trip to Vienna. The couple were typical low-level operatives: American citizens of northern European descent, bored and boring, highly anti-Semitic, fascinated

with all things German, made even more alluring by being
an ocean away. Unlike most operatives, the Whitemeyers
provided their services free of charge. Smug in living a
life of secrets, they did not need the money the *Reich*
would have paid to betray their country.

What brought Peter Whitemeyer out in this Sunday
morning rain was an instruction from his German handlers
that he make contact with a new agent, a man who'd
recently slipped into the country by way of an Argenti-
nean passport. Whitemeyer had been anticipating this
meeting for three weeks. He was nervous; that was just
part of the game. But the anxiety would be worth it if it
meant he could converse with a *real* National Socialist,
someone who'd actually spent time in the *Reich* during
these historic days. As such, he couldn't wait to meet this
man, pick his brain, and ask him of things of *Vaterland*.

Whitemeyer knew very little about the contact, or why
he was in the States. As it stood now, he and his wife
were to house and feed the visitor for one night, provide
him with two hundred dollars in small bills, some gas
rationing tickets, cross-country transit schedules and what
his handlers called "national road maps." The agent, they
said, would look "like a university student."

Whitemeyer arrived at the main rotunda early and had
walked the immediate campus three times already, returning every ten minutes to the agreed-upon meeting place.
It was now nine-thirty. The contact was a half hour late.
Damp and cold, Whitemeyer took up station under the
awning protecting the entrance to the campus bookstore.
The rotunda was empty, the rain getting heavier. Whitemeyer looked down at his magazine, making sure the
cover was displayed prominently.

When he looked up again, a man was standing in front
of him.

He *did* look like a student. Tall, blond, young features,
wire glasses. Handsome, almost attractive. Except for his
fingernails. They were filthy.

He was holding a copy of *LIFE* magazine too.

"A very interesting issue," the young man said to Whitemeyer.

"It's the pictures, I like," Whitemeyer replied, as he'd been instructed to do.

The young man was carrying a suitcase; Whitemeyer quickly took it from him. "You're hungry? Tired? Thirsty?"

Willy Skass smiled.

"All three," he said.

WHITEMEYER'S HOUSE WAS LOCATED ON THE edge of the south campus, near the river and the pines of Maudsley Woods.

He'd been tenured early at the university, and the house, elaborate for academic standards, was a reward to himself. Three stories covered in ivy, an antebellum design with a porch bearing faux Roman columns holding up the roof, it was once the university's library annex.

His family was still at church when he and Skass arrived, driving the half mile or so in Whitemeyer's spiffy Oldsmobile. They spoke sparingly during the ride. The contact was indeed weary, Whitemeyer supposed, and like all operatives, understandably tight-lipped. This would change, Whitemeyer hoped, with the help of a few brandies and perhaps a cup of hot potato soup.

The maid met them at the door. She hustled Skass's suitcase up to the spare bedroom while Whitemeyer ushered his guest directly into the den. This room was an impressive display of red mahogany, well-stocked bookshelves, and cheap but large paintings. The far wall was dominated by an enormous fireplace. Though it was not even ten A.M., the offer of a brandy was accepted, thrilling Whitemeyer. He lit a pipe and both men settled down in chairs pulled close to an already roaring fire.

"I realize I can't ask you about your mission, per se," Whitemeyer told Skass. "But any morsel you'd be willing to share, would stay close to my vest, I promise."

Skass grinned and sipped his brandy. "Actually, I know very little about it," he replied. "Even less than you, I'm sure."

Whitemeyer took the mild compliment with a long puff of his pipe.

"Well, of course, I recognize the need for the hush-hush," he smiled back. "But your means of entry? Well laid out for you, I trust?"

"From Berlin, to Lisbon, to Buenos Aires, to Mexico City, Havana, Miami, Baltimore to here. Yes—expert in planning."

"That they are," Whitemeyer beamed. "Or should I say, *we* are?"

Either Skass did not hear him or didn't get the rib; either way he did not laugh. Whitemeyer changed the subject.

"And your accent sir—"

"Call me Willy, please—"

"Thank you. And I'm Peter to you. Is it your own? It sounds a bit Commonwealth."

Skass smiled again. He was enjoying the brandy more than his host, but doing well to keep that fact secret.

"It is the result of many hours of training," he lied. "There's a language school in Hamburg. I spent February there, perfecting what you hear. I hope I can pass for a South African, if not an American. Beautiful place, Hamburg . . ."

"Yes, we hope to travel there when—well, when matters are settled . . ."

Skass went on: "I assure you I would be quite pleased to converse in pure German with you, except I'm under orders not to do so. With anyone. You understand, of course? All that preparation, and should I slip . . ."

Whitemeyer winked at him. "Understood, again."

He refilled their brandy snifters. His guest was charming but evasive. Should he probe deeper, or let it rest and talk about the weather? The mid-morning brandy emboldened him.

"Do they send you over unarmed then?"

Skass shook his head.

"My suitcase, upstairs. It contains several hidden panels. Inside I have an assortment of weapons. Two pistols. One that is silent. The other can fire a projectile containing acetamine poison. Are you familiar with that?"

Whitemeyer anxiously shook his head no. Finally, some news!

"It acts on the central nervous system," Skass explained. "Extracted from a type of squid, I believe. Mimics a stroke, kills its victim almost instantaneously."

"From a squid you say? Fascinating . . ."

"Yes, it is. Last autumn, I was allowed to visit a technical school built for our special agents. I saw many innovative weapons and communicating equipment on display. Some of the best minds in the *Reich* work there."

Whitemeyer was flush with pride now. Not at what Skass just told him, but because the German agent apparently felt he too was a full-fledged National Socialist. It was the reference to "our special agents," that had him soaring.

"I also have an assortment of knives in my bag," Skass went on, staring into his half-empty brandy glass. "I'll be happy to show them to you, if you wish."

"I certainly do," Whitemeyer gushed, refilling their glasses.

But just then, a noise came from the outside hall. Voices, high and female. A shuffling of feet and the front door closing again. Whitemeyer sank back into his seat, instantly annoyed. It was the family: his wife, his daughter and their young son, returning from church.

Without warning, the sliding doors to the den opened, and Whitemeyer's wife came in. She was tall, slender, a brunette. An attractive woman of forty-four, well dressed in a Sunday suit and hat. Her name was Ellen.

Whitemeyer was furious upon seeing her. She was well aware that the contact was coming to stay with them, and he considered her barging in to be dangerous and rude.

Skass jumped to his feet and bowed deeply as she stood before them, smiling but nervous. Whitemeyer began sputtering an introduction, but Skass beat him to it.

"I am Willy," he said, taking her hand and bowing deeply again. "Your home is lovely. Thank you for allowing me its comfort."

"It's our pleasure," she replied, forcing herself to be nonchalant—after all, that's the way one should be on these occasions, isn't it? "And you've seen the campus? Do you think you might matriculate someday?"

Whitemeyer was so incensed, he nearly interrupted her. She shouldn't be talking to him like this!

But again, Skass was quicker. "All of the surroundings are so pretty, how can I resist?"

He was looking deep into her eyes when he said this. And she even deeper into his.

"You must meet the children. Children!"

Whitemeyer was nearly blue with rage. Yet no one was paying attention to him. A young boy of six walked into the room, stuck out his hand and vigorously shook with Skass. He was dressed in his Sunday best as well. This was Carl, their youngest.

"I have model airplanes," the boy squeaked. "We can look at my collection anytime."

"I would like that, young man," Skass replied, a little hastily.

Behind him was a teenage girl, still growing, a smaller version of her mother, right down to the lily-white dress.

She curtsied for Skass, but barely looked at him.

"I'm Annie, welcome to our home."

Skass performed an exaggerated bow.

"As lovely as your mother," he lisped.

Ellen let out an embarrassing guffaw. Both children turned red and quickly left the room. Whitemeyer was glowering at her.

But he could not let it show.

"A brandy, dear?" he asked her with forced sweetness. She finally took her eyes off Skass and turned to him.

"A brandy? Now? I think not, Peter. It's Sunday morning!"

SKASS HAD HIS BOWL OF SOUP AND A CUP OF weak tea forced on him by Ellen Whitemeyer. Then he went up to his room for a nap.

When he did not reappear by 5 P.M., the time the family would have dinner, Whitemeyer, who'd spent much of the afternoon seething in his den alone, became concerned.

He rang for the maid who then fetched his wife, and in the den, reflected in the pale glow of the dwindling fire, they had a tense conversation.

"You do not wake a guest from a nap, or ever," she was telling him. "It's just not done, Peter. Particularly considering who he is."

"But it is dinnertime," Whitemeyer insisted. "On the Continent, it is acceptable to lightly rap on a guest's door. It's almost expected. Especially on a Sunday night."

She put on her most hardened face. Still, she looked pretty.

"I will not be party to offending a guest, especially this one. That's really all I want to say. We will hold off dinner until he comes down."

"And if that is eight o'clock, or nine, or ten?" Whitemeyer shot back. "He is leaving early in the morning. When will I have my time to talk to him?"

"*Our* time," she corrected him—she was just as anxious to talk about Germany as her husband. "And that conversation will just have to wait until after dinner."

Suddenly a yelp came from the hallway. It was the maid.

Whitemeyer and his wife rushed from the den to see the servant pointing up the spiral staircase, apparently too stunned to speak. And sure enough, she had reason. Slowly descending the stairs was their son, Carl. He had both hands stretched out in front of him and it appeared at first that he was carrying two small candles.

But actually the tips of his index fingers were on fire. Mrs. Whitemeyer let out a yelp herself.

"Don't worry, Mother," Carl was saying, calmly toeing his way down the long staircase, his eyes transfixed on the twin flames engulfing his fingers. "It's a trick Willy just showed me . . ."

When he reached the bottom step, the boy took a deep breath and with much drama, blew on his fingertips and extinguished the flames. Then he clapped his hands together and let out a great laugh.

"Wasn't that *keen*?" he roared.

Husband and wife were still speechless when Skass appeared at the top of the stair and hurried down to engulf Carl in a massive bear hug.

"He awoke me for dinner," Skass told the parents. "We've become great friends!"

Horrified, both adults began to offer apologies for their son, though still quite baffled by the fire trick.

Skass waved their concerns away. "I would have slept for days," he said. "And that would have been very rude."

He picked up Carl in a flurry of arms and legs and proceeded to carry him triumphantly into the dining room. The maid had quickly recovered and was just laying on the first course.

Whitemeyer's face beamed slightly, finally punctuating what had been for him a gloomy afternoon.

He bowed slightly and smiled at his wife.

"After you, my dear," he said.

DINNER WAS A WHOLE LAMB SERVED IN A GAL-lon of greasy mint gravy.

The day was still dark, and with the growing evening, Whitemeyer asked that all the dining room candles be lit. This gave the meal an oddly romantic glow.

Skass insisted on carving, methodically inspecting a set of sterling knives before selecting the right one. He did an expert job, rendering the lamb into sixteen perfectly cut pieces. He proved to be a fine conversationalist as well, though reticent in spots, just as Whitemeyer and his wife would have expected him to be. He was after all, an espionage agent, a spy. And, in some regard, so were they.

The children were fascinated with him, especially Carl. He was seen several times during the meal examining his fingertips, wondering himself how it had happened and whether his digits would spontaneously combust again. Twice during dinner the children had left their seats to watch more closely some small hand illusion Skass had offered to perform. The children came to him, both White-meyers noted, a charming lapse in dinnertime manners. The man was remarkably comfortable to be around.

The meal finished, the children were exiled to the kitchen for ice cream while Whitemeyer, his wife and Skass took their coffee in the den. Brandy was dispensed. The rejuvenated fire sent a rich glow around the room.

Once the maid had left, Whitemeyer pulled his chair closer to Skass, effectively checking his wife's line of sight.

"So please, tell us," he began, "what *are* the present conditions inside the *Reich*?"

Skass managed his warmest grin of the night.

"Well, let me ask you this," he replied. "What do *you* think they are like?"

Whitemeyer put on his best concerned face.

"*Challenging*? We hear of the bombing raids, of course, and the change in the situation in the Atlantic."

Skass let out a great "Ha!" It was loud enough to startle both husband and wife.

"*And where do you get this news?*" he roared.

Whitemeyer quickly regained his composure. "The *New York Times*. The *Herald*." he said.

"The radio too," Mrs. Whitemeyer added.

Skass laughed again. It sounded a bit drunk.

"Well, I *do* have some news to give you," he said with a slurp of brandy.

Whitemeyer and his wife leaned in closer to him.

"Not one Allied bomber has ever penetrated the *Reich*'s airspace," Skass declared boldly. "Anything you hear to the contrary is desperate propaganda on the part of the Allies."

Both Whitemeyers looked perplexed. She spoke first: "You mean all these stories, these reports we read of Hamburg, Frankfurt, Berlin, in flames. They are *all* lies?"

Skass nodded confidently. "Every last one of them."

Husband and wife looked at each other. A whiff of disbelief went through the room. Skass sensed it immediately.

"Skepticism is healthy . . . and wise," he said. "But let's look at the facts. The Jews control the newspapers, both here and in England. Jews are pathological liars. Naturally they do their jobs well."

"Too well," Whitemeyer said.

Skass leaned forward. The fire was waning a bit.

"I have traveled the *Reich* extensively in the past year," he said softly. "I can truthfully report that I did not see one instance of bomb damage or any signs of war at all. All of this unpleasantness is taking place not within the *Reich,* but in other parts of the world, which, I might add, are quite some distance from the fatherland."

He slurped his drink again.

"Now, as for the Allied bombers themselves—well, I can tell you I have seen the French countryside littered with them. And I'm sure this is true in Russia and Africa and wherever they attempt to get at our resources. They try—we must give them that. But they just don't succeed. Our fighter pilots are that good."

Another gulp of brandy. Whitemeyer quickly replaced it.

"You have heard reports of thousands of bombers and fighters being manufactured in this country every month, correct?" Skass asked them.

Both husband and wife nodded.

"Think of this then: Why would the Allies need so many, if they were actually winning this war? Why would there be such a priority on replacements, if our pilots weren't shooting them all down?"

The logic was twisted yet it was beginning to have an effect on Whitemeyer. Planting false stories would not be any great task for Allied propagandists, he supposed. And news photos could be doctored easily enough. He felt his chest swell. Could it be true? Had the *Reich* been winning all along? And it was little more than distortions and lies the Allies had been feeding the American public? It would not be the first time one side in a war believed it was winning right up to the moment of defeat. Witness Germany in the last world conflict.

"The situation in the Atlantic is no different," Skass went on. "I spent many days on the high sea, one period of time aboard one of our fastest battle cruisers. Let me assure you, I saw no ship, no plane and I dare say no bird, fish or serpent that was not securely within the realm of the *Reich*."

A long silence. The fire crackled a bit. Peter Whitemeyer wanted to believe—it was his wife who was still skeptical.

"But these battles we hear about," she said. "D-Day. Italy. The Bulge. Can they *all* be a Jewish fantasy as well?"

Skass did not miss a beat.

"War is about battles," he said. "And all these things— they have happened. But again, they have transpired *outside* the Reich. Even the Jewish controlled press cannot deny that."

He raised his glass in a toast and looked deep into her eyes again.

"We are preserving the victory," he said with a wink. "And doing well at it."

A long gulp of brandy now. Ellen had been won over.

"And within the *Reich* itself," Skass continued. "Our artwork flourishes. I attended not one but two operas in Hamburg my last week in country. The museums rival only our athletic stadiums in size, as do our universities and our hospitals. It really has been an amazing renaissance."

"And the clothes!" Mrs. Whitemeyer gushed. "What are the women wearing?"

Skass's face turned an appropriate pink. "I am no expert there," he said. "But I must say, I see more of the ankle in the *Reich*'s these days . . ."

All three laughed at this, Whitemeyer himself a little too hard.

Mrs. Whitemeyer repositioned her chair so that she was now the closest to Skass. "This unpleasantness is almost over then?"

"It is on schedule," Skass replied softly. "And while the day our fleet rides into New York Harbor might not be next week, it is certainly no more than a year or two away."

Mrs. Whitemeyer indicated with the wave of her hand that her husband should refill Skass's snifter. Miffed, he did her bidding.

"And I'll reveal one more thing," Skass said, testing the new pouring. "The *Reich* has developed a line of wonder weapons that are truly mind-boggling."

"My God, like an atomic bomb?" Whitemeyer blurted out.

Skass hesitated, but just for a moment. "Bigger. Better. More fantastic than that."

Now it was Whitemeyer who was mesmerized. "Of course, we hear whispers about the V-Ones and V-Twos . . ."

Skass nodded slowly. "And the V-Threes? and Fours? and Fives?"

"My goodness, you've seen such things?"

"Indeed I have," Skass boasted. "These are the things that ensure our eventual victory."

Skass winked and put his hand to his lips.

"Beyond that, I really cannot say any more."

But both Whitemeyers wanted him to. She made another movement for Whitemeyer to fill their visitor's glass. But Skass stood up instead, stretched and yawned.

"All this wonderful brandy," he confessed. "I'm afraid it's made me sleepy again. A gift I suppose, as I have to leave so early tomorrow."

He bowed deeply.

"I bid you good night . . ."

The Whitemeyers protested, but it was no use. Skass began moving toward the door and they knew once unseated, a guest must always be allowed to leave. That's how things were done.

Crushed, Whitemeyer opened his desk and drew out four envelopes. One contained two hundred dollars in small bills, another two months' worth of gas tickets. The third held a half dozen Rand McNally road maps, each devoted to a specific region of the United States. The fourth was thick with cross-country train and bus schedules.

"Are you sure this is all we can do?" Ellen asked Skass.

"You have done too much already," he said, turning to her.

He held her hand and kissed it, bowed and kissed it again. Then he took the envelopes and shook hands with Whitemeyer.

"I will see you in the morning of course," the professor said, slurring his words slightly. "I feel a restful night coming on too."

Skass turned to go, then stopped and looked back at them.

"There is one more thing," he said. "And that is, no matter what happens, you can never, ever tell anyone I was here. The *Reich* expects that from you . . ."

For the first time that night Whitemeyer actually touched his wife. He draped one arm around her and the other around Skass and whispered: "And the *Reich* shall have it. By our word, we will never talk of this.

"No matter what happens."

* * *

PETER WHITEMEYER ACTUALLY SPENT A REST-
less night.

His alcohol intake had worked against him, providing
an insomniac headache in between fits of sleep.

His wife slept soundly as always, as far away from him
as possible, and wrapped in her own set of blankets. For
much of the night he lay motionless, wary of not waking
her. His expansive bedroom looked twice its size this endless night. The rain had continued, and the wind was
blowing, and at various times, both awake and asleep,
Whitemeyer thought he heard odd noises coming from
down the hall. He dreamed that his young son had crawled
into the room asking not for a glass of water as he was
wont to do, but demanding bandages instead.

Whitemeyer watched the sky slowly begin to brighten
around five A.M. then fell into one last bit of sleep.

When he awoke again it was six-fifteen. Panic swept
through him. Skass was to leave about now, and Whitemeyer would miss his opportunity to see him off. He leapt
from bed and dashed into the bathroom. No time for a
bath, just a wash of the face, a cold shave, some greasing
for the hair. Then it was silently into his clothes of the
day: dark trousers, a white shirt, blue tie, and socks.

A brush of his shoes took only another few seconds,
and then he was ready to go down. His wife woke up as
he touched the doorknob.

"Do not disturb our guest again!" she shot at him sleepily.

"He has already gone," Whitemeyer told her. She rolled
over and went back to sleep.

Whitemeyer quietly left the room and stepped out into
the hallway. He could hear the maid downstairs, and
smelled the coffee brewing. Good, she at least had prepared Skass a farewell repast. Whitemeyer put his ear first
to Carl's bedroom door and then Annie's. He did not want
the children interfering this morning either. Both rooms
were as still as tombs.

Whitemeyer scurried downstairs, stopping only at the

landing, so as not to let his guest see him hurrying. He pretended to check for the morning paper first, quickly opening the front door and shutting it again, knowing full well the *Record* wouldn't arrive for another two hours yet.

Then he walked into the kitchen. The maid was sitting at the table, her back to him, sipping a cup of coffee. She heard his steps and jumped to her feet, startled to see him. Even on the earliest mornings, Whitemeyer never came down before seven A.M.

"What is this?" he barked at her. "Our guest has not risen yet?" It was the only explanation he could fathom for the maid's insubordinate behavior.

"He has already left," she blurted out in reply. "He has been gone nearly an hour."

Whitemeyer's face dropped a mile. He checked his watch. It was 6:35.

"He left *before* six?"

The maid was tugging at her apron and trying not to cry.

"He did, sir. He said he was going out to find a taxi. I offered to call for one, but he asked me not to. He left at quarter to six."

Whitemeyer was devastated. Just like that, his hero was gone. No hearty farewell, no muscular handshake. No well-said, well-done. Just gone. An ugly rage was building toward the maid.

"Did he say *anything* before he left?" he demanded of her.

"Not a thing," she replied hastily. "Except of course a thanks for the hospitality."

"Oh, he did say that, did he?"

"Yes, most definitely, sir . . ."

Whitemeyer slumped into a kitchen chair.

"Well, that's a small something, I suppose."

* * *

WHITEMEYER TOOK HIS COFFEE INTO THE DEN and, lacking anything else to do, began reading the previous day's newspapers.

His headache never went away, and the coffee wasn't any help. At about 7:15, he heard his wife go out for her usual early morning constitutional. He was in no mood to wish her good-bye. His life had become dull and restless again, now that his Nazi was gone. Even the excitement of getting caught harboring a spy no longer provided a jolt. Skass had said a German victory was still two years away. Whitemeyer sighed as he read about some fictitious bombing raid on the railroad yards at Bremen.

"I cannot wait that long," he thought aloud, eyeing the brandy bottle though it was very early in the morning. "I will not."

Just then he heard a rumpus in the hallway. It was the usual bustle of the children getting ready for school—or so he thought. The doors to the den slid open and Whitemeyer looked up to see his wife standing there in her raincoat. Her face was absolutely white. Her hands were dripping with blood.

"My god, what have you done now?" Whitemeyer shouted at her.

"Annie . . ." was all she said.

3

IN THE SPRING OF 1945 THERE WERE TWO FBI offices in Manhattan.

The Bureau's main office was located downtown at Foley Square. Agents here handled a multitude of ongoing wartime investigations, including routine espionage cases, reports of enemy activity in ports up and down the East Coast, security checks at military and industrial facilities— all while keeping an eye on domestic criminal activity as well. It was a lot of work, and thus a small army of G-men occupied the offices at Foley Square, even though its location was supposed to be classified. The federal contingent was actually so large (and well paid), its presence had an affect on the local economy. Food, coffee, liquor, and cigarettes cost nearly twice as much within a two-block radius of the "secret" location.

There was however another much smaller FBI field office in Manhattan—and this one really was top secret. It was located at 834B Seventh Avenue, between 53rd and 54th streets, one floor up from the old Stage Deli. This office was called the SWS—for Special Wartime Service. It handled Nazi sabotage cases, many of which FBI higher-ups deemed too sensitive for distribution to their regular field offices. The SWS office was manned by just a dozen agents and their assignments were relayed directly from Bureau headquarters in Washington. By design, SWS had little to do with any other FBI assets in New York City.

Or at least that was the idea when the secret unit was created in 1941. The truth was, despite repeated attempts, the Germans never succeeded in establishing a solid sabotage network in America, as they had during the first world war. Either bungling or intrigue at the top of the German High Command were the most probable explanations for this. But now, with the war in Europe rushing toward a conclusion, the conventional wisdom said the Nazis had all but given up trying to destroy targets on American soil.

Still, in its four years of existence, the SWS office had investigated nearly two thousand cases of *suspected* sabotage in the eastern United States. A gasoline fire at an aircraft assembly plant in New Jersey, poisonous chemicals leaking into a reservoir upstate, a wrench found in a machine making parts for tanks in Hartford—they all had to be checked out. And just because the fire was due to careless smoking, the reservoir the victim of a faulty valve, and the wrench left as a reminder to the plant foreman from a recently terminated employee, this didn't mean full investigations were not conducted. They were, with mountains of paperwork and hundreds of man-hours to prove it.

In the end though, it turned out to be much ado about nothing.

SENIOR AGENT JAMES "BIG JIM" TOLLEY WAS the person in charge of the New York SWS office.

He was a huge, barrel-chested Irishman, six foot four, forty-eight years old and weighing nearly three hundred pounds. A Camel cigarette usually drooping from his lips, he looked tougher, braver and smarter than he really was. His booming voice and steely blue eyes, though, led few people to question his authority, his wisdom, or his diet. The truth was, he might have been the least ambitious employee of the FBI, if not its biggest.

A twenty-two-year veteran of the Bureau, Tolley was a headquarters good boy who'd been awarded the SWS post by J. Edgar Hoover himself. It was not a brilliant choice. During the rather desperate times in 1942 and early 1943, when German U-boats were sailing just miles off the east coast and it seemed like there was a Nazi saboteur lurking around every corner, Big Jim Tolley had spent much of his time in the burlesque houses on 42nd Street. He had private tables in more than a half dozen of them and there wasn't a maître d', bartender or dancer within a six-block area who didn't know him on a first-name basis.

Yet somehow, Tolley had been able to squeeze everything he could out of his manpower, giving his staff free rein and slaving his agents to check every lead, douse every suspected fire, and most important, assure every government official who asked that the situation was under control. With a great assist from the Germans, the war years just slid right by.

In fact, as of December 1944, Tolley's men had spent most of their time compiling lists of suspected communists in New York City.

THIS PARTICULAR MARCH DAY HAD STARTED out as usual for Big Jim—with a cup of coffee and an enormous jelly roll from the deli downstairs. His second-floor office window looked out on to bustling Seventh Avenue, and he liked nothing better than to eat his breakfast and enjoy the view below. This included keeping tabs on the pretty girl who ran the laundry directly across the street. She was probably no more than twenty, a redhead, and a dead ringer for Betty Grable. Big Jim had already tapped her phone once, just to hear her voice during the most mundane of business conversations. He'd also installed a secret camera just below his windowsill to snap pictures of her whenever she was looking especially sweet. A confirmed bachelor, though, Big Jim had once confided to a drinking buddy that this was as close to love as he ever wanted to get.

Just three bites into his confection, his morning ritual was disturbed when the phone rang. A glance at the desktop switchboard told him the call was coming from Foley Square. Tolley stopped eating and put down his coffee. A call from the Square usually meant more work for SWS, especially these days, when it was well known that the antisaboteur squad was carrying a very light caseload. Tolley was not too anxious to pick up the phone then.

But it kept ringing and ringing and finally, answer it he did, only to find his initial fears had been right. Pleading shorthanded as usual, Foley Square had a case that needed looking into. It was a day-old murder on the campus of Princeton University, over in New Jersey. Nothing directly connected with any war-related investigation, but one that called for a Bureau presence nevertheless. Could Big Jim spare someone to handle it?

Tolley's first inclination was to say no. The SWS office was actually shorthanded too. Tolley's men had been in constant motion for nearly four years. Many had forfeited vacations, put off sick days, and even worked weekends, just to maintain the hectic pace of checking every tick and tock Washington sent their way. Now that the assignments were barely trickling in, the G-men at SWS had been catching up on their days off. Even the secretary was on vacation.

"Homicide isn't the type of thing we do around here," Tolley told his counterpart in the downtown office. "Besides, is this really a federal crime we're talking about?"

"We've got a stolen taxicab sitting in a train station just outside Philly," the man from downtown explained. "There's blood on the seats, and it might have been used by the killer right after the murder. The driver is missing but the vehicle was definitely driven across state lines. So, at the very least, that's a violation of the Dyer Act. Also, Princeton is on the list of priority national security sites because of the egghead research they do over there. So take your pick. Either way, it could be federal."

"Still sounds pretty iffy to me," Tolley told him, looking to see if his laundry girl had arrived yet. She hadn't.

"Well, it *is* iffy," the other agent replied. "Truth is, they just need some hand-holding over there. The local police are in over their heads. The campus cops don't even carry weapons. If a G-man showed up, looked around, made himself known, just for a day or two, well . . ."

"Everyone would feel better . . ."

"And sleep better," the agent added.

A pause.

"So, can I send you the file?"

Tolley glanced at his bare work roster and realized that if he allowed the case to be transferred to SWS, he might have to go over to Princeton himself—an unacceptable situation.

Big Jim relented nevertheless. It was a nice day, he was in a swell mood, plus it was good politics to do Foley Square a favor now and then. "OK, I'll see what I can do," he said.

He hung up, finished half his jelly roll, then buzzed for his number two man, a senior agent named Leo Spank. Spank came in, sat down, and helped himself to one of Big Jim's cigarettes. Tolley told him of the request from Foley Square. Spank rolled his eyes.

"We'll have to send the janitor," he said. "Because besides you and me, he's the only one left."

But then from the outer office came the sound of a typewriter clacking away.

"Well," Spank amended. "Besides the other guy . . ."

THE OTHER GUY WAS SPECIAL AGENT JOE Copp. He was very well-known inside the FBI; at one time he was its third most decorated agent. When he joined the Bureau in 1931—it was called the Division of Investigation back then—he was a rock-jawed, handsome college boy with a slightly twisted nose and jet-black hair. Once known as a very natty dresser, Copp was what Hoover liked to call "all-American clean." In fact Copp looked so much like a G-man, his face had adorned the cover of the Bureau's recruiting manual in 1933.

Copp was legendary amongst his peers for his busting of several Midwest bank-robbing gangs, including the notorious Denton-Hatfield crew, a job he completed almost single-handedly. Everyone inside the Bureau knew the story. The Dentons, as they were also called, preyed on small towns in Kansas, Missouri, and Oklahoma from 1933 to 1935. Though not as well-known as Clyde Barrow's outfit or the Dillinger Gang, the Dentons were no less ruthless. They killed twenty-four people during their nearly three-year crime spree, including two federal agents, a half dozen bank tellers, several bank guards and many civilians, one being a five-year-old boy run down during one of their getaways.

As with most gangsters of their ilk, the Dentons showed no remorse from their crimes or mercy for their victims, especially if they were law officers. Like the Barrows, the Dentons thought small, hitting only banks or grocery stores in tiny isolated towns, far from the big cities. Perpetually short on ammunition, they preferred beating their victims with rifle butts or hammers whenever possible. When the bullets flew though, the Dentons did not discriminate as to who got shot. They were, by far, the bloodiest gang in the west.

During one robbery, at a bank in tiny Southfield, Kansas, the gang massacred five people after the elderly guard tried to resist. Two of those killed that day were expectant mothers who already had nine children between them. In an earlier stickup outside Red River Falls, Oklahoma, gang leader Jake Denton shot the bank teller between the eyes simply because he didn't like the color of the man's tie. That set a nasty precedent. Of the two dozen people killed during the gang's reign of terror, eight had been shot between the eyes by Jake Denton.

Transferred to the Chicago FBI office in late 1934, Joe Copp was told to track down and eliminate the Denton-Hatfield crew. A veteran of a half dozen similar pursuits since 1931, Copp knew it was useless to chase the gang through the backroads of the Midwest. The Dentons were known to have a number of safe houses and hideouts, and whenever things got too hot, the gang would always head south, to Mexico, where they could lie low for a while before heading north again.

But this didn't happen too often because the Denton gang were experts at dispersing after a crime and then reforming just before the next one, a tactic their contemporaries never really mastered, leading some to their downfall. This talent made catching the Dentons by conventional means almost impossible.

How did the various gang members know what small town to be in, at what time and on what date? Skullduggery by phone was impossible because the FBI had tapped the lines of all of the gang members' families and associates. Same with the mails, as all correspondence surrounding the gang was routinely intercepted and read. Still, there was a definite pattern to their crimes and once on the job, Joe Copp vowed to noodle it out. He gathered as much information as possible on the gang, compiling Bureau reports, eyewitness accounts, tear sheets from detective magazines, and newspaper stories. Copp developed a personality essay on the gang's leader, Jake Denton. One thing Copp knew going in was that Denton, like Barrow and Dillinger before him, craved publicity. Jake had even shortened his name from Dehnstenhoffer just so it would fit into a headline. Copp surmised then that he was a prolific reader of newspapers.

He also knew that Denton considered himself a mastermind—but was he really? Or was he just the smartest lug in a jar full of screws? Copp didn't know. But in an effort to stay on top of the case, he'd festooned his office with mug shots of all the Denton gang members, along with teletype news reports on their latest exploits and maps pinpointing their crimes. This was all very unusual for Copp's colleagues in the Chicago office. Up to that time, agents were expected to keep their areas neat and tidy, their walls adorned only by a framed picture of Director Hoover and a small American flag—and that's when they were even in the office at all. Back then, agents were strongly encouraged to move about the people, to be seen, to be heard. To put a face on the fabled G-man.

Copp took a different tact with the Dentons. The first five weeks on the assignment, he stayed firmly planted behind his desk. It took lots of reading, lots of research, lots of cross-checking, coffee, and smokes—but finally he caught on to the Dentons' pattern. And it was rather ingenious: The gang would rob the same bank exactly one year to the day it had been hit by one of four other gangs: the Barrows, the Dillingers, Pretty Boy Floyd or Machine Gun Kelly. The pattern was nearly foolproof. With the publicity given to those veteran crews, there was no shortage of what crimes they had pulled, or where or when. The Denton gang members would assemble near the targeted bank a few days prior to the one-year anniversary, eyeball the job, and then go in shooting.

By cracking the code, Copp had answered another question as well: Jake Denton *was* sort of a mastermind. The beauty of his plan was in its simplicity.

But Joe Copp was better.

ON FEBRUARY 27, 1935, COPP BEGAN TO LAY HIS trap. After the Dentons knocked off a bank in Lancaster, Oklahoma, a place visited by the Barrows exactly one year before, Copp arranged for no long pursuit—and plenty of headlines for Jake Denton to feed on. He also made sure that every newspaper in a five-state region played up the anniversary of the Barrows next subsequent crime—a stickup in Low River Junction, Missouri, on May 4, 1934. With dozens of stories on that famous holdup blowing around the Midwest, even a year after the fact, it was probably the loudest bank robbery Clyde Barrow and his crew ever pulled. There was no way Jake Denton could have missed it.

When the Denton Gang drove into Low River Junction on the morning of May 4, 1935, Copp and nine other FBI agents were waiting for them. Copp was disguised as the bank guard; his men were dressed as civilians. Jake Denton walked in, announced the holdup and called out the name of his gang. But when he turned around to shout instructions to his crew, he discovered the barrel of Joe Copp's revolver pointing directly at his own pronounced brow. Copp pulled the trigger and blew off Jake Denton's face. A fierce gun battle ensued and when the smoke cleared, three of Denton's men plus Jake himself were dead. Four others, waiting near the getaway car outside, escaped. One of these men was Jake's brother-in-law, Clem Norton, the lookout, who was seriously wounded in the gunfight.

The surviving gang members drove all night, winding up in West Ridge, Missouri, around dawn. By this time, Clem Norton was near death. Stringy Hatfield, now the leader of the decimated gang, went into West Ridge and woke up the town's elderly doctor. Claiming a friend had been hurt in a car accident, Hatfield took the physician from his bed and brought him to the gang's hiding place.

Joe Copp found the doctor's body the next day; it had been thrown into a ditch alongside Highway 65, head bashed in with a hammer, the bloody trademark of Stringy Hatfield. Clem Norton's heavily-bandaged body had been dumped beside him. The doctor was eighty-one years old at the time of his murder and left seven adult children, thirteen grandchildren and five great-grandchildren. He had suffered 103 separate fractures to his skull.

Exactly one month and two days later, what was now simply called the Hatfield Gang struck at a bank in Deerfield, Kansas—a well-known Dillinger target. Again, Joe Copp was waiting for them. This time he had a full company of lawmen with him, including twelve U.S. marshals, four squads of National Guardsmen and a dozen armed World War One veterans deputized for the occasion. The Hatfield Gang never even made it to the front door of the bank. They were mowed down like dogs in a brutal cross fire, which, as reconstructed by the Bureau's fledgling crime lab, involved the firing of no less than 1,285 bullets, more than half of which found their way into some part of a gang member's flesh.

J. Edgar Hoover himself declared the Denton-Hatfield Gang finished after that—but this was not quite so. The day of the Deerfield clash, Stringy Hatfield did not accompany his men to town. Claiming his ulcer was acting up, he remained behind at the gang's hideout, and thus avoided their fate. When the gang failed to return, he put two and two together and fled.

Joe Copp devoted the next six months to his pursuit. Shorn of his gang and their firepower, Stringy, who was actually a large man, over six feet tall and weighing more than 220 pounds, took to robbing gas stations and whorehouses, frequently hopping freight trains to get from one place to another. Spurred on by the needless murder of the elderly doctor more than anything else, Copp memorized train schedules and set up ambushes all over Oklahoma and Texas, but Hatfield always managed to slip through his fingers. When the killer disappeared into Mexico in the winter of 1935, the Chicago office called off Copp's crusade. By this time, just about all of the prominent bank-robbing gangs of the early thirties were either dead or in prison and the Bureau was turning its attention to other matters. Joe Copp was given a half dozen citations, promoted to field supervisor, and reassigned to Reno, Nevada—to investigate illegal gaming.

Eight years passed, but Copp never forgot what he'd seen in the ditch that dreary bloody morning. He kept a picture of the doctor and his extended family inside his jacket pocket, just so what Stringy Hatfield had done would never be far from his heart. And when, in July of 1943, he heard that Stringy Hatfield had killed again, Copp took two weeks' worth of sick time and, without consulting his superiors, began tracking the killer once more.

The onetime bank robber had committed a different

kind of murder this time. Slipping back into the U.S. in the spring of 1943, Hatfield had somehow found work on a locomotive crew hired out by Southern Union & Freight. The rail company had secured a contract with the U.S. Army to transport German POWs from receiving ports in South Carolina to prison camps in Texas. The segregation laws being what they were in the southern states, whenever the prison train passed through Louisiana and it was time to feed the prisoners, the German POWs were allowed to eat in the train's dining car—something the Negro soldiers guarding them could not. One such night, when one of the soldiers got into an argument with the conductor over this contrary situation, Hatfield intervened and, reportedly in a drunken rage, killed the black soldier by cracking his skull open with the butt of his own rifle.

Copp was an expert at figuring road maps and determining the shortest distance between two points, and he could drive fast, especially at night. So he traversed the country and arrived in the Louisiana town nearest to where the murder had happened just three days later. After interviewing the train crew, he picked up Hatfield's trail right away. Eschewing motor vehicles and riding the rails as he knew Hatfield would do, Copp headed south, toward Mexico. He finally caught up with his prey in the little border town of Esperago, Texas. The man was just seconds away from splashing across the Rio Grande and making it to safety.

Confronting the killer at a dilapidated filling station not twenty-five feet from the Mexican border, Copp emptied his revolver at Hatfield, with no result. A fistfight ensued, during which much of the interior of the ancient gas station was destroyed. In the course of this battle, the massive Hatfield grabbed a long screwdriver and began stabbing Copp. Desperately reaching out for a weapon of his own, Copp found his hand wrapping around a large ball-peen hammer—an irony not lost on him, even at that precarious moment. Sheer will and the hammer's blows allowed Copp to finally prevail, subduing Hatfield, but not before the killer sustained several fractures to the face and jaw, eight broken ribs, a snapped clavicle and two crushed testicles.

Copp brought Hatfield back to justice, and it seemed as though the Bureau could indeed finally close the book on the marauding bank-robbing gangs of the thirties. But after his trial and a sentence of death, Stringy Hatfield did a very strange thing: He hired a lawyer and filed a lawsuit against the Bureau claiming Copp used "excessive battery" in his apprehension. The Bureau had never faced a criminal rights suit before, and had the matter quietly reviewed by a member of the highest federal bench. When the judge indicated that due to recent constitutional interpretations the Bureau might well lose in open court, Hoover himself authorized a hush payment of one thousand dollars to Hatfield's family and a reduction in sentence to life without parole.

That was the beginning of the end of Joe Copp's career. Hoover was furious that the Bureau could have been embarrassed in such a manner—and that meant someone had to take the fall. In a matter of hours, Copp went from poster boy to scapegoat. It was only because he had secret admirers high up inside Bureau headquarters that he wasn't canned immediately. He was put on two years' field restriction instead, which, when complete, would bring him to the age of forty-one. At that time, he would be forced to retire, with only a fraction of his rightful pension.

Essentially then, Copp was sentenced to twenty-four months of office work to be served at the most inconspicuous Bureau office possible, followed by a less-than-honorable dismissal, and most likely abject poverty soon afterwards.

As it turned out, his prison was the secret SWS office in New York City.

*   *   *

BIG JIM TOLLEY LIT A CIGARETTE AND CALLED
Copp into his office.

The disgraced agent did not look so much like a bro-
chure cover these days. His nose had been punched in so
many times, it was no longer handsomely twisted, but
now just crooked and flat. His right leg still contained
pellets from a shotgun blast he'd taken in '33. His left
arm was known to stiffen periodically, a reminder of another gunshot wound he'd suffered in 1937. Both neck
and forearms retained the scars of his hand-to-hand combat with Stringy Hatfield. Even his hearing was starting
to fade, the result of being too close to so many guns
going off during his career. He looked and walked and
talked like a man in his fifties. Yet he was only thirty-
nine years old.

He'd been in this second-floor hell for fourteen months
now. During that time, he'd kept to himself, never con-
versing for very long with his colleagues. Arriving
promptly at eight and leaving promptly at five, Copp's
days consisted of typing out overdue field reports, filling
in investigation forms for the other agents and, when necessary, answering the phone.

Now standing before them, Big Jim handed Copp the
notes from his conversation with Foley Square. Copp read
them in silence. A young girl had been murdered in
Princeton. The suspect had probably fled across state
lines.

"What's this have to do with me?" he asked.

Spank stole another of Tolley's cigarettes. A warm
breeze came in from Seventh Avenue; spring was arriving
early.

"Big Jim wants you to take a ride over to Princeton,"
Spank said, casually lighting the Camel. "Be seen, you
know, by the faculty, the campus cops, and especially the
civilians. Ask some questions, review the case a bit, make
like someone's on the job."

Copp thought they were kidding.

"You're putting me back in the field?" he asked Tolley directly.

"Just temporarily," Big Jim replied. "And it's only because we are so short staffed around here that I'm making this exception. Just between us girls."

Copp almost smiled.

"But don't go crazy with this, Joe," Spank warned him. "The police over there are convinced the guy who did this is long gone. It's been almost a couple days now and, you know, we just don't have the wherewithal at the moment to go off half-cocked chasing after him, especially with all the overdue reports you have to write. So, just do a 'hello and good-bye,' and then come on home."

Copp looked at the bare report again.

"So this is not a real case you're sending me out on," he said.

"Nope," Tolley told him. "It's just a walk-through. We're fibbing them a bit, but that's the best we can do. If a girl gets killed in Jersey—that's really someone else's problem these days. Five years ago, maybe someone here would have jumped on it. But things are different now. This office has got more important matters to attend to."

He took a huge bite of his jelly roll.

"So, just take a spin over there," he continued, licking his fingers clean. "They'll be thrilled to see you I'm sure. Make like you're looking to see if anything leads anywhere. But if you can avoid discussing the specifics of the case, all the better. And don't let them turn anything over to you. Duck soup? OK?"

Copp took a long time staring at the page of notes. Wheels were turning.

Finally he said: "Duck Soup? Sure thing."

4

JOE COPP ARRIVED ON THE GROUNDS OF Princeton University bright and early the next morning. It was Wednesday and traffic coming over from New York had been light.

He looked good and felt good for a change. He'd grabbed a haircut and shave after leaving work the day before and still smelled of Bay Rum. He was wearing his best G-man suit—blue, double-breasted with pinstripes—which he'd stayed up to nearly midnight cleaning and pressing himself. His shoes were new and expertly polished.

His only stop this day was Princeton's Department of School Safety, an office located in the subbasement of the university's maintenance facility. Copp was to have a private talk with the head of the campus police, but word had got out that a G-man was coming. When Copp arrived at the works barn, he found a crowd of maintenance men and female students waiting outside for him. Many had cameras and autograph books in hand.

Big Jim had been right; they *were* thrilled to see him. A visiting FBI man was big news anywhere, even at Princeton, a place that had its share of famous names and faces. And why not? The public viewed G-men as both mythical heroes and comic-book characters. They'd busted the bank-robbing gangs in the last decade and the Axis in this one. The newspapers were always full of them. Be he a field agent or a paper-clip manager, few civilians would pass up the opportunity to see a real live G-man. Copp spent the first twenty minutes of his visit shaking hands, signing autographs and having flashbulbs popped in his face. Though he was careful not to show it, he enjoyed all this immensely.

Finally finding his way to the safety office, he sat down with the boss of the campus cops, a man with the unfortunate name of Keystone. Most of his tiny police force was on hand too, some in suit coats and ties. They spoke very little about the killing itself, this because, as Copp would learn, none of them had actually seen the body or the working crime scene. The Princeton city police had been the first to arrive, and they'd sealed off the area immediately. They did know the girl's name was Annie Whitemeyer and that she had been stabbed sometime in the early morning hours, apparently after leaving her house to walk to a nearby pond. "Wrong time, wrong place," was how Keystone put it. "I guess the poor kid never had a chance."

As ordered, Copp let fly with just enough bullshit for everyone in the room to think the Bureau was keeping an eye on the case. He praised the campus security men for their expert handling of what had transpired and asked that their final report be sent to him when completed. Then he signed a few more autographs, posed for pictures and got a lively tour of the university grounds. Along the way, he gave some quotes to a local newspaper reporter who had been tailing him for the entire visit. A big story in the next day's edition was a sure thing.

When Copp finally left, the campus guards gave him a horn-honking escort back to the highway. The day was over and he'd fulfilled Big Jim's instructions in spades.

And it all might have ended right there.

Except . . . it had been such a long time since Copp had done anything like this. Between his recuperation from the fight with Stringy Hatfield and the time he'd already served in his suspension, Copp hadn't been out of the house in nearly two years. He had liked getting back into real clothes and having a real shine on his shoes. To see again how people lit up when they saw a G-man, how anxious they were to shake his hand, to slap his back. No surprise he hadn't limped all day and his arm did not stiffen once.

Yeah, Copp had missed these things.

Driving back to Manhattan that night he knew he wasn't ready to go back inside.

Not just yet.

HE GOT TO THE SWS OFFICE VERY EARLY THE next morning, long before Big Jim, Spank or anyone else had arrived.

Leaving a vague note about seeing to one last detail, he promised to be back in by noon. Then he drove back over to Jersey and into the city of Princeton itself. He had reassured the campus cops, why not the city police too? At least that was his scheme. The regular precinct cops were bowled over when he walked through the door. He asked to see the police detectives assigned to the university murder case and was ushered into the chief's private office straightaway. Over peanut butter snaps and coffee, Copp learned the Princeton dicks had no suspects, no witnesses, no motive and no leads in the killing, except for the taxicab found in Philly, which was way out of their jurisdiction. They too spoke very little about the actual murder, and Copp did not encourage them to do so, knowing this would make Big Jim very happy.

When the time came, Copp delivered the same message as the day before, that the Bureau was concerned, monitoring, interested in the eventual outcome of the case. He commended the city police on their professional handling of the crime and the meeting concluded with the cops asking him for pictures and autographs. They even offered to give him a ride in their new squad car. Copp politely declined. His plan was to get back to Manhattan by noon, his brief fling with the outside world finally concluded. But then the chief of police himself hurried in, alerted to what was happening in his office. He insisted that he and his captains take Copp to the best restaurant in Princeton for lunch. It was so uncharacteristic for Copp to accept, he surprised himself when he said yes. The Princeton cops seemed mildly shocked too.

Over bad steaks and warm Moxie, the cops peppered him with questions not about the murder case but about chasing bank robbers out west. Copp did not disappoint them with his replies. He told the Denton Gang story, leaving out the part about Stringy Hatfield, of course. He touched on several other of his gangbusting exploits as well. This was not like him. To go on so much about his career, in front of people he barely knew, he felt like an old hen doing it. But this was probably the last time he'd ever get to boast while still a G-man. So why not jive them a little? The lunch wound up stretching past three hours. By that time, the Princeton cops were beginning to look a little bored.

It was right after the dishes were cleared away that everything took a left turn. The cops announced they had something for him. Copp would have bet a fiver it was either a watch or a bottle of booze, both of which he would have to decline. They handed him the file for the Annie Whitemeyer murder case instead. Not a carbon copy—the original file.

It was an awkward moment. Copp hovered over the table for a few seconds, not sure what he should do. There was no way he could refuse it, that might tip off the Bureau's less than noble motives. Yet he could not take permanent possession of the file either. Big Jim would kill him if he did. The best he could do was accept it graciously, lock it up for a few days, then return it. Then he could finally fade away.

He promised to review the file and messenger it back to Princeton by the weekend. The chief indicated they were in no hurry to get it back. Copp got his escort to the highway, this time with flashing lights and wailing sirens.

By the time he got back to Manhattan, the SWS office was closed for the day.

*   *   *

HE WENT HOME TO HIS WEST SIDE WALK-UP,
cleaned his face and hands and started making his usual
dinner for one.

His place was small, but well-appointed, meaning he
had enough stuff to fill all four rooms. This was only
because, when the sky fell in, he'd been able to ship some
furnishings bought in his glory days to New York at the
Bureau's expense. Sometimes he wished he had just the
walls to stare at, though. The movables were comfortable,
but they never failed to remind him, at least once a day,
of how things used to be.

He sat down with a piece of leftover pork, a bowl of
peas, and a cup of coffee. He had no newspaper to read,
as he usually did during meals. So he took his first bite
of meat and flipped open the Whitemeyer file.

The first thing that fell out was the photo of the murder
scene. Copp nearly threw up on his plate. It was the most
gruesome picture he'd ever seen. The young Whitemeyer
girl hadn't just been stabbed to death—she'd been hung
upside down, sliced open, and gutted. Portions of her flesh
had been ripped off. Many of her internal organs were
missing and bite marks could be seen all over the body.
The photo's tag line said she'd been raped—*after* death.

Copp pushed his meal away from him. *What was going
on here?* This was not the routine murder case everyone
at the Bureau thought it was. This was something horrible
and sick. He checked the photo's time, date and location.
Everything matched. He held the photo closer to the light,
slowly turning it upside down. The girl's eyes were open
and she was staring directly into the camera, one last gasp
of surprise frozen on her face. Even in death, she just
couldn't believe what had happened to her.

Those Princeton cops had really played him for a
sucker, Copp thought now with a grim laugh. The horrible
method of killing. A postmortem rape. *Cannibalism?*
They wanted nothing to do with this; it was way out of

their league. That's what prompted the call over to Foley
Square in the first place, not knowing that two Bureau
chiefs would get involved and handle the thing like yesterday's trash. But when Copp showed up for his double
dip of forehead buffing, the Princeton cops saw a golden
opportunity to wash their hands of it completely. So, they
wrapped it up, put a bow on it and gave it to the Bureau—
with Copp as their delivery boy. He had to give them
credit. This time the rubes proved to be a lot smarter than
he.

Laying the gruesome photo aside, his fingers eagerly
went to turn to the file's written report—but that's when
he stopped himself. *He couldn't do this.* Not again. He
stood up and walked out of the kitchen and looked out
his living room window. The sun was just beginning to
set and a deep red glow washed over his face. His leg
began to throb.

He'd faced this problem before. Since being banished
to SWS, he'd come across a few case files that at the time
seemed to indicate authentic Nazi sabotage attempts. And
he'd made the mistake of reading these files cover to
cover. Naturally this led him to examine the circumstances, look for patterns, formulate opinions, and then
dream up ways to counter whatever was happening. One
particular case had to do with a Shell oil plant over in
Bayonne. The leads all pointed to someone flaming the
place over Armistice Day weekend. Another had to do
with a B-25 going down off of Rhode Island. Again, the
thing smelled fishy, and Copp had stayed up three nights
in a row trying to put the pieces together.

But then, inevitably, the crash would come, that moment when he realized he was just wasting his time trying
to be useful. He was persona non grata at SWS, a secretary in pants and no more. Hoover had declared it so himself. Copp couldn't offer any theories to his colleagues.
No one would listen to him, even if he did.

That's why he could go no further into the Annie
Whitemeyer file. If he looked beyond the crime scene

photo, if he read the actual file itself, he knew what would happen. His teeth would sink right into it—and he would not want to let go.

So, nope . . . not this time. He would not be fooled again. He walked back to the kitchen, stuffed the grisly photo back inside the folder and sealed it shut. Then he locked the file away in his bedroom desk.

Tomorrow, still tightly sealed, he would put it on Big Jim's desk and await the crumb-spewing tempest.

COPP NEVER FINISHED HIS SUPPER THAT NIGHT.
He threw his meal away, washed up the dishes, then retired to the living room to read. But concentration was impossible. He tried the radio, but nothing on could hold his interest. He shined his shoes. He made new coffee. Still, he felt ill at ease. Even a pipe could not calm him.

He found himself eyeballing a bulging photo album which contained stacks of his old newspaper clippings as well as his most famous field reports. He took it off the bookshelf purely on impulse. Maybe a crime he'd worked in the past was similar to this Princeton killing. But in the next second, he knew this was just a poor excuse to go back down memory lane. No way would he have forgotten an act so ghoulish. There was no doubt about one thing though: the case locked away in his desk drawer had the potential to be a big one. A career-maker. The savage killing of a young girl, by persons unknown, on the campus of one of the most prestigious universities in the world? It already sounded like another Lindbergh case, right down to the befuddled local cops. This was a job that any G-man worth his salt would jump on.

Leaving his personal debris spread out on the floor, Copp poured himself a glass of milk, leaned against the sink, and let his mind wander. Was there any way he could push this furlough, this temporary reprieve from his field suspension, just a bit further? What if he threw one more day at this Princeton thing? He could argue that he was just fulfilling Big Jim's instructions to the supreme—that he was trying to make the FBI look *real* good. But you see Big Jim, your brainstorm backfired and the Princeton cops loved the Bureau *so* much, they threw the whole case in our lap, and . . .

Copp shook these thoughts away. Big Jim would eat him like a clam with that line of crap. If he had actually followed Tolly's order to the letter, he would never have gone back to Princeton the second day. And the file would still be sitting in the Princeton chief's private office, slowly slipping from memory, eventually to collect dust, unless of course the killer struck again. Copp poured his glass into the sink, picked up all his old war stories and put them away. He couldn't imagine when he'd ever want to look at them again.

SEVEN O'CLOCK FOUND HIM CLEANING HIS RE-volvers. He had three, and not one of them had collected a speck of dust since the last time he'd oiled them. By seven-thirty he was polishing his Bureau badge. The gold had actually become tarnished in some spots, but with a lot of rubbing and effort, Copp had it gleaming once again. He was keeping busy, but the wheels would not stop turning. He *did* know how to track down bad guys. He was an expert when it came to chasing someone on the lam. If he were somehow able to catch this guy . . .

That's when the phone rang. It was his weekly long-distance call from his folks in Pennsylvania. As always their voices cut through the static like knives to his heart. They had no idea what had happened to his career—he'd led them to believe that his move to New York was a promotion of sorts, a transfer to the biggest city in the world. But boy, was he dreading the day, not too far off, when he would be jobless and have to tell them the truth. More than once he'd caught himself thinking that maybe they'd be dead before he was finally kicked out of the Bureau.

Or maybe he would be.

The phone conversation was pleasant; his father talked about the war, his mother about her winter apple jam. But Copp hurried them off before they could begin their ritual of telling him how proud they were of him, and how they were still singing his praises, after more than a dozen years, to all who would listen. He had to run, he told them; he was working on a very special case. They sent their love and said good-bye.

The connection broken, Copp could barely hang up the phone, his arm was so stiff.

HE CLIMBED OUT ONTO THE FIRE ESCAPE AND lit another smoke.

It was dark now, storm clouds were flying over his head. The street below was deserted; the glow coming from midtown was rather dull tonight. What would these streets look like three months from now? Or in six? Returning GIs, sailors and airmen, moving fast, scooping up the jobs, the girls, neither of which was good for an old man like Joe Copp. He let out a long troubled stream of smoke. He'd certainly picked the wrong time to go out of style.

He allowed the bitter memories to leak back in now. He'd been a damn good agent once. Hoover himself had said: "Joe Copp is the best boy we have." And who had reason to dispute God, least of all Copp himself? That statement alone should have been enough to hang his hat on; his past performance should have counted for something. But when he'd tried to defend himself after the Stringy Hatfield mess hit the pan, to a man, his superiors cut him to pieces with lectures about how things had changed, in the country and inside the Bureau, since Copp went out west to Reno and fell off the edge of the world. Chasing bank robbers and beating them to within an inch of their lives just wasn't the modus operandi anymore. Snooping on ordinary citizens and chasing Commies was.

In the end Copp was disgusted with his former friends and colleagues. Every last one of them, reading from the same script.

No, bringing Stringy Hatfield to justice was the worst thing he could have done. With no trial of his own, and a deal made behind closed doors, he'd become a has-been in a matter of a few hours. There was no crueler blow for him. As a kid, all he'd wanted to do was grow up quick and become a government agent. Throughout high school and in college, he actually began to smell it. Then, finally, making the grade and getting his badge . . . The Bureau had been his whole life. His dream come true. But that dream came back to take one huge bite out of his ass— and when it did, it hurt a lot worse than any gunshot wound.

HE CLIMBED BACK THROUGH THE WINDOW AND checked the time.

Eight forty-five. Still a while before he could start thinking about going to bed. He tried the radio again, but the news was brief: Roosevelt was on his way to Colorado, a drought was expected in Kansas. Significant gains on all fronts, both in Europe and in the Pacific. The weather for the foreseeable future: rain.

He could now listen to a concert from Symphony Hall, or hear a debate on whether to regulate personal aircars now, before they flooded onto the postwar market. Or maybe, he could take just one more peek . . .

Before he knew it, Copp found himself in his bedroom, unlocking his desk drawer and slipping out the Princeton file. In a child's game he did not open it. Instead he reached inside, telling himself that it would be OK to look at whatever he might pull out—but nothing more. With two fingers he reached in and snagged another batch of photos. He steeled himself; did he really want to look at more gruesome pictures? Suddenly the rules he'd made up didn't seem so convenient.

But he had to go through with it, and to his surprise, these were not photos of the grisly murder site at all. They were family pictures, portraits of Annie Whitemeyer in happier times. As a Girl Scout. Singing in her church choir. Helping run a Red Cross cake sale. She had been a beautiful young girl. Haunting eyes, shy smile. Any deep thoughts, about life, about boys, about her parents, all locked away in the back of her mind.

That's when Copp felt a tingling sensation begin to fill his skull. His stomach growled angrily. Looking into those eyes, at the age of ten, then maybe twelve, then maybe last week . . . it was just too much for him to take. Had his parents not called. Had the shine on his badge not been so faded. Had these pictures of young Annie Whitemeyer not fallen out—his life would have been very different. But it was too late now. The walls were closing in and there was nothing he could do to stop them but this.

He unraveled the file's tie cord, lit a cigarette and sat down to read.

THE FILE WAS SPARE, JUST SIX PAGES OF TYPED text, less the photos. The cover-page summary began with a statement from the first Princeton city cop on the scene. He'd found the sixteen-year-old girl hanging upside down, her ankles tied to a low branch with bedsheets, her wrists bound with a bathrobe sash. Her pale blue night-gown had been torn away and she'd been slit from abdomen to rib cage. Some of the resulting gore had been lined up in a neat row beneath her body. Some, like her liver, her stomach, her tongue and breasts, were unaccounted for, as were long patches of her skin. Bite marks were evident over ninety percent of her body.

Right away Copp's intuition told him that someone on the Princeton campus had murdered the girl. A maintenance worker. A professor. Maybe even a student. It seemed to make the most sense. The girl had been torn open, true. But what the crime photo showed was not a butchering, but a dissection. Copp studied the picture with his magnifying glass. The incisions on Annie White-meyer's skin were sickeningly precise. Surgical. That's why the image of a person who worked in a laboratory came to him. Someone familiar with sharp instruments. Someone who knew how to slice things up. Someone close by . . .

But Copp was forced to dissolve this theory with the next page. Here, he read that shortly after the girl's body had been discovered, the Princeton city cops, plucky fellows, had spread out and questioned just about everyone on campus. They were helped in what normally would have been a massive endeavor by a quirk in the academic schedule. The killing had happened on the first weekend following ten days of exams. By tradition, the campus was empty of students for the next week as most went home or into New York City for a bender. Many of the staff members were gone as well. Those people who had remained on campus had either spent the morning in the library or in bed, and the vast majority had done so in the presence of others. The Princeton cops stopped their canvassing only after learning the taxicab had been found in Philly, but not so soon as to determine that just about everyone on university grounds that morning had a solid alibi.

All this seemed to give credence to the theory put forth by the Princeton dicks on page three: that the killer was someone just passing through. A hobo. A drifter. A freight hopper. In fact the Princeton cops' preliminary report began with the declaration: "There's a good chance the perpetrator of this criminal act is more than a hundred miles away from here by now."

But this was wishful thinking and Copp knew it. How many hobos found their way onto the campus of Princeton University, where they are then able to catch a young girl away from her house in the early morning hours, cut her up with the precision of a surgeon, and then leave the scene—in a taxi? Copp was not buying that one, and he didn't think those coy dicks in Princeton were sold on it either.

With the next page, it got stranger. The Princeton city cops had kept a log of all persons who'd been at the murder site after the girl's body had been found; this was standard procedure. In this log were the names of all city police officers on the scene, plus the coroner, a police photographer, two ambulance drivers and the man from the funeral home.

But here's where it got peculiar: the names of the girl's family were not in the log. The parents had seen the body, of course—the mother was the one who found it and the father arrived even before the police had been called. But after that, both parents had stayed away. No helpful information mumbled from a state of shock; no desire to be with their daughter's remains to the end. When it came time to ask the parents routine questions, the Princeton police had to go looking for them. The mother had hurried to the campus chapel with her son. But the father, it turned out, had gone shopping—for hats. Three hours after his daughter's body had been discovered, the Princeton detectives found Peter Whitemeyer in a local haberdashery, trying on fedoras.

Nor did the family's odd behavior stop there. As the Princeton police continued their rather meek investigation, the Whitemeyers—husband, wife, son, and maid—disappeared. They had been planning to get away even before the gruesome fate befell them, they had told friends. So after quickly burying their daughter with no memorial service, they left town.

To go on vacation.

5

PRINCETON UNIVERSITY

THE WEATHER FORECAST HAD BEEN RIGHT. IT
rained all over New York and New Jersey that weekend.

The heaviest precipitation came on Sunday night. A
definite chill was in the air, with any hint of early spring
long gone. The weeping willows dotting Princeton's
grounds turned gloomy in the dark rain. Foggy, cheerless,
unlit—the campus looked cold, inside and out.

Around nine o'clock, two pinpoints of light split this
gloom. A car was coming down the main university con-
course, moving very slowly, wipers swishing, engine rum-
bling, headlights piercing the fog and rain. It was an
Oldsmobile, nearly new, black with a gray top and gigantic whitewall tires. Four people were inside. Turning south
at the rotunda, it followed another narrower roadway
south, toward Maudsley Woods. The car slowed down
just before the trees began and took a right onto the driveway that led to the Whitemeyer home.

The people inside the Oldsmobile did not notice another car parked beneath a swath of drooping willow
limbs about two hundred feet away. This second car was
a Pontiac, black, slightly bent, seven old bullet holes rusting its right rear fender. The car had been waiting here
all day, indeed it had been parked in the same spot for
most of the past three days. Whenever the wind would
blow, it made a whistling noise as it passed through the
fender's perforations.

The big Olds went down the long gravel driveway and

rolled to a stop in front of the ivy-covered house. A woman dressed in a maid's uniform climbed out from the driver's side, scampered around to the right rear door and pulled it open. A man, a woman and a young boy stepped out, huddled beneath an enormous umbrella. They hurried up the front stairs of the house, leaving the maid, unprotected, to carry in the luggage.

Lights gradually popped on inside. Smoke began wisping from the chimney. Upstairs, shadows told of the rituals of unpacking. Having parked the car in the garage nearby, the maid went in by the back door. A cat appeared soon afterward, dashing through the rain to do several days' worth of business in the wet shrubbery.

That made it official: the Whitemeyers were home. Back from their vacation, they'd been gone for nearly a week.

Watching from the shadows nearby, the dark figure in the whistling Pontiac extinguished a cigarette and checked the time. It was 9:05 exactly.

THE WHITEMEYER HOUSE WAS JUST BEGINNING to warm when the front doorbell rang.

Padding out from the kitchen, her gray hair still damp, the maid answered on the second chime to find a man in a long overcoat standing on the door stoop, dripping wet.

"Good evening, ma'am," he said. "May I speak to the man of the house?"

The maid let him in without a word. She picked up a small house phone and had a quick, whispered conversation with someone. Then she opened the door to the den; inside, the fire had already gone out. He should wait here until Mr. Whitemeyer came down.

The maid left, closing the door tightly behind her. Only then did Joe Copp dare take a breath.

This was not like him. He felt wrong. Dirty. Uncomfortable. Three days of sitting in his car, close to the lily-clogged river, with his smokes and his joe—all that was one thing. But to actually make entry into a domicile where he really had no business, with no warrants, no backup, not even a pair of handcuffs. Christ, he was in deep now.

Copp wasn't even sure he was an FBI agent anymore. He'd called in sick on Friday, leaving a message with the overnight that made no mention of his two days in Princeton. On Saturday he failed to contact the office at all, a violation of the requirement that all active Bureau agents, whether they were busting bad guys or shuffling papers, call their office at least once during off days. Sunday had brought the same kind of insubordination. The truth was, Copp had nothing to say to anyone at the office. He was an unauthorized agent working an unauthorized case. It was not something he wanted a long conversation with Big Jim about.

What's more, it had not been a pleasant stakeout. The rain had been nonstop, the dampness had been painful for his bad leg, and he'd been forced to do *his* business in the woods. Today had been an especially long day, with the fog creeping in around noontime. By early evening, his smokes began running out. It was sad in a way—there was a time when Copp had lived for this sort of thing. His car reeked of the smoke and spilled coffee from dozens of stakeouts. But between his ailments and the uncertainty of his job—he was so sure that he was going to be fired on Monday, he'd already penned a letter of resignation—sitting in a parked car for three days in the cold and rain just didn't seem glamorous anymore.

Still, the time had not been wasted. He'd spent it studying the Annie Whitemeyer file up and down. He could recite it by heart now, he'd read it over so many times. He'd analyzed and reanalyzed all of the statements, taken and made, from everyone connected with the case. He'd studied the floor plan of the Whitemeyer house, the layout of the actual crime scene. He was intimately familiar with all of the photos of the young victim, both when she was alive and otherwise.

Despite all this, the murder was no less sickening than he'd found it in his apartment that previous Thursday evening, the night he dove headfirst into the case and forgot to come up for air. Some of the statements written by the Princeton city police were incomprehensible, and their grammar was atrocious. It had taken him almost all of Friday just to sort it all out. He'd even diagrammed the case, using the back of an empty doughnut bag as a canvas. The resulting drawing looked like an octopus whose appendages stretched off into infinity.

It was just after noon on Saturday when his data finally became set. That's when Copp was able to begin his search for some link, some key that would tie it all together. Every crime had a plot to it, a script that the bad guys and the innocents played out. But like a puzzle, the importance of events was sometimes unrecognizable until that last piece fit into place. So what was that piece in this horrible crime? What link pulled this one all together? He spent hours looking for it.

And on Sunday morning, after much coffee, many cigarettes, a lot of aspirin, and too little sleep, he finally figured it out. He knew who killed Annie Whitemeyer. And it wasn't a hobo or a drifter, nor someone who worked on the campus. It was her father, Peter Whitemeyer himself. Copp didn't know why, he didn't know when or even how. But when all the other factors were eliminated, two things pointed to the father's obvious involvement. The man had proximity to the victim and his actions afterward were just too bizarre. It had to be him. Copp was sure of it. And he was ready to stake what was left of his career on it.

That's why he was here.

THE DOOR TO THE DEN OPENED AND PETER Whitemeyer walked in. Hands in pockets, but still quite stiff, he looked just how Copp had imagined him. Regal, graying, stern. A nasty professor-type. But no doubt he was weak when pushed. That was just fine with Copp. He was sure if it ever came to blows with this guy, he could knock him out with one punch.

He lifted his badge up to eye level. Whitemeyer lowered his reading glasses to look at it.

"I'm Special Agent Joe Copp. Can we have a moment to talk?"

Whitemeyer didn't seem a bit surprised that an FBI man was standing in his den. But clearly he wasn't happy about it. He didn't indicate that Copp should sit down, or even take off his very wet coat. Instead, he folded his arms tightly across his chest and hid his hands from view.

"This is about the investigation, is it?" he sniffed. "I wasn't aware the federal government had become involved."

"Well, it has."

"And you've been assigned to this case?"

"Yes, I have," Copp lied. His eyes were starting to water a bit now.

"Well, I don't know what you could possibly do for us," Whitemeyer told him dismissively. "The local police have been quite thorough, thank you."

"But still far from a solution," Copp replied quickly. "I was wondering if you recalled anything about the morning your daughter was murdered. Something that might have come to you, while you were away. On vacation."

Copp let that last word hang in the air for a few seconds. Whitemeyer seemed stung. He pretended to think a moment.

"No, nothing," Whitemeyer finally answered, trying to light his pipe. "But certainly, if we do we'll get in touch and . . ."

"We still don't know how she got out of the house." Copp cut him off. "Was it her habit to leave the premises, in the early morning? In her nightclothes? Alone?"

Whitemeyer glowered at him. "Certainly not!"

"Her bedsheet was used in the crime," Copp pressed. "How did it get out of the house? It doesn't make much sense that she'd be walking around with it."

Whitemeyer's face drained of color. He began to stumble.

"Well, unlike the police, I believe she was taken . . . from her room . . . sometime in the night."

"You suspect a kidnapping, then?"

Whitemeyer was totally flustered now. He took off his glasses—and that's when Copp felt his heart sink. The man's eyes were stone dry. And his hands—they were sissified, feminine. There was not enough strength in them to kill.

This was not good. Copp had worked a lot of interstate homicides before being sent to bust the Denton Gang. From this experience, he'd developed a foolproof method of IDing a killer. It was a certain look the guilty party had when he realized he was caught: a watering of the eyes, a darkening of the brow, a tensing of the hands, especially if the victim had been strangled or stabbed. Copp had seen this revealing look many times, usually just before beating the suspect to a pulp. But he could not see it now—and in that instant Copp knew that he'd been wrong. Whitemeyer did not murder his daughter.

But still, something was very fishy here.

"I have no idea what the circumstances were," Whitemeyer was stammering on, looking everywhere except into Copp's eyes. "A kidnapping. A murder. What difference does it all make now? Our daughter is dead. And your questions are opening up old wounds again. So, I thank you very much for your time, but . . ."

He began ushering Copp back out the door, but Joe stood his ground.

"How about Mrs. Whitemeyer? Might she have remembered something while you were away?"

"No, I haven't . . ."

The voice came from behind them. They both turned to see the lady of the house standing in a doorway which led into the den from a back hall.

She was out of her traveling gown and wearing a long

white frock. She was attractive for her age and, Copp imagined, probably quite striking in the right moment. Her voice was soft and shallow, but adamant. Her eyes were teary. Copp wondered about her hands.

"We really did tell the police everything," she continued, walking to within five paces of her husband, but no farther.

"How about the maid?" Copp asked them both. "The police report stated her room was closest to your daughter's. Perhaps she saw something? Heard something?"

"That was a mistake," Whitemeyer mumbled. "Our maid's quarters are quite some distance away actually. And she knows nothing. Nothing at all."

"Did the local police speak with her?"

Husband and wife shot a glance at each other.

"No, no, they didn't have a chance . . ." Mrs. Whitemeyer replied.

"She does not speak English," the husband interjected. "Not in an understandable fashion anyway."

Copp made a big production out of retrieving his notebook and writing down something important. Actually, he just scribbled the words: "Lying about the servant. Maybe."

"I'm sure the local police already asked you this," he began again. "But just to be certain: did you see anyone lurking about your property that day? Any strangers, drifters about?"

Both husband and wife stared at the floor.

"No," they said in unison.

"Anyone from the university—a colleague, maybe someone in the medical arts department—stop by?"

"No . . ." again in unison.

Copp paused.

"And you had no visitors that evening? No overnight guests?"

A moment's hesitation.

"No . . ." they finally spoke, again together.

Copp just stared back at them. *What was going on here?*

"How about your son?" he asked. "Has anything come back to him?"

"He recalls nothing," Mrs. Whitemeyer snapped.

Copp turned his x-ray vision on her. True, her eyes were wet, but also very angry. And sad. He looked closer. Just as he had made killers before, he'd also looked into the faces of many grieving relatives. And that's sort of what was happening with Mrs. Whitemeyer now. But not exactly.

"How's the little fellow holding up?" Copp asked her softly.

"Like his mother, not too well," she replied.

At that moment the son himself toddled into the room. He was in his pajamas and sniffling. Two heavy bandages covered the tips of his index fingers. He hurried past his father and into his mother's arms.

"And now he's awake!" Mr. Whitemeyer exploded.

It was time to go. Copp knew these people did not pass his test as murderers. But could they be . . . *accomplices*?

He didn't know.

Nodding politely in Mrs. Whitemeyer's direction, he followed the husband out of the den and to the front door. Copp had previously scribbled his home phone number on a piece of notebook paper. He handed it to Whitemeyer.

"I work out of the Bureau's special Manhattan office," he told him. "But it's best that you call me at home—that is, if there's anything you need."

Whitemeyer graciously took the number, huge relief on his face that Copp was finally leaving. This was another indication that all was not on the level here.

"Thank you," Whitemeyer said, unlocking the front door. "I will do that."

Copp turned to go.

"One moment," Whitemeyer stopped him. "Did you say your name is Copp?"

Joe froze. "Yes, it is . . ."

Whitemeyer actually smiled, weakly. "Is that German by any chance?"

Copp shook his head no. "It's short for Coppelli. Changed at Ellis Island."

"Ah," Whitemeyer said. "You're Roman then?"

"Italian," Copp replied with a shrug. "Or halfway anyway. My mother was Irish."

Whitemeyer thought about this for a moment, then carefully folded the piece of paper and slid it into his shirt pocket.

"Half Irish, half Italian," he murmured as he opened the door for Copp to go. "I guess there are worse things to be these days."

6

WILLY SKASS KILLED FIVE MORE PEOPLE IN THE week following Annie Whitemeyer's murder.

His favorite was a female child in Philadelphia. After the rather routine disposal of the greasy taxi driver, Skass had been almost giddy when he took her. It would be one of his quickest killings ever.

She was blond, in a school uniform, waiting in the train station for her parents after a half day of classes. Skass asked her to help look for his missing dog. She agreed. A short walk from the station, down to a stream and the work was done within ten minutes. This one he buried in a ditch with some leaves, returning to the train station in time to witness the parents' arrival and the beginnings of their frantic search, always a thrill for him. Skass simply stepped onto the next train west and left the area, long before the police were ever called. They would not find her body for nearly five days. Just like the girl in Princeton, she had tasted like fresh cream.

A boy in Pittsburgh came next. He had been more difficult. He was a runaway and a Jew, but he hung out with a gang of young toughs in a seedy bus station downtown. Skass had a hard time isolating him from the pack. It took nearly two days, during which he slept in the bus station with the youths, buying them food and liquor and putting up with their childish behavior before finally getting a chance to take his prize.

This he did at his leisure. He'd rented a cheap hotel room and took fourteen hours to torture, dismember and consume the boy, who tasted bitter. Skass slept soundly afterward, though, then took several hours packaging up and disposing of what remained and cleaning the room. It was a lot of work for what in the end was not a very satisfactory result.

Still, he left Pittsburgh in a homicidal mood.

THIS WAS NOT LIKE HIM. MORE THAN ONCE HE'D likened his lurid activities to the smoking of a cigarette, good until that first puff. True, for him the drive to kill could be as intense as the human need for water. The longer he went dry, the more thirsty he could get. But usually it was the hunt that provided the most titillation. Once his prey was snared, hard work had to be done. He was always very conscientious to do right by his victims, holding some sort of communion with them during the various stages of dismemberment. But in reality, once their lights went out, the excitement always began to drain away. Guilt and the drudgery of cleaning up usually followed; these could leave him deflated for long periods afterward. Or at least that's how it used to be. Because since coming to America, something was different about him. Even if the girl was especially sweet, or the boy unusually vulnerable, he'd found himself wanting to begin a hunt within hours of the last one, be they successful or not. This was a totally unexpected allure of this New World, this accelerated pace. Back in Europe, such desires sometimes took weeks, even months to return.

What was happening to him? Why had he changed so? Why was he so thirsty all of a sudden? Certainly the roundabout journey he'd endured to get to America held part of the blame. There had been no passage on a German navy super-cruiser as he had told the Whitemeyers. Instead the five-week voyage had taken place on a Turkish steamer out of Lisbon, traveling *east* to Argentina, with dozens of stops in between. The trip had provided not one minute of comfort for him. He'd spent the entire journey in the company of old men, grizzled farts that made up the crews of oceangoing steamers these dangerous days. To a man, the crew disgusted him; never once did it cross his mind to take one. Thus, he supposed, the rampage since his arrival on solid ground. Or maybe it was just that America was bigger, better, more spread out. Full of opportunity for every twist of mind and soul.

But beyond that he couldn't explain it. And soon enough, he gave up trying.

IT WAS TRUE THAT HE ATTENDED A SPECIAL agents' school at Klopstock Pension, Hamburg. But Hamburg was not a lovely place these days, and he got to see very little of it anyway, as he'd been locked up in a cell for the entire three-week training period. Any lessons the Gestapo instructors chose to teach him took place inside his cell with no less than four armed guards looking in on him, twenty-four hours a day.

Most of what his handlers passed on to him had to do with surviving in a strange country with the possibility of police curiosity always within the next step—things that Skass knew very well anyway. He'd received some basic gun training, which was good, as he was awful with guns, and in fact hated them for the obscene way they violated flesh and bone. He was made aware of the intricacies of the American telephone system; undoubtedly he would have to make some long-distance calls during his stay. It was a procedure he had to know.

He'd been equipped with some standard tricks of the spy trade as well. In addition to two revolvers and the poison darts, he was given a box of wooden matches that were actually tiny pencils, a fountain pen with a hidden compartment to insert messages and a package of specially treated paper on which to write invisible correspondence. He was never sure exactly what he was supposed to do with these things—and no one ever really told him—but the point was moot. He'd lost all of them on the trip over.

He'd also been schooled in some American history, with a broad approach to baseball facts, which he immediately forgot. He learned some basic civics of American life: don't criticize, don't judge, don't ask too many questions. Above all, try to be friendly and approachable at all times. Again, these were things he was already an expert in.

His teachers had emphasized that American authorities, as opposed to those in Germany, were actually rather passive. They were not usually looking for trouble as many German police were. They were also characterized as being rather slow, especially in small towns and rural areas. In the event he fell into police custody, Skass was told two things: either cooperate fully while looking for the most likely means of escape, or, if possible, create a diversion and leave the area quickly. Unlike Germany too, the U.S. did not have an integrated crime reporting system. Nor did it have a national police. Each municipality operated independently, and this was to his advantage, his Gestapo handlers said. Should he get away from the local authorities and put more than fifty miles between himself and the point of his arrest in a few hours time, the chances the local authorities would find him were almost nil.

So be amiable, be low-key, be observant, know the local constabulary, and don't commit even the smallest of crimes. These were the points the instructors at Klopstock Pension had repeated to him over and over again.

Still, Skass chose to ignore them all.

The young couple in St. Louis he'd taken almost on a whim.

It was the wife he was after when he made a polite request for a ride from the bus station to the YMCA. But, impressed by his manners and humor, they'd invited him home for dinner, and then when he tried to leave, insisted on his staying over. That's when Skass knew he'd have to kill them, just so he could sleep that night. All it took was a bottle of wine and a knife from the carving table. The man went begging, his throat cut over the bathroom sink. The woman acquiesced to her rape, and the false promise that he would spare her. He dined on her for several hours before finally dozing off. She had tasted salty. Or maybe it was the wine.

Waking early the next morning, he didn't clean the house, didn't bother to hide anything. Instead he simply took the couple's car, another clear violation of his Gestapo handlers' orders, and continued driving west.

PART TWO

7

SOUTHEAST KANSAS

IT WAS GANG LEADER JAKE DENTON HIMSELF who once called the Kansas town of Carson Bend too small to rob.

The place was tiny, even by Midwest standards. Barely two hundred people lived here; the local cattle outnumbered them ten to one. Downtown was two square blocks with a dozen wooden structures, split right down the middle by little-used Route 99. Surrounded by high, flat, unending prairie, Carson Bend was literally the only place for a hundred miles around.

The town existed for only one reason: its small railway station. Basically a waiting room attached to a fuel tank, Carson Bend had rooted itself around this unimpressive rail stop back in 1852. Four trains still went through every day: two in the morning, two at night. Many were carrying troops these days, soldiers moving east from the west coast or west from the east. On the rare occasion a troop train would stop in Carson Bend for water or fuel, the citizens would gather to feed the soldiers doughnuts and coffee.

But most of the time, the trains just rumbled through and kept on going.

THIS PARTICULAR EVENING HAD ARRIVED HOT and dry. There were no clouds. No wind. The temperature was hovering near eighty. This was very unusual weather for Kansas; daily rain showers, or even snow showers, were more typical in mid-March. But the state hadn't seen any significant precipitation in six weeks. It was so dry around Carson Bend the range cows were showing their bones. The few birds in the area had flown away, and the crickets were getting extremely loud, especially at night. These signs were clear; another drought was on the way.

This was Saturday night and normally Carson Bend would have been locked up tight by six o'clock. But not tonight. People were in the streets and they weren't talking about skinny cows, birds, or crickets. They had congregated in front of the barbershop, near the bank, and on the steps to the saloon. Everyone seemed to be whispering. The town was abuzz with rumors.

It all began when two U.S. Army officers showed up, unannounced, the previous Thursday. They had taken rooms one street over from the railroad station at the Sunset Hotel. Later that day, the army men were spotted in Bee's Diner, the only restaurant in town, having a hushed conversation with the sheriff in the back booth. An hour later, Carson Bend's tiny fire brigade received orders to go on twenty-four–hour alert.

In a place where seeing more than three seed salesmen at once was an event, these were big doings. Eventually a preposterous story began making the rounds: A very important dignitary traveling by rail would be passing through Carson Bend early next week. This VIP's train was scheduled to stop briefly at the rail station to refuel. The military men were in town to direct security measures needed for the visit.

And who would be aboard this train? One name was on everybody's lips: President Roosevelt himself.

The sheriff, the army officers and the firemen spent all day Saturday denying that anything like this was in the offing. Still it was not such an unlikely scenario. Two of the President's grandchildren were known to be attending camp at Cheyenne Bottoms, Kansas, not three hundred miles to the west. They had traveled there by train two months before. Furthermore, the President was spending the week in Colorado, seeing to political affairs. So was the grandfather going to pick up his grandkids for the train ride back to Washington and stop in Carson Bend along the way?

As it turned out, that's exactly what was going to happen.

In fact, this presidential side trip had been in the planning for months.

THE OFFICIAL WORD CAME LATER THAT NIGHT, long after the crowd downtown had drifted home. A phone call around eleven o'clock woke the town's only newspaper reporter. It was from the sheriff. He suggested the reporter come over to the fire station right away.

The reporter arrived to find the sheriff, his deputy, the visiting army officers and the entire thirteen-man fire brigade on hand. The army men sat him down, made him sign a loyalty oath and then let him in on the secret: President Roosevelt's train was indeed going to pass through Carson Bend on Monday, now only a day away. It would stop at the railway station just long enough to top off its fuel tanks, take on water and then depart. Approximate length of stay: six minutes. And while there were no guarantees, there was a chance the President would acknowledge any townspeople who came out to see him.

The army officers told the reporter he could release the story on the impending visit in the next day's edition of the town's tiny newspaper, the *Prairie News*. There would be restrictions though. The Wartime Powers Act allowed the army to impose complete secrecy surrounding the President's movements. So, in this case, only the *Prairie News* could run the story. No other newspaper in the state would even be told of the visit, not even in the capital, Topeka. This meant the *Prairie News* reporter would not be permitted to make his daily farm reports to various newspapers around the state. Just to make sure the news blackout stayed in place, the military men had already disconnected the town's long-distance telephone switchboard and had impounded the post office's telegraph key. For the next forty-eight hours, no news of any kind would be allowed out of Carson Bend.

The reporter agreed to all the conditions and scampered off to do his work. Five hours later, the *Prairie News* hit the street with a special Sunday edition announcing the big story.

By the end of early church services that morning, most of the town had heard about the presidential visit. By noon everyone else had too.

Including Harry Strum.

STRUM WAS THE RICHEST MAN IN CARSON Bend.

He owned the bank, the feed bin, the drugstore and the Hi-Lo filling station. He held the mortgages on just about every house in town and his 1939 Cadillac Fleetwood was equipped with the only air conditioner this side of St. Louis.

A squat man with soft features and little facial hair, Strum had an old-lady look about him. Still a bachelor at fifty, he lived with his four cats in a big Gothic-style house on North Hill, the closest Carson Bend had to a fashionable part of town.

There were two things everyone knew about Harry Strum: he loved money and hated people. He was said to be worth at least eighty thousand dollars, yet he had no friends, no relatives, not even any mild acquaintances. The fence that surrounded his grand house was widely assumed to be electrified to ward off any intruders. There were supposed to be special hiding places in his basement and attic as well. Most people in town knew him only by curt nods whenever they met on the street, which wasn't very often. Even at the bank he kept to himself, arriving before dawn every day and running things from behind a locked office door, just him and his cats.

It was well known that Strum had bought his way out of the draft in World War One, using money left to him by his wealthy father. So not a Halloween went by when someone didn't sneak up to North Hill and throw a dead chicken up on his lawn or paint a long yellow streak across the bank's front window. The citizens of Carson Bend could never be accused of having short memories.

For the most part though, the townspeople tried to avoid Strum—and he went out of his way to avoid them. It was an accommodation that worked for both sides.

STRUM FIRST LEARNED OF THE PRESIDENTIAL visit when he drove downtown just before noon on Sunday.

He found the main street awash in red, white and blue bunting. The rail station was blocked off by some ancient hitching posts. Store owners were sweeping their sidewalks, cleaning their windows, painting their doorways. The people in the street seemed inordinately jovial, yet just about everyone was carrying a gun. And there was a huge crowd inside the jailhouse. And American flags were flying everywhere.

Strum had no idea what was going on. Certainly the war wasn't over. Or was it?

He pulled up in front of Pearson's newsstand and went in to wordlessly retrieve his reserved copy of the *Chicago Tribune*. That's when he saw the headline in the *Prairie News*, screaming in twenty-bold type: FDR TO VISIT CARSON BEND!

He quickly read the story—the words came off the page like daggers to his heart. Stunned for a moment, Strum finally paid for his paper, hurried back to his car, and roared away. Real spy work makes you want to crap your pants a lot, someone once told him. That's how Harry Strum felt right now.

Though the citizens of Carson Bend attributed Strum's unneighborly behavior to greedy eccentricity, this was only partially true. Strum had something else to hide: he too was a German operative, a so-called "Z-agent." His code name was Hourglass Six. He'd been working for the *Reich* since 1938.

Strum was not a Nazi; he didn't have to be. It was a simple quirk of geography that made him valuable to the Germans. Carson Bend lay 117 miles north of Wichita, site of the Boeing Air Works, one of the largest bomber manufacturing plants in America. This huge facility had been churning out *Flying Fortresses* since the war's beginning. Strum's regular assignment was to drive down to Wichita once a month and spend a few days counting the number of B-17's lined up on Boeing's production ramp ways. For reporting that figure back to his contact in Havana, he received twenty-five dollars. Like many U.S. citizens who had gone to work for the Germans, Harry Strum was in it strictly for the money. And his cover was near perfect. Who would ever suspect the richest man in town of selling out his country for a measly twenty-five bucks a month?

Other than his observations down in Wichita though, Strum's espionage activities had been nonexistent. He was told four years before that if he was ever needed for anything further, the *Reich* would be in touch. What was troubling him now as he drove at high speed back up North Hill was he'd received just such a message three weeks before. It came in a package mailed to him from Havana. Inside was a booklet of postcards, supposedly from a cousin visiting the Isle of Pines, and a magazine, printed in Spanish, extolling the virtues of Cuban sugarcane.

It was the magazine that held the secret message for Strum. To the casual eye, nothing would have seemed amiss about the publication. But by holding each page up to the light, a pattern of pinpricks emerged in certain letters within the text. It was simple really. Put together all the letters with the pinholes in them and you had your message.

It took Strum a few hours to write down and arrange the several hundred letters into an understandable form. When completed, the directive told him that another mission was being planned for him and that he should stand by for further instructions. At the time, Strum had been excited by the news. Obviously if his handlers wanted him to do more than ride down to Wichita and count planes once a month, that would mean more money for him.

But with this rather incredible news that the President was coming to Carson Bend, Strum's stomach had turned to rock. Of course his pending assignment had something to do with this presidential layover. It would have been too much of a coincidence if it did not. Courage and steely nerves were not his long suits; his handlers knew this because he had told them at the beginning he wasn't interested in any heroics, just in making money.

So what exactly did the Germans have in mind for him?

ONCE HE ARRIVED HOME, STRUM LOCKED every door and window in his house. And while it was not true that his property was electrified, burglar alarms were installed at every means of entry. He activated all of these devices now with haste. Then he pulled all his shades and sat in his darkened living room, alone.

He thought locking himself away from the world might settle his anxiety, but he was mistaken. It only gave him more time to think. Up to this point, the spy game had been easy to play. Drive down south for a few days, count aircraft on a runway, make a phone call to Havana, collect twenty-five dollars. He was well aware he could be shot for these enterprises, but it all seemed so unlikely that he'd ever get caught, he chose not to dwell on the downside. But getting mixed up with this presidential thing? He wanted no part of it.

Panic, his constant companion, began to set in. He left his chair and for the next four hours scoured his house for any evidence that might link him to the Nazis. He'd foolishly saved all the envelopes in which he'd received payments from his Havana contact over the years. Wrapped in a rubber band inside a drawer in his desk, he took them to the stove and burned each one of them individually to ash. Then he mixed the ashes with the last of his kerosene ration and burned them in a bucket outside his back door. Then he buried the remains.

Next he destroyed seventeen notebooks he'd filled with meticulous, overly ambitious observations down at the Boeing plant. These books were like his children, they were the history of his ill-gotten money. But he knew they had to go. Too big to fit in his stove, they went into the furnace with a shovelful of coal.

Then began a long search for any *indirect* links with the *Reich*. He went through his library and took down any book even remotely Germanic. *Travels Through Northern Europe. Prussian Influence on Viennese Poetry.* A book on Fritz Lang. Everything had to go. Even his Lindbergh books. This burning took place in the furnace as well. Four shovels of coal and a cup of precious gasoline did the trick.

It was evening by the time he'd sanitized the house to his satisfaction. Gradually Strum began to calm down. He made himself a sandwich and heated up some milk. Settled into his living room chair again, he bathed his forehead with ice cubes and felt his stomach slowly unwind. Maybe he was reading this thing all wrong. Just because Roosevelt's train was passing through town, that didn't absolutely mean his German handlers were planning an assignment connected to it, did it? It *could* all be a coincidence. If he could just make it through the next twenty-four hours and let the damn train go by, maybe he'd swear off the cloak and dagger stuff for a while. Or maybe not.

His mind somewhat eased, he took off his glasses and

leaned back in his chair. Outside, the crickets were in full chorus. A warm wind blew in his window. It almost felt like summertime. He began to doze off.

The siren woke him a minute later.

THIS WAS NOT THE TOWN′S PUNY FIRE SIGNAL going off. This was a patrol-car siren, coming up the hill, from the direction of town. Strum was out of his seat like a shot. His panic returned.

How did they find out?

He began running through the house, foolishly dousing every light, at the same time realizing this was probably the worst thing he could do. By the time he got back to his living room window, the patrol car had stopped in front of his house and two men had emerged. One was the sheriff of Carson Bend, Clay Boone. The other was his deputy, Sammy Silk. They looked up at his house and drew their guns. Strum shrank back from the window.

He was caught.

Next came the stomping up his front steps, then the doorbell rang. Strum nearly fainted. He reached for his cats, but they were long gone. The bell rang again. He somehow mustered the strength to shut off the alarms and open the door.

"Officers? Is there something wrong . . . ?"

The lawmen stared back at him for a long moment. Boone was the older, more powerful looking of the two. Early forties, rugged but pleasant face, with a bit of Gary Cooper around the eyes. He was a real cowboy. Deputy Silk was not. He was smaller, younger, darker, and nowhere as handsome. The proverbial ninety-pound weakling. Silk held the distinction of being the only Jew in Carson Bend. Strum did not care for him.

Both men were wearing dark green uniforms with strap holsters crossing their chests and cowboy hats pulled low over their eyes. Their pistols glinted in Strum's front porch light.

"Anyone been acting suspicious up here tonight, Mr. Strum?" Boone asked him.

Strum was frozen in place. He could barely speak. "What do you mean, 'suspicious'?" he croaked.

Silk spoke up: "There's a drifter in the area. He stole some stuff in town, then he might have headed up this way."

Strum was so immediately relieved, he nearly did crap his pants. These men weren't here for him.

"A drifter?" he began stuttering. "Way up here?"

"May we search your backyard?" Boone asked.

Strum smiled thinly. "By all means . . ."

The lawmen went off the porch and circled around back. Strum hurried through the house, scattering his perfidious cats to the cellar. He went out the back door, locking it behind him.

The lawmen were inspecting his shed. The structure was big enough to house Strum's car, his garden tools, and a little-used workbench, with more room to spare. They played their dull beams through the small windows and between the cracks in the door, but found nothing. Silk left to search a tiny patch of old cornstalks nearby. Boone went into the shed itself and played his light up to the tiny attic. Strum was a few steps behind him.

"What's happened, Sheriff? Can you tell me?"

"Mam's grocery store was broke into around four this afternoon," Boone replied. "Somebody swiped some food. Then, about a half hour ago, a stranger was spotted coming up this way, climbing over the sage hill."

"Is that right?" Strum replied, taking a long look at the sheriff. For a moment, he thought he detected alcohol on the lawman's breath.

"Well, these drifters come and go, isn't that right, Sheriff?"

Boone did not reply. He looked a bit distracted, but not in a bad way.

"But in any case," Strum went on, "I'll be sure to double lock my doors and windows."

Boone put his light right up in Strum's puffy face. The sheriff's eyes were very bleary.

"Please do that," he told Strum.

Deputy Silk walked up and both lawmen moved toward the front of the house. Strum went back inside and indeed locked all his doors again. Then he coaxed his cats out of hiding and watched from his darkened bedroom as the two lawmen slowly moved down the street, Silk in the patrol car, Boone on foot, searching the road on either side of them.

Only after the patrol car disappeared down the hill did Strum's heart rate return to normal. He waited another ten minutes, not moving. Finally he went downstairs, rearmed his alarms, poured himself a thimble glass of sherry and gulped it down. Then he collapsed into his chair, his cats taking up sentry positions around him. It was his second panic of the day and the twin episodes had left him exhausted. He closed his eyes.

Strange about Boone, he mused sleepily. He'd never thought of the sheriff as someone who drank on the job . . .

That's when Strum heard a footstep out in his hallway. He opened his eyes to discover a man had walked into his living room and was standing not five feet away from him. He was tall, blond, with wire-rim glasses and very dirty fingernails. It was as if he'd appeared out of nowhere.

He was holding a copy of *LIFE* magazine to his chest.

"I particularly liked this issue," he said to Strum. "Didn't you?"

8

LATER THAT EVENING

IT WAS JUST PAST TEN O'CLOCK WHEN THE small convoy of military vehicles rolled into Carson Bend.

The three troop trucks were carrying a twenty-six–man detachment from the Kansas National Guard 1st Division, stationed in Madison, 130 miles to the west. These soldiers were not regular army. They were standbys and second reservists, men who for various reasons had not been sent overseas, and now, never would be. This was as far away from Madison most of them had been since the war started.

The soldiers were in Carson Bend ostensibly to provide security for the President's six-minute layover. They were equipped with M1 rifles, but the weapons were not loaded. Nor were the soldiers carrying ammunition. The presidential security detail forbade live rounds within five hundred yards of the chief executive unless specifically authorized. Only the lieutenant in charge of the National Guard detail had access to a loaded gun, but he kept it locked inside the jeep's tire repair kit. So really, the soldiers were here to perform as a presidential honor guard and nothing more.

They were met at the town hall by the mayor. The military vehicles followed his car to a field about two hundred yards west of the train station, a place called Neshowa Bluff. The troops disembarked and set up pup tents, using their trucks' headlamps for illumination. Once camp was set, they dined on pie and coffee, courtesy of Bee's Diner.

When this late chow was concluded, two soldiers were selected by the lieutenant to stand watch over the trucks and equipment. The rest of the men were told to go to sleep.

THE REPORTER FOR THE *PRAIRIE NEWS* ARRIVED at the encampment about ten-thirty.

He was Dan Rush. Twenty-five years old and newly married, a palsied knee had kept him out of the service, but four of his brothers were scattered all over the Pacific. Rush had a brief talk with the detachment's lieutenant. He told the officer he was gathering information for stories he planned to do twenty-four hours after the President's train left town. Interviewing the guardsmen from Madison seemed like the natural thing to do. The lieutenant agreed to let him talk to the pair of soldiers on watch.

They were Leo Olsen and Ernie Dowd, both privates, both blessed with flat feet. The soldiers were sitting with their legs over the edge of the bluff, joshing and laughing. They looked like characters from a Bill Maudlin cartoon, right down to the faded green uniforms, dented helmets and the day-old beards.

They had set up a portable radio and were listening to dance band music. It was loud and heavy with tremolo. The lieutenant approached them, Rush a few steps behind.

"This guy from the newspaper wants to do a story on you dopes," the lieutenant told the soldiers.

"Go on!" Dowd yelled back at the lieutenant. "Us?"

"Yeah, why us?" Olsen asked.

"Because you're the only ones still awake," the officer replied. "That's if anyone can sleep with that racket on . . ." He nodded toward the radio.

"Man, you got to get with it, lieutenant," Dowd said, snapping his fingers to the music. "That ain't racket. That's Jimmy Dorsey . . ."

The officer reached over and snapped off the radio. Suddenly the night air was filled with a symphony of crickets.

"Look, just try to sound intelligent for this man," the lieutenant told the soldiers. Then he turned to Rush. "Feel free to push either one of them off this cliff at any time."

With that, the lieutenant disappeared back into his tent. Rush walked over to the soldiers.

"Whadda ya know, guys?" he asked them.

"You heard the looie," Olsen replied. "We don't know from nothing."

Rush sat down next to them, letting his legs dangle over the side of the bluff as well. It was a clear night, still warm, moonless, cloudless with a great wash of stars overhead. The valley spread before them looked spectacular. The Neshowa Bluff was one of the highest points for miles around. It looked out on a great plain that stretched from Emporia in the north, down to Taterville in the south.

"Best view in Kansas," Rush told them.

"No argument there," Dowd drawled.

Rush took out his notebook and asked the men their opinion on serving as part of the President's honor guard. Both replied it was a privilege, though they'd only been told about their assignment shortly before arriving in Carson Bend. He prodded them, but that's really all they had to say about the matter.

Not much of a story there. Rush changed the subject.

"Well men, the war is almost over, and you two will probably not see action after all. Does that bother you?"

"I feel bad about not going overseas," Olsen admitted.

"Ditto," Dowd added.

"But," Olsen went on. "I think twenty years from now, I'll be sure glad I didn't."

"Double ditto," Dowd agreed.

"What do you hear from overseas?" Rush asked them. "Any news from relatives? Friends?"

"My uncle is in a supply dump somewhere in Belgium," Dowd said. "He wrote and said the army is going to have so much damn equipment left over when the war ends, they'll have to sell all of it to us civilians. Jeeps, tanks, airplanes. Real cheap, too. Like fifty bucks for a tank. I can't wait to buy myself a Sherman."

Olsen just laughed at him. "What are you going to do with a Sherman tank, Ernie? Shoot gophers?"

"No, I'm gonna plow my fields with it, clear my woods . . ."

"And an airplane? Want one of those too?"

"Sure, for crop dusting . . ."

Olsen laughed again. "You can't even drive a jeep, never mind a tank or an airplane."

"You'll see wise guy," Olsen said. "What about you, Mr. Reporter. Ever want to drive a tank? Or deliver newspapers from a P-51?"

But Rush wasn't paying attention. He was staring at a strange light that had appeared in the sky. It was bright red, neon almost, and moving about forty-five degrees above the western horizon. It seemed to be coming right at them.

"Wow, what is *that*?" he asked, pointing to the glowing object. Both soldiers saw it too.

"Probably a B-17 taking off from Boeing," Dowd said.

"No—I've seen plenty of B-17's fly over," Rush told him. "They don't look like that . . ."

The red light was getting closer.

"Man, that thing is really moving," Olsen said. "Maybe it's a secret weapon or . . ."

Suddenly the red light shot right over their heads and then went straight up. In less than two seconds, it disappeared amongst the stars.

"Well, I'll be damned . . ." Rush whispered. "That must have been a comet or something."

"Seeing a comet brings real bad luck," Dowd told them. "That's what my grandmother used to say. It's an omen that someone famous is about to die. Ain't that right, Leo?"

"Comets don't go straight up," Olsen said gravely.

They were quiet for a few moments; Rush had heard of people seeing strange things in the sky over this part of Kansas, but he'd never believed them, until now. He took out his pack of Camels, offered one to each soldier and lit them up. All three were still searching the sky above them looking for any sign of the strange object.

"Now that you mention it, I did hear an interesting thing from overseas," Olsen finally said, letting out a long stream of smoke. "My cousin just got back from France. He said before he left, all the talk over there was that we were linking up with Germans. To fight the Russians."

Dowd looked over at Olsen like he was a man from outer space.

"What did you just say?" he asked him.

Olsen repeated his claim and added: "He says we're not hitting the Germans so hard anymore so they can throw everything they got against the Russians on the eastern front."

Dowd was incredulous.

"Are you crazy?" he asked Olsen.

"Just telling you that's the word over there."

"That the U.S. Army is teaming up with the Nazis?"

"Yes."

"To fight the Russians?"

"Yes . . ."

Dowd looked over at Rush. "Can you believe this guy? Four years of high school, three years in the guard and he *still* doesn't know his history?"

"Actually this would be current events, I think," Rush corrected him.

"Well, he doesn't know that either," Dowd said.

He turned back to Olsen. "Let me educate you, my very dopey friend. The Russians are our allies. They're on *our* side. The Germans, also known as the Krauts, are the bad guys. They're the ones trying to take over the world. Now the way a war goes is like this: we've been killing them faster than they've been killing us. That means we are *winning* the war. Does the pea in your skull understand that?"

Olsen just shrugged and puffed on his Camel.

Dowd went on: "OK, good. Now, do you think after four years of us battling the Krauts that any good American would want to get buddy-buddy with them? I'd almost go so far as to say that no one in our government would even want to talk to a Nazi—converse with one, like when they finally surrender—without pulling out a gun and shooting the son of a bitch right between the eyes. With all the misery they've caused? To do anything less would be treason."

He reached over and, with a wink to Rush, knocked on the side of Olsen's helmet.

"Hello? Is there anything in there?" he began calling in his friend's ear. "Why in the world would we turn around, team up with our enemy and fight one of our friends?"

Olsen just shrugged again and flipped his expended smoke off the side of the bluff.

"Because things change," was all he said.

9

THE CARSON BEND FIREHOUSE WAS THE OLD-
est building in town.

It was built in the late 1760's, nearly a century before
the railway station, as a way point for intrepid explorers.
It was a simple two-story structure, all wood, with a pronounced lean to the east. After it had been made into a
fire hall, the second level was used as a hayloft where
feed was stored for fire horses. The loft was dark and
empty these days, home to bats, rodents and God knows
what else. No human had been up in the belfry this century, so the fire chief claimed, the guano was that bad.

The first floor of the firehouse was not much better.
The creaky planking was just big enough to hold the
town's Mack pumper, plus a century-old hand tub. The
truck bay smelled of oil, grease, old hay, horseshit and
rubber. Even cigarette smoke could not dull the combined
odor.

So just why the army selected the firehouse to hold the
planning sessions for the presidential visit, no one really
knew; it was at the exact opposite end of town, the farthest
building from the rail station. Nor was it ever explained
why these meetings had to be held so late at night. But
on this evening, one last gathering had been called by the
army. They wanted to brief the town officials on the final
details of the President's visit.

SHERIFF BOONE AND DEPUTY SILK WERE THE
first ones to arrive for this meeting. Both had been work-

ing since early that morning. Silk was tired and sweating. Boone was as high as a kite.

Like just about everyone else in town, Boone had been anticipating the presidential roll-through since first learning about it. Up to that point, he had led a very ordinary life. In his 43 years, he'd never traveled more than 150 miles away from Carson Bend. Short of shaking hands with the Almighty himself, Boone couldn't imagine any other day being more exciting than the one coming up.

The day he'd just completed had been a strange one though; as if nature had to throw him a curve ball before he could have some real fun. It began when he woke up with a terrible head cold. It had come on him literally overnight. His wife, a traveling nurse and former Miss Dairy Queen of southeast Kansas, left him a bottle of Paracol cough medicine before going off to work Sunday duty down in Wichita County. She'd left instructions for him to take two spoonfuls after breakfast and then again after lunch. Unfortunately, Boone didn't know the difference between a teaspoon and a tablespoon and wound up consuming one third of the bottle after breakfast. Paracol is a morphine-based medication. He drove the half mile to town without a problem. But after he climbed out of his patrol car, it felt like his feet never touched the ground again.

He skipped church services and instead gave the patrol car its best wax job ever. Then came the search in the very musty basement of city hall for barricades that could be used to close off both ends of the rail station once the President's train had arrived. What they found were a couple of old hitching posts, long wooden shaved poles that looked terrible and were twice as big and twice as thick as needed to do the job. Still, the army demanded the train station be secure on both sides, so Boone and his deputy set them up and slapped some red, white, and blue bunting around them, in hopes they'd blend in.

At nine o'clock, after church had let out, the mandatory weapons roundup began. As ordered by the army, all citizens had to bring their guns to the jailhouse where they would be held until the presidential train left town. The problem was just about everyone in Carson Bend owned more than one gun, lots of folks had many. By five minutes past nine, the tiny jailhouse was overflowing with guns and people. Boone and his deputy were quickly overwhelmed just trying to make space for them all. Moreover, each weapon had to be tagged, assigned a number, have a lengthy army receipt filled out in triplicate, and then a handwritten deposit slip filled out by the owner.

The process of documenting the townspeople's firearms took much longer than anyone could have guessed. Noon-time came and they were still inventorying guns. Boone could not complain though. He drank another third of the cough medicine for lunch and let the next few hours just float away.

The weapons tally finally ended around four. By this time the lawmen were nesting a small arsenal of shotguns, hunting rifles and revolvers. Boone's plans were to go home, warm the dinner his wife left for him, then sleep for two hours before coming back for his late shift. Silk planned to sack out inside the jail itself. But minutes before they were to go off duty came the news of the break-in at Mam's grocery, brought to them by Mam herself, who burst into the jailhouse demanding her gun back. Boone just couldn't believe it; it was almost as if the Paracol was playing tricks on him. What were the chances that on its busiest day since the Denton Gang rode through some twelve years before, Carson Bend would experience its first ever storebreak?

It was true that drifters passed through town on occasion, much less now then during the Dust Bowl years a decade before. It was not unknown for these lonely travelers to filch a loaf of bread when Mam pretended she wasn't looking. But usually they would get right back out on the road again and move on.

The incident at the town's grocery wasn't that simple.

The store's back door had been jimmied right off its hinges by someone using a sharp instrument, its thick glass window breaking in the process. And while the thief had access to twenty-odd shelves stocked with food, only a cake of pepperbread and some sour pickles were taken—this, even though a cigar box full of money was sitting wide open in plain view. Even more baffling, the break-in occurred in broad daylight, while the street right out front was filled with people cleaning, decorating and hanging about. Yet no one saw or heard anything. It was all very odd.

Boone and Silk feared that if the army found out about the small crime, it would nix the President's train from stopping in town. With all the hard work and excitement going on, that would have been a disaster. So the two lawmen spent their dinner hours searching every unoccupied building in town and beating the thistle patches along the highway for a half mile in both directions, trying to find the curious burglar. But to no success.

Even though he hadn't coughed in more than twelve hours, Boone drank the last of the Paracol around six, washing it down with a cup of very strong coffee. Night fell, the second shift started, and then came the report of a stranger climbing over the sage heading toward North Hill. Boone and Silk raced to the scene and conducted their search, then beat the thistle all the way back down to town again.

But nothing was ever found.

THAT'S WHY BOONE AND SILK WERE THE FIRST to arrive for the firehouse meeting. By the time they had given up on their fruitless search, it was 10:45—too late to do anything else. So they drank stale coffee and tried not to breathe too deeply as the others drifted into the station house meeting: the lead army officer, the head of the Boy Scout troop, the mayor, and finally the fire chief himself.

The officer in charge of the presidential advance party was a major named Alvin Pusser. He was a tall, sunburned Georgian, regular army and pleasant enough. But he was a real by-the-book guy. So for the first thirty minutes of this red-eye gathering, he reread the policy paper for security measures pertaining to domestic presidential visits, citing regulations, chapters, and subheadings of the Wartime Powers Act. Had it not been for all the coffee and Paracol he'd ingested that day, Boone would have fallen asleep five minutes in. Truth was, he was still flying without wings.

Luckily, no mention of the break-in at Mam's was made by anyone. By eleven-thirty, Pusser finally got around to details. The President's train was still scheduled to arrive precisely at noon tomorrow and depart at 12:07. It was expected that at least two hundred people would be on hand, all of them crammed into the tiny railway station. This is where the crowd control would come in. A citizen's gallery would be cordoned off on the station's platform side. The National Guard troops would hold both sides of the tracks while the train was in the station. The thirteen-man fire brigade would form a line separating the citizens from the presidential carriage, which would be the last car on the train. The firemen would be told to turn out in full gear, in case one of the train's wheels became locked and a fire had to be extinguished.

Boone would anchor the firemen's line closest to where the end of the train would stop. Indeed, the President's carriage would come to rest right in front of him. The mayor would be at his side. Both men were told to hold a salute just in case the President should actually show himself from his window. The school band would be permitted to play as the train was entering the station and when it was leaving but not while it was standing still. The Boy Scouts would distribute small American flags to the crowd shortly before the train arrived; all citizens were expected to wave them enthusiastically.

As Pusser droned on, Deputy Silk began fidgeting in

his seat. Boone knew why. Everyone in the room had been given a job to do when the train arrived—everyone except Sammy. His name had not been mentioned at all.

Boone felt his buzz dull a bit. Sammy was a great guy. Solid, dependable, and a friend to just about everyone in town. He just happened to be the only Jew west of Topeka. Occasionally that worked against him. Now Boone could smell it coming sure as the first frost. The army was going to assign Sammy to some out-of-the-way post, just to keep him out of sight, and there wasn't much anyone could do about it. But Boone discovered the Paracol had given him an added shot of grit. He decided if Sammy got the shaft, he would refuse to cooperate with the army any further, no matter what the consequences might be. It was the least he could do for his colleague. Boone glanced around the fire hall and wondered if any of the others might be thinking the same thing.

But as it turned out, Major Pusser had a surprise for them.

Once the army officer finished reading his briefing document, he took off his glasses and let his eyes fall on the slight deputy.

"You are Samuel Silk?" he asked.

The deputy nodded uncertainly.

Pusser glanced back at his notes. "Well, it appears we have a special assignment for you."

Here it comes, thought Boone.

"Deputy Silk," Pusser drawled. "It seems you've been chosen to meet the President himself."

Six sets of eyes stared back at Pusser. *What did he just say?*

The army officer explained: "The president's people want one of the citizens to meet Mr. Roosevelt during the stop—to present him with a carton of his favorite cigarettes. Yesterday we gave the Secret Service a list of names of everyone in town of voting age. Deputy Silk, you are the person they selected."

Silk looked over at Boone, then at Pusser. He was flab-
bergasted.

"But why me?" was all he could ask.

"You're Jewish, Mr. Silk," Pusser asked. "Correct?"

"I am . . ." Silk stammered. "But . . . I haven't been to
services . . . since . . ."

"Since he moved to Kansas," the fire chief said, to the
laughter of the others.

Silk laughed too. It was true though. There were no
synagogues within two hundred miles of him.

"Well, Mr. Roosevelt thinks it would be swell to get a
photo of you and him and the cigarettes—I guess as part
of some get-out-the-Jewish-vote thing," Pusser said. "But
it makes you a very lucky man. So I suggest you take a
bath, get a haircut, and press your uniform. Tomorrow is
going to be a big day for you."

Silk collapsed back into his chair, his face pale with
astonishment. He was smiling, but totally overwhelmed.
He whispered over to Boone: "I just hope they don't find
out I didn't vote for him."

That's when the mayor cleared his throat.

"Excuse me, Major, but really, don't you think it more
appropriate that *I* present the cigarettes to Mr. Roosevelt?"

Pusser asked: "And what heritage are you, Mayor?"

Now the mayor began sputtering. His name was Horst
Heindzschelt.

"I'm of German stock," he replied. It was the worst
thing he could have said.

Pusser grinned. "Any more questions?" he asked, giving them all a sly wink. Just about everyone around the
table winked back.

All except Boone.

His attention was elsewhere at the moment. He was
staring up into the rafters of the hayloft, squinting against
the darkness. Was he finally going nuts? Was the cough
medicine really playing tricks on him now?

Or was there a pair of eyes staring down at him from
the floor above?

He looked away. This was *too* crazy. The space from which the eyes seemed to be glowing was no more than two feet square, too small even for a child to crawl into. And who would be nutty enough to climb up into the old hayloft anyway, with all the bugs and rats and bat shit?

No, this was stupid, Boone told himself. He'd just finished a very long, strange day, and the cough syrup was now burning a hole in his brain. He rubbed his eyes, took a long, deep breath, and looked up again.

The eyes were gone.

10

CHURCH BELLS WERE RINGING.

That's what finally woke Harry Strum this clear Monday morning. Even before opening his eyes, he smiled; a rarity anytime of day. At that moment, caught in semi-slumber, Strum's body felt unusually warm. His mind was unnaturally at ease. He was unafraid, for a change.

He wished now that he hadn't burned his books. He wished he'd somehow avoided those few hours of semi-hysteria the day before. Everything was fine now. Willy was here. He only needed to shelter him for one night and the payment he would receive for his trouble would be substantial. Willy had told him so.

It was important that the *Reich* know where President Roosevelt was at any given moment. That's what all the hubbub was about. Willy was simply here in Carson Bend to do reconnaissance on FDR, just another set of eyes among many reporting along the way. Beyond that, it was all very top secret and Strum couldn't have cared less anyway.

"They aren't paying you enough to know any more," Willy had told him with a laugh. "But who knows? Someday, they might."

It was exactly the right thing to say. Nothing put Harry Strum more at ease than the promise of more money.

But something else had happened to him the night before. Something extraordinary. Something all his money could never have bought him. For the first time in his life, Strum had actually made a friend. And that's why he was feeling so different this morning.

As he recalled it now, he and Willy had sat out on the front porch, drinking wine from Strum's modest collection and talking. Just talking ... Willy was absolutely fascinating. Charming. Disarming. He loved cats, show tunes and Lindbergh. He spoke well not just of Germany, but of the United States too. As their words drifted up into the night, Strum felt almost a lifetime of anxiety slowly drain out of him. He was a kindred spirit with this very witty man. And they had so much in common. Strum had been raised by frugal, educated, loving parents. So had Willy. Strum had been misunderstood all his life. So had Willy. They got along so famously, they'd even made plans to tour Hamburg together once the war was over. A shooting star soaring overhead seemed to seal their newfound friendship. How strange it was that they should meet like this.

Strum yawned smugly now. He thought of the people down in Carson Bend, scrubbing their little windows and sweeping their ordinary dirt. *A coward? A man with no friends?* If they only knew.

But what time was it? He'd already counted fifteen peals from the church bells and they were still going strong. He finally rolled over and threw the blankets off him—only to discover something very unusual. He was naked. Now *this* was strange. Even on the hottest of nights, he always wore heavy pajamas. Why not last night?

He sat up—and suddenly his head began to hurt. Then his stomach. Then his lower extremities. The bells kept ringing, but now they were little hammers pounding on his skull.

He was hungover, badly. All the symptoms were there, they'd just been hiding until this moment. How much wine had they consumed last night? Strum couldn't remember—and that brought up a slight problem. Even the smallest glass of spirits tended to make him giddy. After three or more glasses, he tended to black out.

Maybe there had been more to last night than he could remember.

He got out of bed and painfully steadied himself. An odd smell seemed to be coming from downstairs. He took two small steps and stubbed his toe. Next to his bed he saw the empty wine bottles. They were scattered like bowling pins, six of them, just about all the wine he had. Strum's heart crashed. He had no memory of drinking *that* much. He sat down on the edge of the bed and put his hands to his head. More things were coming back to him, bit by bit.

Willy had left for a while, sometime around ten; Strum remembered looking at his watch on his way to the bathroom and returning to find his newfound friend had disappeared. But he was back soon enough. Then what happened? Did Willy show him a magical trick of some kind? Something involving rope?

Strum slowly got to his feet again and took another sniff. The crass scent of burnt food reached his nostrils again. It was coming from the kitchen, but what was it? Something had just been cooked. Burned to a crisp, in fact.

"Willy? Are you down there, my friend?"

Strum knew he should get properly dressed. He staggered over to the bureau, but again almost tripped over something. At the foot of his bed were two neatly folded white towels. Beside them was the biggest kitchen knife he owned.

Then Strum looked at his right wrist and saw there was discoloration running across it. He turned his hand over—the red raised mark went around it. Suddenly it began to burn and sting. He examined his left wrist. The same scraped-raw ring was there too.

"Willy? Are you awake yet, old man?"

He looked at his wrists again. *Rope burns.* It was a rope trick—he remembered now. At some point, Willy had tied him to the bed. As part of a game. Strum looked back down at the knife. But how was *that* involved?

He got another whiff of burning meat.

"Willy, old man? Is that breakfast you're cooking? I'm not much of a breakfast man, really . . ."

Strum nervously put on a shirt and socks and ran a hand through his very thin hair. The church bells never stopped ringing. He looked at the bureau clock.

My God, he whispered. It was nearly eleven-thirty. He never slept this late!

He left the bedroom, closing the door behind him. Inching his way down the hall, he peeked into the guest bedroom. His stomach did another flip. The bed was still made, straight and square, just as he had prepared it. He could tell it hadn't been slept in at all.

Strum gulped hard. "Say, Willy, you wanted to be in town this morning, I thought? Forget the breakfast, I wouldn't want you to be late . . ."

Strum continued toward the back stairway. That's where he found the first clump of hay. It was wet, and wreaked of a musty smell. Another clump was on the top step of the back stairway. Another, three steps below. They too smelled awful and very old. Why was there hay in his house? Had his kitties dug it up somewhere and brought it to him? That seemed unlikely. They'd never displayed any feline gift-giving instincts before, not even with the occasional dead mouse. And where were they anyhow?

Strum piled the straw neatly on the top step, then slowly went down the stairs and into the kitchen. The odor still lingering confirmed a recent meal preparation. The frying pan on the stove still held simmering gravy. The oven top was splattered with grease. A plate containing a pile of stringy meat and bones, a piece of pepperbread and a half-eaten pickle sat on the table. This was very peculiar. Strum was a strict vegetarian. He never kept meat in his house.

"Willy? Are you about, man? Did you go shopping this morning?"

No reply.

That's when Strum noticed an unidentifiable liquid leaking out of the bottom of his waste bucket. He walked over to it and lifted the lid.

The burnt remains of his youngest cat were lying at the bottom of the pail.

11

CARSON BEND WAS CROWDED AGAIN.

Two hundred people—all turned out in their Sunday best. All here to see Mr. Roosevelt. Main Street was a mess of hay trucks, cattle trucks, old jalopies and horse-drawn wagons. The sidewalks were filled with children. Playing guns, pulling balloons, up to mischief. Many were unattended. Different noises filled the small downtown. The hum of the crowd. The school band rehearsing, badly. The unmuffled engine of the fire truck. Above it all, kids screaming.

Sheriff Boone took it all in and asked himself: did this many people *really* live here?

He was standing on the railway platform, adjusting his hat in the reflection of the ticket window. It was now five minutes to noon.

The Paracol had given him strange dreams. Eyes, looking at him from his bedroom closet, from between the tiles in the ceiling, hovering outside his bedroom window. He had thrashed through the night, trying to get rid of them, and by dawn, they were gone. Now on this clear and beautiful morning, Boone felt great. His hair, known to be unruly at times, was set into place with Wildroot. His face was clean shaven like never before, courtesy of a new razor. His uniform jacket was smartly creased and fit perfectly. His chaps, high leather boots and headgear were all spiffy too. He looked a lot like the cop on the Burma Shave billboard.

As the seconds ticked down, many things were bouncing between his ears. Would there be another day as important as this one for the rest of his life? He doubted it. His wife was down in Wichita again; she would be just about the only citizen of Carson Bend to miss what was about to happen. This was his only real disappointment. Sammy Silk, hair freshly cut, body diligently washed, was more excited than Boone had ever seen anyone—he'd lost the deputy in the crowd a long time ago. The day was perfect. Not a cloud in the sky and the sun was so unusually warm, it felt like summer.

Boone had taken the time earlier that morning to practice his salute. It had to be as crisp and self-assured as the crease in his pants. He wanted it to say something. This piece of Kansas is covered, Mr. Roosevelt. With your world of problems, you do not have to worry about our little place. We are with you. That's what his mom and dad would have told him to do. They were both long gone now. But they would be proud of him this day. His wife too. He would make sure of that.

He checked his watch. Two minutes before noon. The church bells were pealing with more fervor now. Apparently no one had told the pastor when he could stop. Boone walked to his position at the far end of the platform. The mayor was already there, dressed in a morning coat, black pants, gray shoes and chaps. He had a top hat on and a wildflower in his boutonniere.

To their right and directly across the tracks from them were the National Guard soldiers, at attention, eyes straight, their unloaded guns resting on their shoulders. The firemen were in position as well, in raincoats and fire hats, their hoses and axes at the ready. The dozens of little American flags had been distributed; some people had stuck them in their hats as a place of convenience while waiting for high noon.

One minute to go. Boone and the mayor nodded to each other. The mayor tugged at his vest, trying to get it to completely cover his sizable stomach.

"Are you excited, Heinzie?" Boone asked him.

"Not any more than you, Sheriff," the mayor replied

through gritted teeth. "Just doing what I was elected to do."

Boone couldn't resist rubbing it in. "Well, I suppose Sammy is excited enough for both of us. Enough for the whole dang town, I'd say."

The mayor lost a bit more of his wind. "Yes, I suppose he is," he grumbled.

Boone checked his watch again. It was now noon exactly. A screech went through the town. All eyes turned left. The school band crashed into an unidentifiable song. Two hundred voices rose at once. Trailing a storm of smoke and dust behind it, the President's train was coming around the bend.

The racket only grew louder now. Boone's ears began hurting him. Standing up front, right on the edge of the railroad track, there was so much commotion, so much *confusion*, his senses just weren't used to it. Suddenly the train was right on top of him. The locomotive massive and black, wheels squealing painfully, steam and smoke venting everywhere, shiny, everything like brand new. The school band was assassinating "America, the Beautiful." The brass sounded like a person choking to death, the tin cymbals like razors across the throat. The crowd roared. Little flags were now like flowers blowing in an artificial wind. Just like that, the train was pulling into the station.

But then came another sound.

Above the train wheels. Above the crowd cheering.

Someone was screaming.

Boone turned away from the crowd and saw a young boy running toward him from the far side of the railway station. He was covered from head to toe with blood. Everything stood still for an instant. Was the Paracol coming back to haunt him again? Boone couldn't believe what he was seeing. His first thought was that the boy had somehow been hit by the train. But how could he be running then?

The youngster literally fell into the mayor's arms. He

was trying to shout up at them. He didn't seem hurt; he was just splattered with blood. So much so, neither man recognized him. The mayor was frozen to the spot. He didn't know what to do. Everyone else's eyes were on the just-arriving train.

Boone grabbed the boy by the shoulders. Only then did he realize the youngster was a Boy Scout, the blood had covered his uniform completely.

"What happened to you?"

"In the bin. *He's dead . . .*"

"Someone was hit by the locomotive?" Boone yelled at the young boy.

The scout began violently shaking his head—but he could not yell any louder. The train was making too much noise. All he could do was point. Tiny trembling fingers indicated the building next to the train platform, Hall's Granary.

Boone dropped the boy back into the mayor's arms and began running. Along the track, beside the steaming train, over kids, around old people, past the crowd altogether. He arrived with a skid at the front door of Hall's bin. Here he found two more terrified Boy Scouts being held away by Nat Stem, the Negro griddle man at Bee's.

Stem could not speak either. He could only nod toward the back loft. Boone drew his unloaded gun. The rumble of the train's engines filled the bin as it finally came to a halt. Three steps in, Boone saw the body.

It was hanging from a hay hook on the overhead beam. Naked, upside down, feet bound with rope, hands tied to the truss. Blood everywhere. Boone thought it was a hog at first. Gutted, its insides falling out, an animal someone had hung in the bin as a practical joke.

But then he looked into the face and dropped his gun to the floor. The eyes were wide open, so was the mouth. Tears, falling upside down, wet the heavy eyebrows and wrinkled the dark forehead. Boone knew this person.

It was Sammy Silk.

* * *

PRESIDENTIAL ASSISTANT GEORGIE STENSON hated trains. They were noisy, cramped, bumpy, and just plain uncomfortable, even this one.

As a result, he was as sick as a dog, and had been since the train left Denver nearly two days ago. His suit was rumpled, his shirt was stained. He had not had a decent bath in two days, and could not expect one for at least two more. Like almost every other presidential rail trip in the past year, this one had been a nightmare from the start.

The chief executive's train, *Lulabelle*, had left Denver six hours late the morning before, this because the President's new wheelchair turned out to be too wide for the train cars' narrow passageways. Getting a replacement chair took time. This meant they had to travel most of the way to Kansas at speeds higher than the Boss liked, he being a fan of slow leisurely train rides. Stenson's motion sickness began to set in soon thereafter.

The delay in Denver had put the presidential entourage in a foul mood. The whole schedule was out of whack. Picking up the Boss's two bratty grandkids had been a chore; neither one wanted to go back to Washington. To make matters worse, Harry Hopkins, the President's closest advisor, had disappeared.

Hopkins was a problem drinker and it was not unknown for him to go on a bat. He also had chronic stomach problems and late-night trips to the nearest hospital were not uncommon either. But many in the entourage believed Hopkins had gone somewhere else entirely.

Wherever he was, it was his job to run the entire show, and in his absence the workload had fallen on Stenson. He'd been forced to do such things as taste the presidential breakfast, bleach the presidential toilet, clean the presidential cigarette holders and comfort the presidential dog so he'd be able to do his business—on a moving train.

Stenson had stayed up late the night before, drinking by himself in his cramped cabin, hoping the alcohol would put him to sleep. It didn't. By eleven that morning, he was exhausted. By eleven-thirty, he was feeling nauseous from motion sickness.

Now it was noon and he had promised himself that as soon as they weren't moving anymore, he would go throw up. But just as the train ground to a halt in Carson Bend, Joe Mullen, the official traveling photographer, caught him going into the lavatory.

"Did you get the Jew his Luckies?" Mullen asked him.

Stenson just stared back at him. "Did I what?"

"The Jew? We need those smokes so we can take his picture with the Boss."

Stenson could only look back at him helplessly.

"The deputy sheriff?" Mullen persisted. "The heebie? The guy who is supposed to pass the Boss a carton of Lucky Strikes and get his picture took . . . didn't Hopkins set that up with you?"

Stenson started to shake his head no—but then it hit him.

"Damn, *is that here*?" he cried, looking out the train window. "I thought that was going to happen in Dodge City?"

Mullen just shook his head. "Jesus, Georgie, we went through Dodge five hours ago."

They stood there for a long second, speechless. Finally Mullen groaned: "Well, the army just left the guy alone back there and I've got to snap a picture of him and the Boss right now, and we have no goddamn Luckies. That's why I came up looking for you."

"Did you say he's back there alone?"

"Yeah, the Secret Service guy was in the crapper—and I couldn't wait any longer. What was I supposed to do? We're only staying here for six minutes."

Stenson just clamped his teeth together and prayed his stomach would not erupt. There was one cardinal rule among the President's entourage: never leave anyone alone with the Boss. Why? Because the Boss was a snob. He didn't converse well with the lowers and found it painful to make chitchat with any outsiders, especially a civilian.

"Jesus," Stenson moaned. "Hopkins will have my ass on a plate . . ."

He pushed past Mullen and began rushing toward the back of the train. Looking through the windows as they flashed by, Stenson could see only farmers in bad suits and fat women in huge dresses, waving flags and cheering. A rather pathetic sight.

He reached the outer door of the presidential cabin to find the Secret Service man had not yet returned to his post. The President's valet was missing as well. Stenson took a breath and composed himself. Then he knocked twice.

"Mr. President? George here, sir . . ."

There was no reply.

He knocked again.

"Mr. President?"

Still nothing.

He tried the door. It was locked.

Stenson felt something gurgle up inside him. This door was never locked. Where the hell was the Secret Service man? How long was he allowed to stay in the crapper?

At that moment, the President's valet appeared. Without a word, Stenson reached inside the man's breast pocket and came out with a set of keys. Then he told the valet to fetch the Secret Service agent immediately. Stenson found the right key and twisted it into the lock. The door to the President's carriage swung open. He looked inside.

The President was sitting on his couch, cape wrapped around him, head slumped forward. He was ashen and unmoving. He looked dead—but Stenson knew better. In fact, he let out a low whistle of relief. The President had fainted. It happened just about noontime every day of late. The only difference now was that he didn't have a bowl of soup under his nose.

Stenson began slowly backing up—a quick and silent

retreat was in order here. He would leave it to the valet to administer the smelling salts. But two steps back, Stenson collided with something. He spun around and was startled to see a man standing right behind him. He was dressed in an ill-fitting lawman's uniform, with a hat way too small teetering on his head. Stenson's first thought was that the man didn't look Jewish at all.

"Do you have the cigarettes?" the man asked Stenson.

Stenson just stared back at him. Where had this man come from? Had he followed Stenson into the presidential carriage? Or had he been in here all along?

"Sorry, there can't be a photo now," Stenson told him hastily. "Time has run out and you'll have to be going."

The man just smiled. Stenson began ushering him out the door. The valet had returned by now; right behind him, still buckling his pants, was the Secret Service agent. Stenson closed the door and then nodded to the agent. The train's whistle was blowing. They'd be leaving within seconds.

"I'll show you the way off," the agent said, leading the deputy away.

Stenson just shook his head and collapsed into the nearest chair. His upset stomach had returned.

"I'm really surprised by people these days," he said to the valet, rubbing his aching midsection. "None so much as that Jewish deputy. Obviously when he woke up this morning, he knew he was going to meet the President. You would have thought he'd put on a uniform that fit him better."

The valet nodded in faint agreement.

"Or at least taken a moment to clean his fingernails," he said.

SAMMY NEEDED ANOTHER UNIFORM. BUT which one?

Three of his deputy's uniforms were hanging inside the jailhouse closet. That's where Boone was right now, sweating a bit, squeezing between the stacks of guns, trying to ignore the incessant pounding on the jailhouse door.

Which one should he take? There was Sammy's winter uniform, a long-sleeved fleece shirt, heavy tie, heavy pants and a parka. But that seemed a bit too much for this warm April day. There was Sammy's summer uniform: short sleeve shirt, light field pants, no tie, no jacket. But it wasn't *that* hot yet. This left what Sammy called his "tweeners"—an untidy combination of a heavy shirt and thin trousers. Boone took this uniform. It would do nicely. He picked up a spare pair of Sammy's cowboy boots and headed back out the door.

A crowd was waiting for him on the sidewalk, maybe two dozen people in all. He knew every face.

"Can I help you, folks?" he asked them.

No one spoke.

"Is this official business?"

Again, no one replied.

"OK, then I have to go . . ."

He began to push his way through the crowd, when one man caught his arm.

"Sheriff? . . . Are you OK?"

Boone stopped and stared at the hand on his arm. He asked again: "*Is* this official business?"

The man let go.

"I guess it can wait," he said.

Boone grinned. "Thanks. I've got to get these clothes over to Sammy. Have you seen him? He's freezing."

Boone began walking again. Across Main Street, around the corner and over the tracks; the President's train was long gone by this time. People were parting the way for him as reached Hall's bin and turned into the entryway. He took a sniff of the air and smelled the scent of fresh blood. That's when he stopped dead in his tracks. He looked at the clothes he was holding—then flung them away as if they were carrying the plague. His heart began pounding, it felt like a balloon about the pop. The sun was so damn hot. It was sizzling, right over his head.

Sammy was dead.

Murdered.

Butchered . . .

Boone dropped to his knees. Then it finally came. Tears, coughing, his nose instantly full of snot. Five minutes in a state of shock was all he would get. Reality came crashing down on him like an anvil now. He knew his life would never be the same.

Someone helped him to his feet and leaned him against the entryway to Hall's bin. Boone wiped his eyes and felt like a complete fool. He looked next door to the railway station, to see just how many people were watching him. That's when he became aware of something. The railway station was empty. Most of the crowd, silent and horrified, had been moved more than a block away. The National Guard troops were aligned in a perfect semicircle in front of him, sealing off all approaches to the granary. The roads bordering the bin and the railroad station were blocked off by the old hitching posts. The fire brigade and Boy Scouts were holding all traffic away from the area.

What had happened here? This place had been a scene of chaos and madness just minutes before. But now it looked . . . well, *orderly*. The situation seemed under control. The immediate area had been transformed . . . into a crime scene.

But by who? Certainly not him.

Boone stepped into the granary's office to find Major Pusser, his face drained of color.

"Sheriff?" the major whispered urgently. "There's someone here you should meet."

He turned Boone around to face a man in a rumpled suit, wrinkled tie and battered fedora. His nose looked recently broken.

He was holding a gold-plated badge up to Boone's very bleary eyes.

"Special Agent Joe Copp," the man said. "FBI . . ."

PART THREE

12

LEO SPANK WAS SITTING IN BIG JIM'S CHAIR, RI-
fling through his boss's desk when Gertrude, the secretary,
walked in.

"Leo? What are you doing?"

Spank didn't even look up at her.

"What do you think I'm doing?" he barked, continuing
to rustle through the desk's drawers. "That bastard is hiding his smokes on me again . . ."

Gertrude reached down to Big Jim's overflowing IN
box, recovered a stale pack of Chesterfields, and tossed
them to Spank. He greedily lit one up, leaned back in the
chair, and blew a long stream of smoke out the open window toward sun-drenched Broadway beyond.

Happy now, Spank turned his attention back to Gertrude.

"OK, so . . . what is it?"

"Where's the boss, do you know?"

Spank shrugged. "Out, eating something, somewhere I
suppose. Why?"

She was holding a piece of yellow paper; Spank recognized it right away as a "Flash Brief," a message sent
via the Bureau's private telegraph system.

"Well, I just got the strangest message from Joe Copp,"
she said.

Spank stopped in the middle of his second drag.

"Copp?" he said with a gasp. "Joe Copp? Really . . ."

"Really . . ."

They hadn't heard hide or hair from Joe Copp in more than a week.

"Where the hell is he?"

Gertrude read over the flash message. "It says here he's in Kansas."

Spank smiled—this was a joke. "And he got caught in a tornado?" he asked her snidely. "With a little dog? And was kidnapped by midgets?"

But Gertrude wasn't sharing his humor. "No, this seems authentic. I mean, he sent it over the confidential wire, using the correct code sequences."

Spank shook his head in some disbelief. Both he and Big Jim had assumed that once they'd allowed Copp out of the office, the somewhat renegade agent had hightailed it for good.

"So, what does he have to say then?" Spank asked her. "What the hell is he doing in Kansas?"

Gertrude began reading directly from the flash message.

"He says that he's tracked down the killer of the White-meyer girl," she said. "He has him cornered in a place called Carson Bend, central Kansas. And that he's enlisted the townspeople and the National Guard . . ."

". . . the *National Guard*?" Spank roared.

"That's what it says," she replied. "He's enlisted townspeople and the National Guard to search for and apprehend the suspect. Then he says he had to cut this message short because he was sending it from the top of a tele-graph pole in the middle of a rainstorm."

Spank just stared back at her.

"And that's it? That's the end of the message?"

She nodded. "It just says: 'More later.' "

She handed the piece of paper to Spank and he read it over himself.

"Jessuz," Spank finally breathed. "I guess everything they said about this guy was true. I mean, we sent him out to New Jersey to show the badge a little bit—and he winds up in Kansas, for God's sake, federalizing the National Guard . . ."

He scanned the message again.

"The problem is, he's broken about a dozen Bureau regulations in the process . . . Big Jim will have a kitten when he sees this."

Gertrude inserted a stick of Beeman's gum into her mouth and started smacking it almost immediately.

"Well, I for one am glad that he's out of the office," she said. "I mean, he was a nice enough fellow. But he really made for a very lousy secretary."

IT WAS FINALLY RAINING IN CARSON BEND.

Dark storm clouds had swept over the tiny town shortly after noontime, seemingly dragged in place by the Presidential carriage and left behind to drown away everything that had happened here.

The sky had become so black, and the rains so heavy, that it was almost impossible to see for more than a few feet in any direction. The electricity had gone out, and a thick fog caused by the cold raindrops hitting the parched flatlands had enveloped the town as well. A strange night had fallen on Carson Bend, even though it was not yet one in the afternoon. The town had not seen a deluge like this in more than a hundred years.

Despite all this, Joe Copp was feeling better than he had in a very long time.

He was currently perched in the pulpit of the town's tiny church, smoking a cigarette, and looking out on a very wet congregation. Though he too was tired and dirty and his suit was rumpled beyond all help, for the first time in a long time, he felt like he was in control of the situation, and thus, in control of his life. It was a sensation he'd sorely missed.

By his order, most of the town's residents were now huddled in the church. Men up back, women and children down front, nearly two hundred people in all. Shocked, frightened, they'd been made deathly quiet by the gruesome turn of events that noontime. Many had seen the deputy's body, and those that hadn't had been told about it by those who had. There was no need for ghoulish exaggeration in those whisperings. The man had been gutted, his insides had spilled out onto the floor. It was enough horror to haunt the little town for years to come.

Yet even in their apprehensive state, a few of the townspeople had asked Joe for autographs. And he did not mind a bit giving them out. Why? Because deep inside he felt that he'd accomplished something that few people currently within the Bureau could have done. He had tracked Annie Whitemeyer's killer all the way from Jersey to here, a dot on the map in southeast Kansas, in less than a week's time.

That's why he'd signed the autographs with gusto. There was none of the fakery of Princeton going on here. He still had it. He had not lost his touch. He felt like a *real* G-man again.

And that was a damn good thing.

BUT *HOW* HAD HE DONE IT? HOW HAD HE FOL-lowed the killer halfway across the country?

By sticking to the methods he'd honed during his gang-busting days. Criminals always had a pattern and they always left a trail, as proved many times over by the Denton Gang and other no-goods Joe had chased. An investigator just had to be smart enough to look for the pattern and sniff for the trail. And hope for a little luck along the way.

Joe Copp's bit of luck came early, with the chance twist of the radio dial. It happened back in Princeton that rainy night a week ago, not two minutes after leaving the Whitemeyers' home. He'd switched stations on his car radio and caught a bulletin on the local Philadelphia news. A missing schoolgirl had been found murdered, her body unearthed near a train station down town. The *same* train station where the taxi from the Whitemeyer case had been abandoned.

Copp felt a jolt in the seat of his pants on hearing the news. Could there be a connection between the two cases? That kick in the ass told him yes. So instead of returning to Manhattan, he drove south, through the rain, right down to Philly, arriving at the local police precinct just after midnight. The third-watch Philly cops were astonished to see a G-man, of course, especially at that time of night. The usual round of handshakes and requests for autographs ensued. But Joe stayed around only long enough to look at the file on the schoolgirl's murder.

Just like Annie Whitemeyer, the victim had been dissected. Her organs had been removed with great precision. Bite marks were evident over most of the body. Large pieces of skin were also unaccounted for. It didn't take much more to convince him: the same hand had been at work.

He left the Philly police to dither with the killing and drove to the crime scene alone. He examined the shallow grave and its surroundings by the first light of dawn. Then he went to the nearby train station and started asking questions.

None of the railway employees on hand remembered seeing any suspicious characters lurking about the day the girl went missing. This came as no surprise to Copp. The killer had simply stepped onto the next train and vanished—just like Stringy Hatfield used to do. Copp studied the train station's weekly schedule. Backtracking to the approximate time of the girl's disappearance, the most likely means of the killer's escape had been a 10:58 A.M. express train . . . to Pittsburgh. Copp immediately began driving west.

It was in Altoona, halfway across Pennsylvania, when he stopped for gas and saw the newspaper headline: STEEL CITY YOUTH FOUND DISMEMBERED. The crime scene was a fleabag hotel on Pittsburgh's rough southside. Copp arrived just as night was falling; the first thing he noticed

was the bus station one block away from the murder site.
Again he introduced himself to the local cops, got what
he needed and went his own way. By the glow of his
flashlight, he found himself studying transit schedules
once more.

Fleeing criminals almost always headed either west or
south—this was another thing he'd learned during his
gang-busting days. The morning the Pittsburgh boy had
been killed, four buses had left the nearby depot. Of those,
only one was heading west—to St. Louis. Again, Copp
drove all night. He arrived in St. Louis the next morning
to find the newspapers full of the "hacking" deaths of a
young couple near the university.

Standing in a coffee shop, a powdered doughnut on his
lips, Copp's body shook upon seeing those headlines.
Two years of humiliation and counting paper clips had
not dulled him after all. He'd followed the right scent.

There was no turning back after that. Copp knew the
right thing to do was to call Big Jim and tell him what
he had done. But surely because of his past record, and
the fact that he'd been AWOL for the past three days, the
Bureau would have relieved him of the case right on the
spot. And by the time they'd revved up some other G-
man to look into the situation, the killer would be long
gone.

No, Joe knew if he had any chance to salvage what was
left of his career, not to mention his self-respect, he would
have to do this one alone.

Damn the rules . . .

But who was he chasing exactly? Certainly not a typical
killer. Copp had investigated many homicides over the
years and they usually fit into two categories: hot or cold.
Dead gangsters, for instance, had a certain coldness about
them. Wrong place, wrong time. Two bullets in the head.
End of story. However, many times passion ruled the murderous hand. During a coke raid in Detroit in '34, Copp
found a woman with exactly one hundred stab wounds in
her—ninety-nine in the crotch, one in her heart. No need

for a psychiatrist to figure that one out. Copp went directly
to the doorstep of her recently-jilted boyfriend and made
the quick arrest. Thus, a hot killing.

But Copp had never seen anything like this string of
murders. Annie Whitemeyer had been rendered so methodically. So expertly. So . . . *delicately*. The girl in
Philly had been taken the same way. After the first two
killings, Joe was sure he was tracking a mad surgeon, one
who was waylaying young girls and slicing them up. Pittsburgh changed this notion; apparently his doctor liked
killing young boys as well. Then, in St. Louis, the theory
got twisted again. The young couple, his neck slit, she
raped then cut apart—the doctor was indiscriminate. He
was neither hot nor cold. He was different.

But St. Louis also gave Copp what he sought most:
what the fancy pants at the Bureau called a modus operandi. To Joe, it was simply the pattern, the criminal's way
of doing things. His doctor seemed to be killing on a
timetable; at least one victim every three or four days.
Almost as if he needed to. Oddly, Copp knew the feeling.
In his younger days, he'd loved all things chocolate, but
knew eating too much was bad for his digestion. Still,
whenever he craved the taste, he would feed the urge and
get sick, only to start hungering for it again after seventy-
two hours or so. Was it the same for this killer? Did he
need to cut flesh and take it every few days, just as Joe
had needed his candy bars?

He didn't know. But at least he had his MO. Now he
needed a definite direction. The suspect was heading west;
that was pretty obvious. The trail of bodies practically
drew a line from New Jersey to St. Louis. But so far his
killings had been in large population areas. And there
weren't many large cities west of St. Louis. Or small ones
either. So where would the killer strike next? That question might've stumped a lesser investigator. But not Copp.
He knew the key to tracking a bad guy in this part of the
country came down to one thing: gasoline.

Getting enough gas and using it wisely was a way of life in the Midwest. With the long stretches of highways west of St. Louis, one could go only as far as the gasoline held out. It was not unusual to see cars abandoned by the roadside, fuel tanks dry, especially in these days of gas rationing. If the killer was still driving the murdered couple's car, then eventually he would need to stop for gasoline. It was as simple as that.

This meant the most important information Copp needed could be found at the filling stations along the way. But which one? Again, here's where his experience kicked in. Ten years before, Copp had chased the Denton Gang all over the Dakotas, Nebraska, and especially throughout Kansas. As a result, he knew every highway, every truck stop, every diner, and cow flea town on the map.

He knew every gas station too.

THE COUPLE'S CAR HAD FILLED UP AT A PLACE near Jefferson City, Missouri, along Route 50. This was about ninety-five miles west of St. Louis, what was considered a heavily traveled piece of road. Human instinct was to get gas not when the tank was almost dry, but when it reached the "low" mark. That usually meant a distance of between eighty and one hundred miles. This was another gem Joe had learned from his gang-chasing days.

Eighty-two miles farther west, the couple's car had appeared once again. This time at a Texaco station on Route 50, just outside Drexel, Missouri, which was located on the Kansas state line. Joe knew the place so well, the owner recognized him when he drove in. Another employee had actually pumped gas for the stolen car's driver, and thus there was no description Joe could get anytime soon. However the owner did know that the driver had left his place and had turned onto Old Route 7, heading into Kansas.

It was the break Joe needed. Old Route 7 was little more than a mail road. At best it was a roundabout way to get to Wichita.

And it had only one town anywhere close to it.

A place called Carson Bend.

JOE HAD FOUND THE COUPLE'S CAR ABANDONED about twenty miles outside town early that morning.

The driver had not left it alongside the road, rather he had parked it next to a cow barn some distance off the roadway. It was positioned in such a way, wheels turned all the way to the right, windows open, as to look like it belonged there. Joe found a bit a cleverness in this. This person was not someone who panicked easily.

He searched the car front to back, top to bottom, but found no blood, no evidence, no clues at all. All he could tell was that the car had probably been next to the barn for about a day or so and that its occupant had probably left on foot.

If this was so, there was only one place within a hundred miles he could have walked to.

JOE HAD TAKEN CONTROL OF THE CRIME SCENE minutes after arriving in Carson Bend.

Where most of the people saw horror in the killing of the deputy, Copp was simply seeing more of the same. The sight of a G-man so quickly on hand eased the situation considerably in those first few minutes after the body was discovered. Even the army officer, Major Pusser, was impressed and told Joe as much, shortly before he lit out of town.

It was now just minutes before one o'clock. The rain was coming down harder, and thunder was shaking the small church to its foundation. The town was in the process of being sealed off by the National Guard. As soon as Joe realized the soldiers were in town, he had federalized them—just like the old days—and sent them to set up road blocks on each of the four roads leading out of Carson Bend. Their standing orders were to stop anyone leaving town and hold them for questioning.

Was Joe still authorized to do such a thing? Without the OK from headquarters? He didn't know, and at that moment, he didn't care. The SWS office knew he was out here now—his treacherous shimmying of the slick telegraph pole had insured that. But it was still impossible to have a two-way conversation with them, so his instincts told him he had to take matters into his own hands and improvise.

He'd deputized the town's thirteen-man fire brigade and about a dozen World War One veterans as well. The vets were good people to have around. They usually knew how to handle a weapon and, having seen the horrors of a gun battle before, wouldn't get spooked at the first sight of blood. The firemen too were not as likely to shy away from a bloody encounter as might an ordinary citizen.

He'd given them all an oath, most of which he'd made up, and then sent them out to collect all of the townspeople.

Though it had been Joe's idea that all citizens come to the church for their own protection, he had another reason for giving this order. Past experience had told him that it was sometimes more interesting to see who *didn't* come to the party, than who did. He was waiting now for the last of the townspeople to be collected, then he and his posse would start looking for the killer in earnest.

JOE HAD DONE THIS KIND OF THING MANY TIMES before, of course. Manipulating local support to bring a dangerous criminal to justice was his forte in the old days. Usually, these operations were cut and dry. Get all innocents into a safe place, then look for the suspect, find him and give him a chance to surrender. If he doesn't agree, blast him to kingdom come.

But there was still one loose end in this one. It kept coming back to Copp every few minutes, and each time it sat a little bit longer in his stomach. It was a simple question really: Was it odd that the killer's latest horrific crime had taken place in Carson Bend just as the President's train was passing through?

The answer was yes, it was *very* odd. But Copp decided not to let this throw him. It was, he convinced himself, just a "parallelism," as his old Bureau instructor would have called it. A simple coincidence. A convergence of two random events, that seemed related, but probably were not. Such things popped up frequently in investigations. The criminal shot dead at the bank was the long-lost brother of the guy who installed the vault the man was robbing at the time of his demise. A woman run down in the street by a getaway car was a sister to the man in Cleveland who sold the auto to the criminals in the first place. There seemed to be a connection, but there really wasn't.

At least in this case, Joe didn't think so.

Why had the killer come here then? Just one more chance at a body along his cross-country spree? Possibly. Or maybe the killer had even heard about FDR's train passing through and thought the event would bring many people together in a small place, thus providing a tantalizing pool from which he could select his next victim. Or maybe the killer had just blundered upon this lonely place on what would prove to be the most infamous day in its history.

But whatever the circumstances, they could always be sorted out later—Joe was that confident in the eventual outcome. His fugitive *had* to be somewhere close by. He was surrounded, confined within a small area, in a torrential rainstorm, with no roads out. He was probably as cold, wet, and miserable as the rest of them. Just like back in his gang-busting days, Copp could sniff the damp air and actually smell the killer nearby. He was that close.

IT WAS EXACTLY ONE O'CLOCK WHEN SHERIFF Boone walked into the church.

He was fresh from a visit to the doctor's office for some smelling salts and a sedative. He was soaked to the bone like everyone else. He was also coughing heavily and still very pale. Copp met him halfway up the aisle and quietly led him up to his command post in the pulpit.

"Are you okay, Sheriff?" he asked the lawman. "It would be a real help if I could rely on you for what's about to come. But I'll understand if you just want to take a backseat on this one."

Boone coughed hard again, but then shook his head. "If it means catching the guy who butchered Sammy, I'll walk through a wall if I have to."

Copp gave him a hardy slap on the back—and almost knocked the man off his feet. He straightened Boone up, then gave him a much milder squeeze on the shoulder.

"Glad to have you aboard then," he told the sheriff.

Several firemen came in soon afterward; they had ten more townspeople with them. The chief indicated to Copp that they'd now rounded up everyone they could find in town.

Copp then asked that the doors of the church be closed and locked. Then he did a count of the shivering congregation. Two hundred and seven people, kids included. He led Boone up to the pulpit.

"You know everyone here, Sheriff?"

Boone's bleary eyes scanned the room.

"Every last one of them," he replied.

Outside the thunder crashed again; a flash of lightning lit up the altar. Copp indicated the gathered citizens again. "OK, take another look," he told Boone. "Now tell me— who *isn't* here?"

Boone scanned the crowd again.

"Well, I don't see Muriel Rivers. But she's as crazy as a bat. Never leaves her house—not even for the President."

"Who else?"

"Pop Crowley, he runs the gas station. He's probably asleep. Probably slept through the whole thing . . ."

"Anyone else?"

Boone did one last pass of the crowd. Suddenly it was very apparent.

"Harry Strum," he said.

"And he is?" Copp asked.

"He practically owns the town," Boone explained. "But he couldn't rub two friends together on a bet. He's nasty, sneaky. A very unpleasant fellow, to say the least."

"Any *strange* behavior?"

Boone thought a moment. "Aside being hated by everyone? Let's see. He doesn't celebrate any holidays—not Christmas anyway. He's cheap as a stone; still has the first buck he ever made—or stole."

"He's wealthy then? Not just richer than everybody else?"

"He's both," Boone replied. "Truth is, though, we don't see him much. He leaves town a lot."

Copp got out his notebook.

"What do you mean?" he asked.

Boone shrugged. "Every month, on the third Monday, he takes off for about a week or so . . ."

"Where does he go?"

Boone shrugged again. "No one knows—or cares. He has the gas tickets because he owns the filling station. He has a big Caddy that looks brand new; it must ride the highways like a ship on a mild sea. He's been doing this thing, well, since the war started. But as to where he disappears to—I've never heard anyone even venture a guess. The fact is, everyone is happier when we know he's out of town."

Joe's ears began buzzing. Suddenly the entire case seemed to come together, right before his eyes. He had a rich guy, someone who had access to gas stamps, had the means to move about the country and who had been disappearing on a regular basis for years.

Could it be that he had tracked the killer—*to his home*? Could it be that the killer actually lived here, in Carson Bend? He would have to be a very sly one for this to be so, Copp thought. Get out to the countryside, stash your car somewhere. Use the trains, buses, maybe even airplanes to carry you to another part of the country to start your murderous vacation. Then kill your way all the way back home again.

It was an outlandish theory—but a theory nevertheless. He began scribbling in his notebook.

"Anything else you can tell me, Sheriff?"

That's when Boone slapped his forehead with his hand.

"Damn it . . . the prowler," he whispered.

"What prowler?"

"Someone broke into the grocery store yesterday," Boone said. "A stranger—or so everyone thought. The last time anyone saw him, he was heading up North Hill, that's where Harry Strum lives. We searched the entire area, including Strum's backyard . . . but never found anybody."

Joe felt his chest puff up even further.

"Let me ask you something Sheriff: this guy, Strum . . . is he a doctor?"

Boone laughed. "Everything but," he said. "He owns the bank, the grocery store, the drugstore, and the gas station."

"But he's not in the medical field?" Copp persisted. "Even as a veterinarian?"

Boone shook his head no. "If he was a doctor, no one would go to him. Even if he was a vet, I wouldn't take my pet flea to him."

Copp lit a cigarette. Boone saw the expression change on his face.

"Hey, wait a minute—are you thinking *Harry Strum* had something to do with killing Sammy?"

Copp replied: "I'm not sure. Not everything matches up, however . . ."

But Boone was shaking his head.

"Look, Strum's an odd duck, believe me. But you just don't know this guy."

"I know just about anyone in this world is capable of murder," Copp cut him off. "*Anyone . . .*"

The truth was, Copp wasn't sure where all of this was going exactly. But a lot of arrows seemed to be pointing toward this guy Strum.

"Where does he live?" he asked Boone. "Where is this North Hill?"

Boone brought him to the front door of the church. Opening it slightly, he pointed through the sheets of rain to the hill located just outside of downtown. It could barely be seen through the murk.

"There's a house up there?" Copp yelled over the wind.

"Sure is," Boone replied. "I just can't believe I didn't think about it before."

Copp gave Boone a mild, fatherly slap on the back.

"That's okay, Sheriff," he told him. "The mind can do funny things, especially during times like this."

Copp studied the house for another moment, then went back inside the church. Funny things indeed . . . He felt like he was at the convergence of several different mysteries, not just one. But he still held tight to his suspicion that Strum might well be his grisly killer. One thing was certain: Joe would know the second he laid eyes on the man. All the signs would be there. He was sure of it.

So it was time to make his move. He asked for an all-quiet from the firemen and vets sitting in the rear pews. They responded with unbridled enthusiasm.

"I need some volunteers to accompany me up to Harry Strum's house," Joe announced. "Who's with me?"

Every last hand went up. Twenty-two men, farmers and firemen, each carrying either a hunting rifle or a shotgun.

"And how many vehicles can I count on to make the climb?" Copp asked them.

Three, was the reply, two hay trucks and the fire brigade's pumper. Joe felt his heart grow warm again. This was the kind of civilian cooperation he'd gotten in the old days. It was good to know this sort of thing hadn't died out, and he told the men so. Every one of them was raring to go.

Except perhaps, Sheriff Boone.

"Strum is so dang rich," he said to Copp as the posse hurried out the door. "Why would he want to kill anyone? What's his motive?"

Copp took a long last drag of his cigarette, then crushed it out on the church's floor.

"Sheriff, I've found that even the most unlikely characters do the most unlikely things sometimes. If Strum is at home and we get into his house, I'll almost bet we'll find all sorts of surprising things—books on surgery, medical operations, things of that nature."

Boone just shrugged again.

"It just doesn't sound like the Strum I know," he said. "But you're the expert."

13

HARRY STRUM'S HOUSE WAS ONLY A QUARTER mile from town.

Getting there would not be easy though. Famous for washing out even in the mildest of downpours, the road leading up to North Hill was running thick with mud.

The sheriff's patrol car would have a hard enough time climbing the slope. The fire brigade's pumper and the two hay trucks would fare even worse.

The small convoy of trucks encountered problems just a few feet up the slippery hill. The drivers had trouble just keeping their vehicles on the road. Before they had even reached the halfway point, the pumper truck had stalled twice and slipped backward, almost colliding with the hay trucks behind it, and the patrol car *behind* them.

Boone had to dodge the pumper as it began to falter. Wildly spinning the patrol car's wheels, he plowed ahead, covering many of those riding in the back of the hay trucks with a shower of mud. Boone managed to get about two thirds up the hill when the patrol car itself began to sputter. Pressing hard on the old Ford's accelerator, the lawman was somehow able to keep his forward momentum going, though the patrol car went up the rest of the slope sideways.

The patrol car and the fire truck reached the summit at the same time. The hay trucks were close behind. They all arrived with one loud back blast from their engines.

So much for a quiet approach, Copp thought.

The vehicles turned left and gained the short road Strum lived on. The citizens, wet and muddy, jumped off the trucks and began heading up to Strum's huge house. They were yelling and screaming, holding their guns high above their heads.

"This thing is turning into a Frankenstein movie!" Boone yelled over to Copp.

Copp ran to the front of the gang of citizens and held his hands high. The crowd stopped.

"If we're going to do this," he told them, "we're going to do it my way. Got it?"

They got it.

He turned to the firemen, still dressed in their heavy raincoats and hats. It was odd to see them carrying guns. The fire chief was out front.

"You and your men, go around back, cover the rear," Copp told the chief. "If anyone tries to go out the back door, give him one command to stop. If he doesn't obey, shoot him."

The fire brigade left, quickly disappearing into the rain and mist.

Copp turned to the World War One veterans.

"Split yourselves up and get to cover on both sides of the house. If anyone comes out a window, give him one chance, then let him have it."

The vets obeyed just as quickly. Dividing into two ragged formations, they too vanished into the torrent.

Copp turned back to Boone and shouted above the rain: "Sheriff, will you cover me up to the front door?"

Boone was soaked and looked miserable.

"Anything to get this over with," he replied.

The rain was getting worse. The wind was blowing near gale. Copp checked his weaponry. He had a full load in his service revolver, a full magazine in his tommy gun.

He nodded to Boone and together they walked through the big gate to the bottom step of the house. Boone took up station here. Copp went up the steps alone. A situation like this actually called for a bullhorn; but he didn't have one. No one did. He would have to use the direct approach.

He reached the porch and shook the rain from his fedora. Then he pulled out his badge with his left hand and brought his tommy gun up on his right.

He took a deep breath. Stay cool, he told himself. If this Strum guy is involved, you'll know it the second you lay eyes on him. The watering pupils, the clenched hands, the deepened brow. Just look for the signs.

He went flat against the door frame and pushed the doorbell. It didn't work. The electricity was still out. Copp leaned over and knocked on the door twice. To his surprise, it opened, very slowly, and a face appeared.

At first Copp thought it was a maid. It took him a few seconds in the low light to realize the feminine puss looking out at him belonged to Harry Strum.

Puffy face, puffy hands, not a hint of homicide in his eyes—in that instant Copp knew he had the wrong man. Again.

The guy he was chasing had done things like overpower a twenty-seven-year-old husband in St. Louis; had made friends with a group of toughs in Pittsburgh. He'd hoisted 90-pound Annie Whitemeyer up and over a tree branch; he'd lifted 155-pound Sammy Silk up to a bale hook ten feet off the ground.

The person facing Copp now looked like he'd have a hard time lifting a five-pound bag of sugar.

Strangely though, Strum was crying. He was holding what Copp thought was a ladies' black-and-white fur hat. But there was blood all over it.

Strum was saying: "Please . . . just shoot me . . ."

Before Copp could say anything, a chilling cry came from behind him. He turned to see firemen and veterans in a mad rush across Strum's front lawn. Slipping in the mud, dropping their weapons, they were all heading back out the gate.

What was this? Copp thought. A mass desertion?

Then Boone ran up the steps and pointed back down the hill. Six columns of thick black smoke were rising above the town. Flames were shooting up everywhere.

"Jessuz . . ." Copp whispered.

Carson Bend was burning down.

He stumbled down the steps, seeing but not quite believing. It looked like the whole town had suddenly combusted. There were actually about six individual fires all forming into one. Long sheets of flame were covering one end of town to the other.

Copp felt his head begin to ache. This didn't make any sense. How could so many fires start simultaneously?

The firemen frantically climbed back on the pumper truck, and, wheels spinning madly, went back down the hill; the two hay trucks carrying the veterans were right behind them. The fire truck's siren sounded mournful as it dissipated in the heavy rain.

Dripping and helpless, Copp wasn't sure what to do. Should he forge ahead and question Strum? Or should he catch up to the last hay truck and go help fight the fire?

He turned to ask Boone what he wanted to do—and discovered the lawman was no longer standing beside him.

In fact he was nowhere to be seen.

"Sheriff?"

Copp looked every which way for him. Where did he go? Certainly not back down the hill with the others. Copp would have seen him in the mad rush. His patrol car was still parked out front of Strum's, and he was not inside it.

"Sheriff Boone?"

This was weird. A moment ago the lawman had been right beside him.

But now . . .

Copp turned back toward the house. A crack of lightning lit it up for a second. Copp shook off a chill. This was the only place Boone could have gone.

"Hey . . . Sheriff?"

Copp took his tommy gun out from under his coat and rechecked the magazine, a very bad feeling going through him. He peered through Strum's front door. The door's curtains were flapping in the stiff wind, but he could see no other movement. It was completely dark inside.

Copp took two steps toward the front door, then stopped. Back in '32, just outside Dallas, while taking in a man who had gone berserk, Copp went through an open front door and got a shotgun blast in his shoulder for the trouble.

He thought for a moment, soaking in the pouring rain. Something was telling him the front entrance was not the way to go this time. He took his flashlight from his pocket, then quietly stole around the east side of the house, heading for the backyard.

On the closely cut grass at the rear of the house, he discovered a set of muddy footprints, far apart from those made by the veterans or the firemen. These prints came up from the direction of the sage hill and went right through the back door of Strum's place. Someone had walked up here from town—and not too long before. The mud from their soles and heels had barely washed away.

Copp climbed the back steps. Off in the distance he thought he heard an animal cry out. Was that a cat? He couldn't tell.

He tried the back door. It was unlocked. He nudged it open. Inside was a kitchen. It was dark and cold. He clicked his flashlight on. The first thing he saw was a box used for holding kitchen knives. It was sitting on the counter, empty.

The kitchen was a mess. Pots and pans were thrown everywhere. Garbage was strewn about the floor. Copp took a sniff. Cigarette smoke, off to his right. He raised his flashlight and found the plume coming from the pantry. Two careful steps and he was next to the walk-in cupboard. Here he found something very strange stuffed under the first shelf, next to an open can of cooking grease. A cigarette pack surrounded by open matchbooks, held together by a doubled-over rubber band. The cigarette pack was open and one cigarette was sticking out about three inches from the top. It was lit and smoldering.

Copp recognized a time bomb when he saw one. This

one was devilishly simple. The lit cigarette slowly burns down and eventually ignites the others in the pack. They in turn burn down and eventually ignite the matchbooks at the bottom. Placed near anything remotely combustible, it was just as effective as a small firebomb with a fuse of a half hour or more.

It was strange though. Copp knew of this device not from his gang-busting days, but from reading antisabotage documents in his spare time at the SWS office. If this device had been allowed to burn down, the grease would have surely ignited and the whole house would have gone up.

Carson Bend was in flames. Had it been ignited by similar devices? If so, did that mean the arsonist had come here, to Strum's house, after leaving the firebombs in the town? The muddy footprints out back seemed to confirm this. But if so, why leave one to smolder here?

He picked up the cigarette pack and threw it into the sink.

Maybe Strum wasn't the killer—but did he know the person who was?

That's when a realization struck him with the subtlety of a hammer between the eyes. He collapsed into a kitchen chair.

Something had been hanging in front of his nose all this time, yet he'd missed it completely. According to Boone, Deputy Silk was to meet the President, hand him a carton of cigarettes and get his picture taken. Yet if the deputy was killed before he ever got on the train, why didn't anyone on the train make a slightest inquiry as to his whereabouts? Boone certainly would have told him if anyone had. Major Pusser would have too. The people on the train didn't think anything was wrong on the ground at Carson Bend. And that could only mean one thing: *Someone* must have gone aboard the train, someone who the presidential entourage must have thought was the deputy.

But who? And why? Would someone actually kill a person just to get their picture taken with the President? And what did all this have to do with the killer he'd tracked to here? For the first time in a long time, Joe's arm became stiff again.

A thud from the floor above him Copp to jump from his seat. Footsteps, right above his head, moving slowly. Machine gun up, he crept into the front hallway.

The living room curtains were still flapping wildly. Behind the front door, a pool of dark liquid sat shimmering. Copp played his flashlight over it. It was blood. Thick and red, a trail of drops led into the living room.

Copp moved his light across the parlor. Next to the couch the trail of blood drops turned into a wide smear, leading up to the stairway. A body had been dragged up these steps, not very long ago. Another sound from upstairs. More footsteps. Moving slowly, trying to avoid squeaking the floorboards.

Then came a noise that froze Copp to the bone. A long slicing noise. Like a wet cloth, being ripped in half.

That was it. The killer—the real one—was upstairs. Copp was sure of it. He could hear him dissecting his latest victim. He looked down at his hands. They were trembling. *Shit!* He swallowed hard. This was not at all like tracking down the Dentons, he thought. He took a deep breath and began climbing the bloody stairs.

At the top was a long dark narrow hallway. Three rooms ran off it. The trail of smeared blood led into the one on the left, the bathroom. Copp inched his way up to the door and directed his flashlight into the small water closet.

The bathtub was thick with blood. Next to the drain a kidney, the heart, and a long bloody tubelike thing had been placed. Each had a bite taken from it. Another body part was sitting atop the bathroom sink. It looked like a blood-soaked grapefruit rind turned inside out. An even larger bite had been ripped out of it.

Copp finally threw up right then and there—it was something he'd been wanting to do since first seeing the Annie Whitemeyer photos. He tried to do it quietly, directly into the toilet. Then he wiped his mouth, closed his eyes and let the moment of nausea pass. Another sound. His gun was up in a flash. Right above him, one floor up. A squeak, a dull thud.

The attic.

That's where the monster was . . .

Copp tried to loosen his stiffening left arm. The tommy gun suddenly felt very heavy. Would he be able to squeeze the trigger if he had to? Past experience would say yes. At that moment though, Joe wasn't so sure.

He crept down to the attic door—and heard another noise. This one from outside; another animal was crying out in pain. Copp listened closer, but the sound quickly died away.

He toed open the attic door and lowered his flashlight. The blood trail led up the half dozen stairs to the top. He went up one step, two, then stopped. Another squeak, another wet ripping sound. His throat tightened. His tommy gun was cocked, his fingers sweating. Another step. Another squeak. Another squeal from the animal outside.

Top step. Copp peered into the darkness. The attic was tiny. A window was open at the far end of it, the silhouette of a person was evident next to the sill. It was Harry Strum. He was hanging upside down, his gut emptied out. Blood was splattering onto the floor like a horse taking a piss. Underneath him were three cats. Throats slit, heads hanging off, their bodies had been haphazardly arranged into pornographic positions. Steam was rising from their carcasses. Copp threw up again.

Next to Strum's body, a window-shade cord was tied to an old pop bottle. The wind was blowing, making the cord tug the bottle against the noisiest floorboard on the attic, ripping the window shade in the process. The resulting sound perfectly imitated someone moving about and doing things most foul.

Then, from outside. A different kind of scream. Very loud. Guttural. Not an animal this time. This was a voice pleading for mercy.

Terrified.

Human.

Damn!

Copp flew back downstairs, trying to avoid the gobs of smeared blood, reaching the first floor seconds later. He tripped going out the back door, picked himself up and scrambled to the garage. But he knew he was already too late. He yanked the door open—and that's when he found Sheriff Boone. The lawman was stretched out on the tool table next to Strum's car, a telephone cord wrapped tightly around his hands and neck. He'd been gutted from his Adam's apple to his groin. A blue foam was bubbling out of him, the residue of the Paracol cough medicine.

Yet he was still alive.

He looked up at Copp and said: "Tell my wife . . . to get me some clothes, will you? I'm freezing . . ."

An instant later, the car in front of Copp suddenly came to life. Wheels screeching, it took off, crashing through the garage's rickety door in an explosion of wood and splinters. Copp fired his tommy gun into the back of the big Caddie as it roared away, but to no avail.

The car went down the driveway, squealed to the left and disappeared down the hill in a cloud of mud and exhaust.

THE FIRE-FIGHTING EFFORTS WERE NOT GOING well down in Carson Bend.

More than half the town was engulfed in flames despite the downpour. The fire station, the church, Bee's Diner and the jailhouse—all were aflame. Hopeless as it was, the townspeople were battling the flames with buckets and hoses and even coffee cups full of water.

Then they saw the Cadillac speeding down North Hill, heading straight for town, and had only one collective thought: This was Harry Strum, guilty as sin, making his getaway. They were sure of it. They dropped their hoses and buckets and retrieved their weapons. When the big Caddy entered the town, they were waiting for it.

The Cadillac roared down Main Street chased by streams of gunfire. Swerving past the burning church, the sheriff's office, the bank. Past Copp's totally engulfed Pontiac. Skidding, smashing, utterly destroying other vehicles.

Halfway through this gauntlet, the car slammed into the porch of the post office where five frightened Boy Scouts had taken cover. All were crushed to death. The Caddie ran the length of the sidewalk, then knocked down what was left of Mam's Grocery. Mam herself was out front fighting the flames with a garden hose. She too was killed instantly.

Those people who got a good look at the driver were astonished to see it was not Strum behind the wheel at all, but a blond-haired stranger with wire-rim eyeglasses. He seemed relaxed to the point of absurdity. Even as he was careening through town, the man was seen steering with one hand and casually picking his teeth with the fingers on the other.

Who was this?

Avoiding one last storm of rifle fire coming from the railway station, the driver made the big left turn off Main Street, roared through the Hi-Lo and skidded out onto Highway 99.

With another screech and a cloud of exhaust, the car sped off into the rain, heading east.

PRIVATES LEO OLSEN AND ERNIE DOWD WERE manning a small roadblock on Highway 99 about four miles outside Carson Bend.

They had been standing out here for almost two hours now, literally in the middle of nowhere. On both sides of them were nothing but bare cornfields and long rows of dilapidated fences. With no shelter from the rain and wind, no way to communicate with anyone, the men had spent the time grumbling about the army and sharing their meager supply of cigarettes.

In fact, they'd just lit their last Camel when they saw the big Cadillac coming over the hill.

"Who the hell is this?" Olsen asked.

"He's on four coals whoever he is," Dowd replied, carefully extinguishing what remained of their precious Camel.

"He doesn't look like he's planning to stop, Ernie," Olsen said. This was an understatement; the big car was bearing down on them at eighty miles an hour. "Are we supposed to halt this thing?"

Dowd looked around helplessly.

"Aren't those our orders?" he asked.

"I guess they are . . ." Olsen said.

The two soldiers reluctantly walked to the center of the highway. The car was now just five hundred yards away and speeding up. It was obvious the driver saw them.

The soldiers raised their rifles into a combat stance—but it was a bluff. They didn't have any ammunition. Their carbines were empty.

The car was just two hundred yards away now and still coming on like a locomotive. "He's definitely not stopping . . ." Olsen yelled.

"Then standing here is not a very good idea!" Dowd yelled back.

"Now you're talking . . ."

Both men attempted to jump out of the way, but at the same time both had decided to pull his buddy along with him. A near-comic tug-of-war ensued as Olsen tried to yank Dowd one way, while Dowd was trying to pull Olsen in the other.

Finally they just let go of each other and dove for safety. Not a second later, the Caddie roared by them, its rear bumper hooking the heel of Olsen's boot and shearing it off, taking along five inches of his skin and cutting him right down to the bone.

Both soldiers landed facedown in the mud. Dowd recovered first and crawled over to Olsen. He was just realizing he'd been clipped by the speeding car.

"*Jessuz*—did you even get a look at him?" Dowd yelled at Olsen.

"He took half my foot with him!" Olsen yelled back.

Dowd got his friend to his knees—only to hear another screech behind them. They turned and saw another vehicle was right on top of them. Lights flashing, horn blaring, it was the Carson Bend patrol car. The driver was hanging out the window, firing a pistol at the Caddilac now about a quarter mile ahead of him.

This time Dowd just managed to push Olsen away at the last instant. The patrol car sped by a second later, leaving a shower of mud and spray in its wake.

"Now that guy I recognize!" Dowd bellowed. "It's the G-man!"

But Olsen wasn't listening to him. He was twisting his handkerchief around his horrendously bloody foot.

"Goddamn it," he cursed. "If they *do* have another war, I'm going to take my chances over there!"

THE ROAD WAS STRAIGHT BUT IT WAS NOT flat. Rather it was a series of small rises and sharp dips.

Every time Copp hit a rise, the patrol car would become airborne. The faster he went, the longer he stayed in the air. The longer he stayed in the air, the harder the old car hit the roadway when it came down again. The harder it hit the roadway, the worse it sounded on the wheels. Four flat tires? A broken axle or two? Surely these things were yet to come.

The patrol car was a bulky old '34 Ford, a bucket of bolts on wheels, and Copp had buried its speedometer long ago. He was traveling at least eighty miles per hour. The car felt like it would fall apart at any moment.

Up ahead, Copp could see the Cadillac going through the same roller-coastering. By Copp's count, he'd shot six bullet holes into the Caddy. One had blown out the back window. He could see the shadowy figure hunched over the steering wheel, twisting this way and that. Copp's instinct told him this person was not a great driver. He seemed to be at the mercy of the Cadillac rather than telling it what to do.

Several times the car had just missed colliding with a telephone pole, a picket of which lined to the right hand side of the highway. But the Caddy had speed—and it was only that the driver couldn't seem to keep the big car straight that Copp was able to gain on him, at least close enough to get a gunshot off. But though he'd made at least a half dozen hits, the Caddy showed no signs of slowing down.

This went on for many miles before Copp caught a break. The Caddy spun out coming off a particularly steep rise in the road. Copp could see a cloud of dust, smoke and sparks as the Caddy came down hard and did a compete 360-degree turn. It was only the mad driver's luck that he wound up facing the same direction he was going before the mishap. He simply recovered his steering, hit the accelerator and was quickly off again.

But the spinout gave Copp what he needed most—time to catch up to the fleeing suspect. When the Caddy screeched away again, Copp was just coming over the rise. He felt all four wheels leave the pavement at once and heard the whistling sounds a two-ton car makes as it hurtles through the air. The Ford came down hard—again. Copp would have sworn it busted a tire or two—but no. He came down violently but intact. And when the smoke and dust ahead of him cleared, he found himself practically on the bumper of the fleeing Cadillac.

Copp's hand was out the window in a flash, firing his pistol over the Ford's hood and into the back of the Caddy. But after two rounds his gun clicked. He pulled the trigger. Another click.

Damn!

He was out of ammunition.

He reached between his legs and came up with his tommy gun. It was expressly forbidden by Bureau rules to fire a machine gun while in pursuit. But this did not stop him. The raps against him were so long now, what difference would one more make?

He would have to be careful though. He wanted to disable the Caddy—not kill the driver. He had way too much invested in this to end the case peeling the unknown killer off a telephone pole. He pushed the accelerator to the floor and brought the Ford right up on the Caddy's bumper. Copp had never driven this fast before in his life. His hands were sticking to the steering wheel—he'd been forced to reach inside Boone's pocket for the patrol-car keys and he was up to his elbows with the sheriff's blood.

They went into another dip, and that's when Copp made his move. He pushed the accelerator so deep into the floorboard the rubber cushion on the pedal snapped off. He lifted his machine gun and fired off a short burst, just enough to blow out his passenger side window. Then he pulled up next to the Caddy and glared across at the killer. The man's features were barely lit by the green-tinted dashboard illumination.

Copp raised the tommy gun and gave it a little flick. His meaning was clear: he was telling the killer to pull over. But the monster was smiling at him . . . and pointing at something straight ahead. A glint of light caught the corner of Copp's eye. He looked forward to see a huge truck was coming right at him. He could read the words *Diamond Reo* on its grill, it was that close.

Why he chose to swerve left instead of right, he would never know, but the reflex saved his life. Had he gone right, he would have sideswiped the Caddy and *then* been crushed by the huge truck. But left he went, sending the Ford sailing completely off the road and down the shallow embankment. Even while airborne, Copp battled the steering wheel, dropping his tommy gun and jamming on the brakes with both feet. The Ford landed hard; his spine felt like it snapped in two. The cloud of dust he kicked up on impact was so thick it blinded him. Somehow he was able to reach the wiper button—the dust cleared only to reveal a huge sycamore tree dead in his path. He swerved right, just missing it, only to scrape a huge scrub bush and then bounce off a large rock. The Ford shuddered once again, but kept right on going. Copp found his foot back on the gas pedal, downshifted, and turned the wheel. With the accelerator once again punched to the floor, he shot back up the embankment and he found himself on the roadway again—just five seconds after he'd left it.

Up ahead, no more than two hundred yards away, was the Cadillac.

Copp accelerated and was soon coming up on the Caddy again. He retrieved the tommy gun and raised it into the crook of his arm. He pulled up alongside the Caddy, ready to send a burst right into the driver's head. But when he went to aim the weapon, he could see no one inside the other car. Copp froze for a second, checking the road in front of him. There was no truck bearing down on him this time. When he looked over at the Caddy again, the driver had suddenly reappeared.

Now this was his first good look, eye to eye, with the killer. And for an instant, Copp thought he had the wrong guy once again. This person looked like a kid—someone still in his teens. Even Harry Strum made a more likely looking killer.

But whoever he was, at this point Copp knew he'd have to kill the guy to stop him. He raised his machine gun again and began to squeeze the trigger.

That's when the killer blew him a kiss . . .

The patrol car's engine began sputtering a moment later.

GASOLINE.

In the end it came down to just three gallons. That's

how much more gas the Caddy had than the Ford. Less than a buck's worth if you had to buy it. But it would make all the difference in the world.

The patrol car started bucking. Then came a sizzling sound from the engine. Copp looked down at the gas gauge. It was deeply below the empty line. The old Ford began to slow down. It didn't take long at all for it to eventually roll to a halt at the side of the long straight highway.

Miles from nowhere.

The last Copp saw of the Caddy its two red taillights were disappearing over the horizon.

He got out and stood there, and that's when everything just came crashing down on him. He was at least thirty miles from anywhere, on a very desolate highway, totally alone. He collapsed, his sore backside hitting the macadam with a painful thud.

Joe Copp's mind was spinning fast now and some pretty ugly scenes were passing before his eyes. If Hoover had made him a secretary because the last fugitive he'd brought back got a little roughed up, what would the Bureau do to him now, after he'd piled up a list of endless transgressions, with absolutely nothing to show for them?

And, while he was on the subject, exactly how many Bureau regulations *had* he broken here? Unauthorized deputizing of civilians, unauthorized federalization of military troops. Not contacting the nearest FBI field office with details of the case. Not calling for backup. Unauthorized use of Bureau equipment. The list went on and on.

Copp began to realize a burning truth, something he'd been denying ever since he'd brought Stringy Hatfield back: Big Jim and the others had been right. The Bureau *had* changed. Ten years ago he would have received a citation just for pursuing the killer this far, no matter what the outcome. Now he'd be lucky if they didn't throw him in the same cell as Al Capone.

Copp's arm was dead stiff and now his leg was beginning to throb. Everything he owned had probably gone up in the conflagration back in Carson Bend. His car. His case journal. Everything.

But all that was paled by one more crushing realization: that, for the third time in as many years, Joe Copp had got it all wrong.

PART FOUR

14

NAVY LIEUTENANT ROD SIPE HADN'T SLEPT IN two days.

He'd flown three ten-hour missions in a row in that time—*triple* duty, but not so unusual these days. Sipe was the commander of a PBY-5 Catalina seaplane. Flying out of the tiny resort town of Newport, his squadron patrolled the waters from the tip of Cape Cod down to the southern New Jersey shore. This was an area encompassing thousands of square miles of ocean.

Sipe's squadron had one mission: find German U-boats and sink them. In four years of operation, their service record was outstanding. Yet even as the war was winding down, Sipe and his colleagues found themselves working longer hours and flying more missions. At the height of the war, his squadron had been stocked with eighteen Catalinas. Now they only had three, with a fourth being used simply for cannibalized parts. The navy considered it unwise to replace the aging seaplanes, especially when hostilities in the Atlantic would be over in a matter of weeks. Fewer airplanes meant more missions the remaining ones had to fly.

IT WAS NOW HALF-PAST MIDNIGHT.

Having just returned from his latest flight, Sipe was stretched out on his bunk, trying to will his muscles to relax. He'd flown so much the previous two days his body felt permanently contorted into the shape of his cramped pilot's seat. As a result, it was nearly impossible for him to get his long, lanky frame into a comfortable position.

He tried to distract himself by thinking about that day coming soon when he would be finally mustered out. He would return to Keene, New Hampshire, marry his fiancée, Karen, buy a big house and stay out of airplanes forever. Thinking these things usually did the trick and put him to sleep. Even now, he could feel his eyelids slowly begin to close . . .

That's when a sharp rapping came on his berthing door.

"Lieutenant? Please wake up, sir . . ."

Sipe opened his eyes. The voice belonged to his plane's crew chief, Avy Dillon.

"What is it, Dills?" Sipe yelled, refusing to move from his bunk. "Is the war over?"

"Not that I know of, sir," was Dillon's reply.

"Then why are you waking me up?"

There was a brief pause. "Because we have to go up again, sir."

"Go up again?" Sipe was instantly furious. *"When?"*

"Right now, sir. And quick . . ."

TEN MINUTES LATER, SIPE WAS WALKING TO-ward his aircraft, practically dragging his parachute and flight bag behind him. Its engines already turning, the plane had been parked at the very end of the base's auxiliary runway, probably the most out-of-the-way place one could get in the sprawling naval air station.

Sipe still didn't know what was up; Dillon's information was very sketchy. Only that they had a special mission to fly and that some kind of VIP was coming along for the ride.

This did not put Sipe in a good frame of mind. The

mention of a VIP meant this had all the makings of a "boonie," slang for a plane ride given to some politician who either needed his picture taken doing something heroic, or simply wanted a lift somewhere. The late hour was puzzling though. Boonies were usually done in the best of weather, during the brightest part of the day.

It was now nearly one A.M.

Two large black cars were waiting near the plane when Sipe arrived. Several SP jeeps were parked nearby as well. The big Catalina had had all its fuselage windows covered with black tarpaper and it was surrounded with armed men in civilian clothes, none of whom looked particularly happy.

What the hell is this? Sipe wondered.

He strode up to the front of the airplane to find his crew already lined up, flight equipment in hand, standing at attention. The base commander was there, as was the air station's intelligence officer. Everyone looked stiff and anxious.

Sipe saluted his superiors. He eyed his men; not one of the five would return his glance.

"Reporting for duty, sir," Sipe announced. "Am I to be briefed?"

The base commander saluted back. "There will be no briefing, Lieutenant," he said.

With that, he turned to the first black car and nodded. An SP reached over and opened the car's back door. A man in an ill-fitting gabardine suit stepped out.

Sipe took one look at this person and wondered if he wasn't dreaming all this. He recognized the guy right away.

It was Harry Hopkins.

SIPE WOULD HAVE BEEN MORE SURPRISED ONLY if FDR himself had emerged from the car.

Everyone knew Harry Hopkins. He was FDR's alter

ego, his legs, his hatchet man. They said when FDR had
a headache, Hopkins took an aspirin. As FDR's first assistant, Hopkins was not just some ordinary politician. He
was probably the second most powerful man in the U.S.

Now he was standing before Sipe, wearing the worst
suit he'd ever seen.

And he looked terrible. It was no secret that Hopkins
had been in and out of the hospital for months for bleeding ulcers, over work, maybe liver damage. He was thin;
his eyes looked way too large for his face. Sipe would
not have been surprised if someone told him that Hopkins
had been raised from a hospital bed to come here, to this
place. If possible, he looked even more exhausted than
Sipe did.

They shook hands uncomfortably.

"Somewhere you have to go, sir?" Sipe asked him.

Hopkins nodded. He seemed nervous.

"Something like that, Lieutenant," he replied.

Hopkins retrieved a flask from his coat pocket and took
a swig. It was not alcohol; Sipe detected the telltale stink
of paregoric.

"Let's get going . . ." Hopkins finally said.

FIFTEEN MINUTES LATER, THE CATALINA WAS
airborne.

Hopkins was strapped into the jump seat behind Sipe.
Two of the armed civilians had climbed on board with
him and were sitting between Sipe and his copilot. One
of these men had a map case; the other a sort of laptop
navigator's station.

Once he'd cleared the air station's operating zone, Sipe
turned to his passengers.

"OK fellas, where are we going?"

The civilian navigator showed him a map of the North
Atlantic. A big red *X* marked a spot about two hundred
miles off the New Jersey coast.

"What's the flight time to that coordinate?" the man asked Sipe.

The pilot did some quick calculating. "Best estimate," he replied. "Two hours."

"Make it in ninety minutes," the man said.

Sipe almost laughed. "Can you arrange a fifty-knot tail-wind?"

The man did not reply. He just sat back and closed his eyes. Sipe looked over at his copilot, who just shrugged.

Then he pushed the throttles all the way forward and turned the big plane to the southeast.

Out to sea.

THEY FLEW LIKE THIS FOR MORE THAN AN HOUR.

Sipe kept his head forward, eyes on his flying, noting that the sea below seemed unusually calm. Hopkins might have fallen asleep; either that or he was not saying much. Not that it made any difference. If Sipe's orders were to fly Hopkins and his two companions anywhere they wanted to go, then he would do just that. The problem was, there was nothing where they were going except wide-open ocean.

At exactly eighty-five minutes into the flight, Sipe felt a tap on his shoulder. It was the civilian navigator.

"We're getting close," the man said.

"Getting close?" Sipe responded. He looked out at the broad expanse of ocean before him—both sky and surface were inky black. "Getting close to what?"

The man thrust another, smaller map in front of Sipe's face. There was a large blue *X* scratched on this one. It approximately matched their present position.

"There . . ." the man said, referring to the marked spot. "We put down there."

Sipe looked back at him. His face was rock hard. There was no doubt about this—he was serious. But landing in the middle of the Atlantic Ocean. With FDR's top aide on board? What was going on?

"Just do it," the navigator told him.

Sipe just shrugged.

"Mine's not to question why," he murmured. "I guess."

THEY BEGAN CIRCLING THE SPOT INDICATED BY the civilian navigator. Sipe's men were at their stations, looking for any floating obstructions that might affect their landing. He trimmed his engines back to half power and lowered his flaps. The sea was running about three to five feet now; it would be a safe, but not exactly smooth landing. They never were.

Sipe turned the big plane around one more time then started his descent. The Cat' began to buck as its flaps caught the stiff mid-ocean breeze, but Sipe's expert touch was able to smooth out most of the rough spots. Down through four hundred feet. Three hundred. Two . . . Then, just as they passed 150 feet, one of his men cried out: "Sir! We have a surface indication off the starboard side! Three hundred yards . . ."

Sipe's hands froze for a moment.

"Chief! Recheck that!" he called back to Dillon, who was stationed at the plane's forward starboard window. "I need an ID, quick!"

"It's a sub, sir!" came Dillon's reply. "A German . . . he's surfacing!"

Sipe didn't even stop to think about it. It was too late to abort the landing. They would have to fight on the surface.

"Arm weapons!" he yelled back to his crew.

That's when he felt the tap on his shoulder again.

It was Hopkins himself.

"That won't be necessary," the man said.

WHAT HAPPENED NEXT WAS LIKE PART OF A bad dream.

Sipe landed the seaplane successfully and was told by the civilian navigator to taxi over to the waiting sub. The German boat was riding high on the surface now and illuminated by its own spotlights. It was what Sipe and his crew called a "Long Doggie," essentially the biggest and the longest-ranging U-boat the German Navy had fielded. Its deck was lined with sailors in heavy-weather gear. Oddly none of them were armed. Neither was the sub's huge deck gun.

Sipe pulled up to within one hundred yards of the sub and then cut his engines. An eerie silence filled the seaplane's cabin. Hopkins got up and was led to the starboard hatchway by the two civilians. Hopkins opened the hatch himself and stared out at the sub through a pair of binoculars. Someone on its conning tower waved; Hopkins waved back. A rubber boat was lowered over the side of the sub and five men—three passengers and two paddlers—put on board. The rubber boat slowly made its way over to the waiting seaplane. Sipe was just able to see the three passengers as the boat passed in front of the nose. These men were wearing gray coveralls, typical of U-boat crew members. But Sipe could tell they were not ordinary sailors. They all looked to be in their late fifties and each had a graying sophisticated air about him. One was sporting a mustache; another a monocle.

"German officers," was the word that slipped out of Sipe's mouth.

"Army, not navy," his copilot quietly agreed. "They don't seem to be enjoying their little boat trip too much."

The rubber raft reached the side of the seaplane and one by one, the three men climbed in. They saluted crisply and then shook hands with Hopkins and the two civilians.

They began speaking in German. One of the civilians began translating for Hopkins.

Dillon came up close to Sipe's position.

"What's going on here, sir?" the crew chief asked him.

Sipe didn't have a clue and said so.

That's when he felt another tap on his shoulder. It was the civilian navigator again.

"OK, let's get out of here," the man said. "And I want you all to remember one thing: None of this *ever happened* . . ."

15

NEW YORK CITY

THEY FOUND BIG JIM IN A BURLESQUE HOUSE called the Old Hennessey Club.

It was located near the corner of 42nd Street and Broadway and known to be one of his favorite haunts. The seven o'clock show had just concluded—that's seven *in the morning*—and Big Jim was having his breakfast. He'd been here since early the afternoon before, eating, drinking, and watching the girlie shows nonstop. He had not bothered to call his office, or even check in, this even though it was just a few blocks away. But no one from the office had tried to track him down either, which was fine with him.

Depending on his mood, he might amble over to the office later this morning. Or maybe he would wait until after lunch. Or even after the dinner shows.

It would all depend on how many of his favorite dancers were working that day.

It was about 7:45 when the two men in black suits and gray fedoras entered the club.

They asked the doorman where Big Jim could be found; the doorman indicated the FBI man's regular table, front and center, right up close to the footlights. The men did not offer any tip to the doorman for this information; that was the first bad sign.

Big Jim was in the process of devouring his favorite breakfast, a meal prepared especially for him by the theater's cooks. It consisted of a massive Holgren sausage, six fried eggs, a quarter loaf of burnt toast and pot of black coffee. The two men walked up to him and, without identifying themselves, advised him to stop eating.

"That is not what you need in your stomach right now," one man said.

Big Jim ignored him.

"Especially all that fried stuff," the second man added. "Not a good idea where you're going."

"And who are you two, may I ask?" Big Jim finally said, sopping up a large portion of a broken yolk with a piece of burnt toast.

"Angus sent us," the first man said.

"I don't know anyone by that name," Big Jim replied, resuming his attack to the huge pork and pepper sausage.

"It's not a person's name," the first man said enigmatically. "You should know that."

Big Jim had had enough. He rose from his seat to his full gargantuan height.

"Must I remind you two that breakfast is the most important meal of the day?" he said. "In fact, my doctor told me that to remain healthy—and alive—and breathing—that I must have my six eggs and Holgren every morning. Now for whatever reason you two blokes have seen fit to interrupt this very important aspect of my morning routine, I don't like it—and I can assure you, my doctor won't like it either."

As he was saying this, Big Jim pulled back the sides of his suit jacket to reveal not one, but two massive handguns hanging in matching holsters just above his substantial stomach.

The two men were not impressed. With the swiftness of a magician, and with no less the sleight of hand, the first man slipped a handcuff around Big Jim's left wrist and then his right. At the same moment, the second man relieved the FBI chief of his pistols. It happened so fast, the only other person in the theater at the time—the morning bartender—hadn't seen a thing.

"Sorry for the strong arm pal," the first man told Big

Jim. "But you have to come with us. Orders from the top. And we were told if you resisted, we had to drag you."

Big Jim began sputtering now. "But you must at least tell me who you represent."

The two men finally flashed ID cards. In the dim light of the theater, Big Jim could read only three letters: OSS.

OSS? he thought. He hadn't spoken with anyone from the OSS in nearly five years. What did they want with him now? And why the rough stuff? And *why* would they care what he was eating for breakfast?

BIG JIM WAS BROUGHT OUTSIDE TO A WAITING sedan, pushed in the backseat, and whisked away. The two men were squeezed in on either side of him; a third man drove. They tore down Broadway, through the Lincoln tunnel, emerging into a light drizzle on the Jersey side. No one was talking. The OSS men sat mute and Big Jim didn't bother to ask them any questions—not because he felt they were trained not to answer, but because he knew they probably didn't know anything to tell him in the first place.

The car traveled along for about thirty minutes, moving ever deeper into the New Jersey hinterlands. The pavement of the roads they traveled seemed to become progressively worse until the driver pulled onto a narrow dirt path and splashed his way through a mile of mud and potholes. Finally they reached a small clearing. Two more black cars were waiting here; an aircraft was waiting as well.

Not many things gave Big Jim pause—but this aircraft did. He knew very little of flying machines. Bombers, fighters, seaplanes—they all looked the same to him. But he *did* know that all of them came with propellers attached.

Yet this plane did not have one.

There was a man in a bright silver suit standing next to the strange aircraft. As soon as he spotted Big Jim's sedan, this man climbed up into the aircraft's bubble cockpit and began throwing switches. Suddenly there was an explosion of noise, followed by an extremely loud, high-pitched scream emanating from the rear of the bizarre airplane.

"What is this?" Big Jim was finally able to blubber out. "*Flash Gordon*?"

But his traveling companions remained mute. They seemed just as surprised to see the strange craft as he was.

His driver stopped the car and Big Jim was pulled out. One of the men from the other sedans approached him. He did not introduce himself, but he too flashed an OSS pass.

"We have orders to get you to Washington as fast as possible," this man told him. "That's the reason this plane is here."

Before Big Jim was able to say a word, he was led out to the shrieking aircraft. It was impossible to speak now, or hear anything or even think clearly. The noise was that loud. They reached the front of the aircraft and a ladder was put in position leading up to the cockpit. The man in the shiny suit took one look at Big Jim and shook his head worriedly. He engaged in a tense hand-signal conversation with the OSS man. The gesturing alone told the tale: no one had told him that Big Jim was, well . . . so big. His top secret jet airplane, known as the XF-80F Shooting Star, was the first of a new breed of jet fighters, still unknown to all but a few within the U.S. government. It had been hastily modified to carry two people instead of one and sent up here to Jersey for this rush-rush taxi mission. The trouble was, Big Jim's bulk equaled two people, not one.

The OSS man simply shook his head; there was nothing he could do. The pilot finally just shrugged and gave him a wave. Big Jim was hauled up the ladder and shoehorned into a very cramped space newly cored out behind the pilot's seat. The fit was so tight, Big Jim had to put his hands over his head while the OSS man struggled to strap him in. This done, the OSS man retreated and the canopy closed down around them. Immediately Big Jim felt deathly claustrophobic.

Then the pilot yelled back to him: "What did you eat for breakfast?"

Again with the breakfast question? Big Jim thought.

He yelled back the components of his morning repast, indicating its overall vast quantity. The pilot just shook his head again and handed Big Jim a large plastic bag.

"Take this," the pilot said. "You're gonna need it . . ."

THE FLIGHT TO WASHINGTON LASTED LESS than an hour.

Big Jim, or more specifically, his stomach, had never experienced anything quite like it before. The airplane sailed through the sky so smoothly, the FBI chief felt no movement at all. It was almost as if the ground was moving beneath him, and that he was sitting still. And therein lay the problem. The speedy flight and the sausages and eggs were just not a good combination. By the time the top secret jet flashed over the Potomac, Big Jim had filled the plastic bag with his breakfast, and just about everything else he'd eaten in the past few days.

The jet touched down at yet another secret AAF base, this one located in the woods near Rockville, in suburban Maryland. Here another black sedan was waiting, engine running, a man behind the wheel. But it took two mechanics, two OSS men, the pilot plus the driver to pry Big Jim out of the secret jet. He was pale and sweaty after this tortuous procedure, and by the end of it, he was in dire need of a drink. The sedan driver offered him a belt from his bourbon flask, but Big Jim turned it down—a first. He took a long swig from an air mechanic's water canteen instead.

Somewhat recovered, Big Jim was put into the backseat of the sedan along with yet another OSS escort. The car roared away.

* * *

THE DASH TO DOWNTOWN D.C. WENT BY IN A blur for Big Jim.

The sedan squealed through the crowded streets, splashing through puddles and running red lights. Big Jim still felt like his feet were not yet on the ground. Through bleary eyes he saw the main gate of the White House flash by. Then the car took a sharp right-hand turn and dipped deep into a garage located beneath a building right across the street from the presidential mansion. It was called the EOB, the Executive Office Building. It served as the working offices for the highest levels of the U.S. Government.

"Christ, I can't go in here . . ." Big Jim told his escort. "I look like hell."

"For once you don't have to worry about that . . ." the man replied.

They soon reached the bottom level of the parking garage, and were passed through an army security checkpoint. The sedan rolled up to a huge steel door and finally stopped. Big Jim and his escort climbed out and were met by two more soldiers. They checked the escort's ID and then walked them up to the steel door. One soldier knocked twice and the door opened immediately. Two more soldiers were stationed here. They too examined the escort's ID card.

Beyond them, Big Jim saw a long, dark hallway—it almost ran the length of the building itself. He and the escort fell into step behind the two soldiers and started walking down the featureless hall. Big Jim was so disoriented by now, he was beyond wondering what awaited him next. In just the past two hours, he'd been kidnapped, strapped into a manned missile, hurled through the air, and now brought to a subterranean chamber located deep beneath the streets of Washington. There was nothing left that could shock him.

Or so he thought.

They reached the door at the end of the hallway; two more soldiers were stationed here. There was another exchanging of ID cards; finally one soldier opened the big oak door. The escort stepped in, Big Jim behind him. That's when Big Jim knew he'd been wrong—that there was at least *one* more surprise in store for him.

The room was small, low lit with an antique table dominating the middle of it. Sitting around this table were eight men. Two were U.S. Army officers, three more were dressed in civilian clothes—and the three remaining were wearing uniforms of the German SS. Big Jim was so bowled over by this incomprehensible sight, he nearly threw up again.

He was ushered into the room, with little notice of his entry taken by the men around the table. The escort put him in a chair directly across from the three German officers and whispered to him: "Just keep your mouth shut, and don't speak until spoken to."

"But why am I here?" Big Jim desperately whispered back to the escort.

But the man was already gone.

Big Jim couldn't help but stare at the faces around the table, again he was astounded by what he saw. To his left was no less than Harry the Hop, FDR's right-hand man. Next to him was Ed Beedy, a member of J. Edgar Hoover's *very* inner circle and Big Jim's boss of bosses. Next to Beedy was an odd-looking man in an all-black suit, with a jaunty red mustache and an unlit cigar dangling from his lips; Big Jim would come to understand this man represented the OSS's super-secret "Futures Division." To *his* left were two colonels, both from Army Intelligence.

But what am *I* doing here? Big Jim asked himself again.

The men around the table had been in the midst of a tense, pressing discussion when Big Jim came in the room. It continued unabated by his arrival. One of the Army Intelligence men was speaking to the German officers.

"Forgive me if I sound like a broken record," he said.

"But are you sure you have not made *any* progress in finding the target's most likely contact here in D.C.?"

The three German officers shook their heads in unison.

"My apologies to you, sir," one replied in near perfect English. "Because it is I who is beginning to sound like a broken phonograph. The truth is that the name of the person here in this city with whom our target would most likely make contact is just not known to us. As we stated before, this person is part of a very loose-knit collection of very low-level operatives. Still the identities of the people on this list is something our Gestapo brothers would never share with us. That's just the way they are."

"It could be one of a hundred people in this city," the second German officer said. "Indeed gentlemen, you have been surrounded by our spies for most of the war."

An uncomfortable moment now descended on the room. Hopkins finally spoke: "We appreciate, with a certain degree of reservation, the assistance you gentlemen have offered us. But please, let us stick strictly to the matter at hand."

Another uncomfortable silence.

"Well, we must attack this thing from the opposite end of the spectrum." Beedy finally spoke up.

Every eye suddenly turned toward Big Jim . . .

Beedy spoke again: "Of the most importance Chief Tolley, whatever you hear in this room can never leave it, understand?"

Big Jim nodded numbly. He was still not quite sure if all this was really happening. Harry the Hop? German SS officers. Here? In the basement of the EOB?

One of the Army Intelligence men passed him a photograph. Big Jim looked at it closely. The photo was of a very unusual-looking man. He seemed both old and young, kind but ruthless, eyes trusting, but with the smile of a felon. Or worse.

"He looks like a bad Hollywood actor," Big Jim declared. "Who is he?"

"His name is Willy Skass," Beedy said. "We have good

reason to believe he is trying to assassinate the President."

Big Jim just stared back at them. "Really? All by himself?"

It was an odd response. But Big Jim had just prevented himself from uttering his first thought, which was: Why? Why would anyone want to kill FDR? The war was almost over and, if one put faith into the conventional wisdom of the moment, the jaunty chief executive had practically won it all by himself. Who would want to kill him?

"Skass is a Gestapo agent," Beedy said, answering the question before it could be asked. "He was sent here about a month ago and has been stalking the President ever since."

Big Jim took a closer look at the photo. "Now that you mention it, he *does* look German."

Everyone in the room did a simultaneous eye roll, including the SS officers.

"He's South African," Beedy told him sternly. "And the fact is, he's a very crafty, dangerous individual and we must find him immediately. He was sent here—actually to a small town in Kansas—to assassinate the President. That much we know for sure. He just missed carrying that off. Now his whereabouts are unknown."

"These gentlemen," one of the army officers now said, indicating the trio of German officers. "Are here to help us find this man, Skass. But it is proving much more difficult than we thought."

Big Jim was shaking his head as if he understood—but his thoughts were actually ones of confusion. OK, so a potential German assassin was on the loose, and three SS officers were here in Washington, helping to get him back. All that was strange enough. But why would these men bring him all the way down here—in a secret weapon aircraft yet—just to tell him this?

"What does this have to do with me?" he finally asked aloud.

Beedy looked over at Hopkins and then back at Big Jim.

"You have a man assigned to your office, Special Agent Joe Copp, is this true?"

Big Jim nodded.

"He was sent out to investigate a murder, on the campus of Princeton University, is that correct?"

Big Jim nodded again. "He went out there, to . . . well, discuss the matter with the local law enforcement, yes."

"Have you seen or heard from him since?"

Big Jim shook his head no. The last he knew, Copp had gone over the hill.

"Isn't that unusual," Hopkins asked, "for an active agent not to call into his office while out in the field?"

Big Jim knew he would have to choose his next words carefully.

"When it comes to Agent Copp," he finally replied, "apparently nothing can be termed 'unusual.' "

He retrieved his handkerchief and wiped his suddenly sweaty forehead. "May I ask why you're so interested in Agent Copp?"

Beedy lowered his voice even further. "Because we believe that this Skass character and the man your Agent Copp might be off pursuing are one and the same. Copp was reportedly spotted in this small Kansas town shortly after the assassin tried to get to the President."

Big Jim let this sink in . . . so old Joe hadn't deserted after all? He'd stayed on the case? A grin spread across Big Jim's face.

"Well, I don't see this as being a problem for much longer," Big Jim told them.

But no one was smiling. Big Jim would have to educate them.

"Well, don't you see?" he said. "You've got this assassin running loose, true, but you've got a guy who is probably the best tracker in the Bureau on his tail. You should read Agent Copp's file. He is a genius when it comes to hunting down fugitives."

But still, no one was smiling.

"We've read Copp's file," Beedy said. "The whole thing—very carefully."

Big Jim shrugged. "So?"

"So, it appears his methods of subduing fugitives are rather 'unconventional.' "

Big Jim smiled. He couldn't help it. It seemed like serendipity to him.

"Well, that's very true," he told them. "Copp can be rough. Brutal even. But what's the problem? If he catches this guy, and let's say in the ensuing struggle, the fugitive gets his scrotum cut off, or his Adam's apple removed . . ."

He let his words trail off for effect.

But Beedy looked like he wanted to come right across the table and strangle Big Jim.

"The problem is," the FBI chief began saying, slowly, "we all want this Skass fellow found alive and in one piece. At any cost . . ."

Big Jim looked back at them, dumbfounded again. This really made no sense.

"Alive? At any cost?" he asked. "But why? You said yourself he's trying to kill the President."

"Why we want this is not for you to know," Beedy shot back at him. "The important point here is that we find Copp and stop him . . . before he finds Skass. In fact, at this point, I'd say Agent Copp is *more dangerous* than Skass."

There now came a long moment, a very awkward silence. Everyone took a deep breath; but no one turned their gaze away from Big Jim. Suddenly he felt very, very small, and the room seemed very, very big.

"So," Beedy said. "Agent Copp. Do you have any idea where he is now?"

Big Jim closed his eyes and saw a bundle of cash sprout a pair of wings and fly away from him; it was his good-performance war bonus, leaving him forever.

"No, sir," he finally murmured. "I sure don't . . ."

16

IT WAS THURSDAY EVENING, AND THAT MEANT
the Portuguese embassy was hosting its weekly diplomatic
reception.

The embassy's temporary quarters were in an ivy-
covered brick town house in Georgetown, a dwelling
which had formerly housed an elite prostitution service.
The residence was honeycombed with bedrooms, parlors,
double-door closets and hidden passageways. Its location
was considered the best in a very tony neighborhood.

The usual crowd was here this warm night. The guest
list included two dozen diplomats and foreign embassy
personnel, mostly from South America; six American military officers, including two who worked in the presidential chief of staff office located on the top floor of the
EOB, plus the requisite gang of unabashed, if low-level,
foreign intelligence operatives. More than a dozen of the
town house's former residents were in attendance as well.

The appetizers included chunk salmon and cheese
buffu. There was a punch bowl filled with Portuguese
wine and literally gallons of scotch for the taking. Cocaine
was available as well. A string quartet played in one corner of the immense dining room, a small army of maids
and kitchen men stood at attention in another.

Besides the salmon being a bit sticky, the talk of the
reception was Countess Maxiree Frederica de'Janiero.
Known to everyone simply as Maxie, she was a beautiful
creature, white porcelain skin, luxurious black hair, educated at three of the Seven Sisters, and still not thirty years
old. Maxie was somewhat of a legend with the Washing-

ton circle elite. She was said to have roasted snake with the bushmen of the Kalahari and wrestled *compancho* with the mudmen of Peru. It was rumored she'd once slept with Wallace Simpson and that Winston Churchill's private phone number could be found somewhere in her purse. As the unofficial hostess for the Portuguese embassy she was known for her elaborate dinner parties and her love of unusual parlor games.

She was also known to be a German spy.

THE BUZZ AMONG THE COCKTAIL GLASSES TO-night was about Maxie's new beau. He was said to be a "roving diplomat," but everyone knew that was a poorly disguised term for an espionage agent, or at least some kind of secret foreign operative. Trouble was, these days, there were so many poseurs about, just about all of them claiming to be roving diplomats, it was hard to tell exactly who was who.

But the whispering in the room this night was that Maxie's new man *had* to be a legitimate intriguist. Maxie was as smart as she was beautiful, and even more important, she was savvy. She could spot a phony at a hundred paces. The consensus among the guests then was that whatever his claim to fame, Maxie's new boyfriend was most likely the real thing.

THEY MADE THEIR FIRST APPEARANCE SHORTLY after nine o'clock.

Maxie was wearing a stunning black strapless gown, her jet-black hair tossed into a million curls. She descended the grand staircase, her new boyfriend at her side, looking not the least bit uncomfortable.

The first guests to greet her were the Brazilian military attaché and his wife. Maxie hugged and kissed both, then turned to introduce her new friend. The Brazilian officer took a quick stock of the man and liked him right away.

His face seemed warm and friendly, his smile was quick. He didn't appear to be at all uneasy, even though a room full of connected strangers was gawking at him and his new lady love.

There was just one catch though.

When the Brazilian officer went to shake hands with the man, he noticed something odd; his wife did too.

Maxie's new beau had terribly dirty fingernails.

AS ALWAYS, MAXIE INSISTED ON PREPARING the dinner's main course herself. So, after formally greeting her guests, and opening the night's champagne, she retreated to the kitchen and began cutting up four dozen freshly killed Cornish hens.

Meanwhile, Maxie's boyfriend entertained the guests with some wonderful, if baffling, sleight of hand. In one trick, he took a wristwatch from the Chilean agriculture minister and put it in an emptied-out sugar bowl located in the middle of the dinner table. Then he had the diplomat sing six bars of his country's national anthem, which he did, horribly off-key, much to the delight of the others. When the song was completed, the Chilean was instructed to walk over to a nearby potted palm and begin digging with a spoon. The man complied—and eventually found his missing timepiece buried deep within the large clay pot, its wristband heavily entwined with roots.

For his next trick, Maxie's friend relieved two of the female guests of their makeup bags. He emptied their contents onto the dinner table, selecting a package of rouge, some lipstick and an eyeliner kit. He gathered up a dinner napkin and poured the contents of the blush and eyeliner powder into it. Then he smeared the inside of the cloth with the lipstick and neatly folded it into a precise twelve-square pattern. He held the napkin over his head, then snapped it open and dramatically pushed it into the face of the Venezuelan consulate general—this for no more than three seconds. When he lowered the napkin again, those gathered were astonished to see the consul's face—his eyes, cheeks, and lips—was made up almost exactly like those of the high-priced call girls.

Dinner, more drinks and dessert soon followed.

It was toward the end of the evening, when, prodded on by the now-drunken guests, Maxie's beau agreed to perform one more illusion.

He requested that everyone remain in their seats and stay perfectly still, the only exception being two Peruvian military officers. The two doors leading out of the dining room were locked. Then the Peruvians were told to stand guard over them—and to shoot anyone who tried to get past.

This done, the beau demanded the lights in the dining room be turned out—but just for a count of three seconds. The lights were flicked off and, in unison, the guests counted to three. When the lights came back on again, Maxie's beau was nowhere to be seen. He was not under the table, nor was he behind the window drapes. The Peruvians swore no one had got by them. The doors remained locked.

Finally, the guests began to search for him. They opened the door to the kitchen—and that's where he was found, hovering over a large garbage pail, gnawing on a piece of discarded game-hen skin.

MAXIE BEGAN THE PROCESS OF BIDDING HER guests farewell soon after that.

All of them had a word or two to say about her unusual, but delightful beau. He's accustomed to retiring early, she had told them all, that's why he was not here at her side, formally seeing them off. Every guest demanded that her funny friend be on hand for next week's reception though, to entertain them again. Maxie laughed away these suggestions, sealing each parting conversation with a lightning-quick air kiss.

With the last of her guests gone by eleven-thirty, Maxie

dismissed the help, then locked the back door and went up to her bedroom. It was pitch-black on the second floor now. She lit a candle, then slowly searched the bedroom's half dozen closets, its bathroom and its adjoining dressing room. Only then was she satisfied that no one else was here. She was alone.

Her "beau" had arrived unannounced on her doorstep exactly one week ago tonight. She had taken him in, as she was supposed to do, in accordance with her being part of the Gestapo's network of Z-agents. And he had proved to be the perfect houseguest. Witty, smart, and willing to engage in any conversation, he soon began fawning over her, making her drinks, bringing her morning coffee and even cooking her dinner on two occasions.

Since arriving though, he'd made an odd habit of disappearing late every night. She had no idea where he went. She had not asked him and he had not offered to tell her. She had assumed these nightly forays were part of his mission here in Washington. But she read the newspapers, and he was always in such a disheveled condition when he returned, around dawn, that she began to suspect something else was causing him to howl at the moon. Something that had little to do with whatever secret mission he was here to see through.

Something that brought a chill to her own fingers whenever she considered it, or sometimes even, a burning sensation to her chest.

So it was that she'd been very anxious to get rid of her guests this night. On cue, her visitor had disappeared once again and all the help had been sent home. For the first time in a week, she was truly alone in the house, which is exactly what she wanted. Now at last came the opportunity she'd been waiting for since her visitor arrived seven days ago.

Checking once again that the door to her bedroom was indeed locked, she retrieved the visitor's tiny travel case from under her bed and began methodically looking through it.

* * *

IT HAD STARTED RAINING AROUND ONE A.M.

It was just a sprinkle at first. But by two, the streets of Georgetown were slick with a cold drizzle. As it came closer to three, a wind blew up and the rain came down heavier. By four, it was a deluge.

Stumbling around somewhat aimlessly through the streets surrounding the Portuguese town house, Willy Skass found himself absolutely soaked to the bone. He'd walked through so many puddles, his shoes now made a squish with every step he took. His nose was running, his hands had begun to ache. He was cold, sick, alone. Miserable. Not even the huge carving knife he kept snugly in his jacket pocket could fool him with a bit of warmth. It felt just as cold as the rest of him.

These were not the best of days for Skass. He'd been in the U.S. now for nearly a month, and, as preposterous as it might have seemed, he was deathly homesick for bombed-out, rubble-strewn Berlin. His old rooming house, even without electricity or water or heat, seemed like some far-off fairy-tale palace now, its decapitated roof, floating in the clouds above the perfect land of the *Reich*. It was just one part of a dream that he'd concocted and was now beginning to believe himself. Even his cell at the prison on Wecht Street now held a nostalgic spot in his heart.

He did not belong here in America. The dark lonely feeling had crept up on him during his drive back east from the disaster in Kansas. The trip itself had been depressing. After filling up the Cadillac near Freestone, Kansas, he'd killed the young boy operating the pumps, but for no good reason. He wasn't particularly hungry at the time and putting distance between himself and Carson Bend would have been the far more prudent thing to do. Even worse, the boy's skin proved tough, his blood bitter.

He drove nonstop to St. Louis, where he caught up with the President's train again. But this time no less than sixteen city blocks around the train station had been sealed off by soldiers and state police. Skass could get nowhere near the presidential carriage.

He frantically drove on to Dayton, where he knew the train was scheduled to make another stop. But once again, soldiers and policemen were out in force and he never got within five hundred yards of it. There had been a reason his Gestapo handlers had selected tiny Carson Bend as his best place to strike, and missing that opportunity had proved devastating to his spirit. Driving out of Ohio, Skass came face-to-face with the possibility that he would not be able to get that close to his intended target again.

He'd arrived in Washington one day after the President's train. He finally ditched the Cadillac and, severely rumpled and unwashed, broke into a men's store in Georgetown and stole enough clothes to last him for two weeks. Then he stole a car and wound up at a YMCA not far from Pennsylvania Avenue. When he felt safe enough in his surroundings, he contacted the last Z-agent on his list: Maxie.

And therein lay another problem for him.

THE MOMENT HE FIRST SET EYES ON HER, standing at her back door, in her nightgown, looking down off the stoop at him, he wanted to rip her open in the worst way, just to see what lay beneath such a great vessel of beautiful hair and skin.

He still felt that way—but something else gurgled up inside his stomach any time he thought of her now. Maxie was different. She was unlike any other woman that had ever come into his life, including his mother. It seemed like nothing could shock her, nothing could suppress her, nothing could throw her for a loop. She was bawdy, ready for anything, any time. Yet he was amazed at the depth of her social graces.

The biggest surprise had come earlier that evening when he found himself enjoying immensely the role of playing her "latest new beau." He was already treasuring those moments, walking down the staircase, holding her warm hand. The most bizarre thing was, she seemed to like him as well. How strange, this feeling! He found himself thinking of her at the oddest times. In the late morning, lying in bed. While shaving. While combing his hair.

But whenever these warm feelings washed through him, it only underscored what amounted to a monumental dilemma for him: If indeed he did tear her open, she would be gone . . . forever.

In other words, she might have been the first woman he'd ever met whom he liked better alive than not so. For the monster he knew he was, did something like this approximate . . . *affection?*

Maybe, maybe not. And Skass wouldn't have known the correct answer if it had bit him on the ass. But whatever he might tag the emotion, it was the reason he'd been walking these cold streets for the past seven nights. He wanted her to stay alive. Had he taken the opportunity, as she had offered to him unconditionally, to sleep in her room, on the couch next to her bed—well, he knew the limits of his temptations and as such there was a good chance that Maxie would not have lived through any night he chose to stay at home.

But now, on this miserable evening, a collision of worlds was happening somewhere deep inside his darkened soul. His mission had been a failure so far, and he had no plans on how to change that anytime soon. He missed his war-torn Germany, yet he knew that once the Gestapo realized he'd botched his assignment, they would most likely track him down and kill him, especially if he abandoned the mission now. So returning to Germany in any fashion was out of the question. Yet he could not remain here.

So all was lost. Skass was in an impossible situation, in a strange land, without viable human contact—except for this beautiful woman who'd managed to haunt him night and day simply by the fact that she was still walking around alive and breathing. He'd suffered such bouts of depression before of course. But in times like this in the past, long before he'd agreed to this foolhardy adventure, whenever he found himself at a very low point, somehow from somewhere, a spark of hope would arrive and hit him on the head. It would fill him with warmth and everything would be good again. But he couldn't imagine where that spark would come from now. In fact he couldn't imagine ever feeling any kind of warm sensation again. Ever . . .

And *all this* was landing on top of one last grim truth. The last person he'd taken was the boy at the filling station in Kansas. That was almost two weeks ago. Just like anyone else, whenever Skass got down on himself, he liked to eat.

And now, foot-sore and soaking, he was getting hungry.

Very hungry.

He slipped through the back door of the town house, got out of his wet jacket, drank a half gallon of warm milk, then climbed the rear stairway to the second floor, his carving knife jammed loosely into his rear pants pocket.

He'd managed to open Maxie's bedroom door without a sound even though it was famous for issuing a very loud squeak. The room was dark except for the light from a tiny votive candle placed in a shallow bowl of water on the nightstand.

He closed the door quietly behind him and slid the knife from his pocket. He didn't want to do this, yet he was compelled to. He had to be fed, and nothing, not even his warm feelings for Maxie, could stand in his way. It was useless to fight the feeling, especially with him plumbing the depths of such a foul mood. At this point, he just wanted to get it over with.

He retrieved a towel from the nearby washstand and slipped out of his very wet shoes and socks. Then the candle flickered and Skass saw Maxie's silhouette. She'd been sitting on the edge of her bed in her nightclothes all this time.

"My sweet," he said to her, surprised he hadn't sniffed her in the dark. "I wish you had gotten some rest. After your hard work tonight at the party, the last thing I wanted was for you to wait up for me."

"It's too hot to sleep," she whispered deeply in reply, even though it was fifty degrees outside and raining and all the windows in her bedroom were closed tight. "Besides, I wanted to know where you went tonight. You left so suddenly."

"Just walking, my kitten," Skass replied calmly, still standing motionless about fifteen feet away from her. "Around the block. Up and down this street. Keeping the enemy away from your doorstep."

"Really? You've been out there, walking guard for me, in this rain?"

Skass took a step toward her.

"On this night and every other night, it would be my honor to defend one as beautiful as you," he said.

"Should I take that as a compliment?"

He took another step closer to her. "If you did, I could die a happy man. Or, you could die a happy woman."

She laughed nervously. "Sometimes it's not the best thing to have our wishes come true."

He took another step toward her.

"But then again," she said. "Sometimes it is . . ."

With this, she reached over and picked up the votive candle, moving it closer to her. It cast enough light now to reveal that she was holding a very large pistol in her hand. It was pointing right at his stomach.

Skass froze.

"Have I ever told you how much I detest guns?" he asked her calmly.

She steadied her hand a bit. "Apparently there are many things you haven't told me . . ."

She nodded toward the foot of the bed where his suitcase now lay, splayed open, its contents arranged neatly atop her cotton afghan. Skass was shocked. These were his most prized possessions: A patch of skin from Annie Whitemeyer's belly. The ring finger from the schoolgirl in Philadelphia. A nipple from the wife in St. Louis.

Maxie raised the gun a little more. "Perhaps now would be the time to fill in some blanks," she told him.

Perhaps it was, Skass thought. He looked down at his hands. They were trembling, a first. He knew this moment was now the lowest of his life.

"I *will* tell you everything," he finally mumbled. "But only with my apologies in advance for anything that might offend you."

SO HE BEGAN. FROM HIS FIRST DAYS IN GER-many, to his initial killings there. He recounted each one, in lengthy and vivid detail. His arrest, his conviction, his release. His mission here. Even as the words were tumbling out of his mouth Skass knew he was making the biggest mistake of his life. Yet he kept on babbling. The monster was a tired man.

He told her about Carson Bend and his activities after it. His failures in St. Louis and Dayton. His lack of any plan to fulfill his mission in D.C.

"And that brings me to the here and now," he concluded. "And so exhausted I could drop."

He took another step closer to her. He was now standing right at the foot of the bed.

And Maxie just stared back at him, the pistol shaking a bit in her hand. She was a foolish girl, but that she'd known since a very early age. She wasn't really that political, she simply loved the excitement of secretly dealing with the Germans, even though their efforts in Europe now looked laughably hopeless. Though it had been her duty to take him in, she was fascinated with Willy nevertheless—in ways he probably never even dreamed of.

He took another step toward her, lifting the knife so she could see its reflection in the bare light of the candle.

Another step closer. The knife glinted again. Skass was now just an arm's length away.

Maxie raised the gun in earnest now, stopping briefly to level it at his upper chest, but then continuing upward until she brought the barrel to her mouth. Then she kissed it and allowed her tongue to run its length and back again. Eating snake with the bushmen was nothing compared to this, she thought.

She reached out and grabbed Skass by the shirt collar and pulled him close to her. He dropped the knife to the floor.

She whispered to him: "Just remember one thing, Willy. The next time you go out hunting for souvenirs, take me with you . . . or I'll fill you full of holes."

17

THE NEXT NIGHT

BOB DOCKS HAD HOPED HE WAS IN FOR A SLOW shift.

He was the dog officer for the southern districts of metro D.C. and had watched with trepidation all day as the rain clouds cleared away and the warm temperatures returned. By the time night had fallen, it was sticky and hot again. This was not good. It was Docks's experience that warm weather always brought out the worst in God's creatures, be they dogs or people. This night would prove no different.

True to form, he spent the first two hours of his four-to-midnight shift chasing down strays from Potomac Park and National Stadium. For whatever reason, since the war started, D.C. had become inundated with stray dogs. These animals sometimes ran together, and inevitably after a ball game at National, the packs would descend on the parking lot to feast on the trash and discarded food. This involved the knocking over of many litter barrels, and that's when the stadium manager called Docks.

On this night, he was able to corral three strays and chase away another dozen or so. The stadium clean-up crew gave him three cold beers in appreciation, and, returning to his tiny office by six, he was intent on eating his supper and enjoying at least one bottle of Pabst.

But no sooner had he unwrapped his sandwich when the phone rang. There had been a very tragic accident over in the southside projects. Docks was needed there at once.

He was told to bring his gun.

THE RIDE OVER TO THE PROJECTS TOOK LONGER than usual. The streets of south D.C. were clogged with army vehicles and staff cars and many intersections were blocked off entirely. When Docks finally reached the scene he was directed by a policeman to an alley which led to the back of a row of tenement houses.

More police were on hand here, most were keeping a growing crowd away from one particular backyard. A few cops had boosted themselves up to the top of the high wooden fence which hemmed in this yard. They were looking down on something inside it.

Docks retrieved his .22 hunting rifle and reported to the police sergeant in charge of the scene. The first thing the cop said to him was: "Have you had your dinner yet to-night?"

Docks just shook his head no; it was an odd question to be asked.

"Good," the cop said. "Because a few of us did—and we all lost them."

Without another word, the cop lead Docks around to the front of the boxed-in yard. Here was a scene Docks had witnessed countless times before. The yard was essentially one big dog pen. It was run down to hard dirt and there were water bowls and chewed-on bones strewn about. A ragged piece of knotted rope looked like it had served as a leash for years.

In the far corner of the yard was its occupant, a good-sized mutt that had at least some German shepherd in him. Ten feet away from the dog was a horribly mangled body. And that was the problem. The police couldn't get to the body because the dog would not let them into the pen.

Docks studied the body. It looked more like a rag doll than human remains. There was so much blood and gore around he didn't realize right away that he was looking at the body of a child. That's when he did throw up a mouthful of bile. He'd never seen anything so ghastly in his life.

"My God man," he roared at the cop. "You people have weapons—why didn't you just shoot the mutt yourself?"

The cop was anticipating the question.

"Just look at him," he told Docks.

Docks gladly pulled his eyes away from the tiny corpse and now studied the dog. He was squeezed into the far corner of the pen, as far as he could get away from the dead body. He was growling lowly, but was also curled up in the total supplicant position, his tail tucked tightly up under his legs. And his eyes were watery. If a dog could cry, this is what it would look like.

"No one here had the heart to do it," the cop finally confessed.

Docks's heart wasn't in it either, but he knew the quickest way to get out of this place was to shoot the dog and be done with it. So he loaded his rifle and brought the dog's forehead into his sight. It was strange, because the mutt raised his head a bit and looked right back into the scope at him, almost as if he knew what was coming.

Docks took a deep breath. The dog barked one more time. Docks pulled the trigger. His bullet went right between his eyes.

Now came the hard part.

Not only had it been Dock's job to kill the animal. It was his duty to carry him away.

The lead cop unlocked the yard's door, and they went into the pen together. Docks had told himself that he would not look at the body again. He would simply put the dead canine in his net and drag him away from here. But as he started to do this, he heard the cop gasp and then throw up again.

"Hey you, come look at this," the cop yelled to him.

Docks reluctantly walked over, just as the cop was turning the tiny body over on its back. Docks then realized the full horror of this moment. This person—it was a young girl of indeterminate age—had not been mauled to death, as everyone had assumed. Rather she had been sliced open, and much of her insides hollowed out. It was so unreal, what lay before them didn't even seem like a human being anymore.

"No dog did this," Docks heard himself say.

The cop was as stunned as he. "Someone did it, *then* threw the body in here."

Docks looked back at the dog he'd just killed. Now he knew why the dog had been acting so strange. *He'd seen what happened . . .*

Now came shouting from the alley. The cop retreated from the pen and Docks went right out with him. They were met by another officer who was both pale and out of breath.

"Next alley over," he told the cop in charge.

They all ran to the next alley to find two more cops standing next to a trash barrel in the middle of an open lot. There wasn't a dog in sight.

"It's another body," one of the cops said, pointing inside the trash barrel. "Looks like another kid . . ."

18

THE NEXT DAY DAWNED OVERCAST AND muggy.

The gray pall hanging above Washington became even darker as news of the horrific double murder began to make its way across the capital. Nearly all of the southside projects had been sealed off by the authorities. Police officials were being very tight-lipped regarding the details of the crime. They were saying only that "Two white girls had been stabbed to death," and that they believed the murderer was still close by.

To this end, the police were searching the basements of every tenement inside the twenty-block crime scene area, convinced that clues to the killings, if not the killer himself, would be found somewhere underground.

Although the murders had happened in his precinct, Patrolman Tom Howley was not assigned to one of the grisly search teams. His station house was just eight blocks away from where the two girls—sisters, nine and eleven—had been found butchered, and every available officer in his district had been called in and put to work on the case. Every one except Howley. He'd been given an assignment clear across the city, a lucky break, or so it seemed.

Because the duty he'd pulled was not much better in his opinion. For instead of tromping through the rat-infested basements of the slums, Howley was going to . . . a baseball game.

*   *   *

THE PROBLEM WAS, HE DIDN'T LIKE BASEBALL.

It was slow, low-scoring and its players were vastly overpaid. At six foot four inches, and nearly 270 pounds, Howley was more of a football guy. Yet here he was, assigned to National Stadium for a pre-season exhibition game between the Senators and Boston. A huge crowd was on hand. Not only were the grandstands filled to capacity, there were throngs of spectators gathered along the foul lines on both sides of the field.

Howley didn't like crowds very much either; they made him feel edgy and claustrophobic. Yet, scanning the stadium now from his vantage point behind the Senators' dugout, he estimated there had to be at least forty thousand people on hand, probably many more. He felt a shudder go through him. At that moment, he wished he was back at the precinct, doing paperwork, cleaning the jail cells or even searching for the child murderer. Anything, he thought, would be better than this.

Still, he had to wonder: How many of that forty thousand were here to see the ball game and how many where here to see the President? That's what this was all about. As one of the biggest cops on the D.C. police force, whenever the President went to some kind of public function dealing with large crowds, Howley would invariably be called on to do security duty. The protection of the President was the main job of the Secret Service, of course. But the D.C. police were frequently called on to supplement their efforts, especially in wide-open forums like ball games or war bond rallies.

So it was Howley's bulk that made him a natural for presidential crowd duty, and he absolutely hated it.

It was almost enough to make him stop eating his usual 5 to 7 doughnuts a day.

Well, almost . . .

THE GAME WAS READY TO BEGIN WHEN FDR was finally brought onto the field.

As usual he arrived by his specially-designed touring car. It emerged from the gate in right field and slowly made its way down the foul line to the presidential box, which was located to the left of the Senators' dugout. The car rolled to a stop, FDR waved to the crowd and the crowd cheered back. Then taking a cue from the Secret Service agent in charge, the stadium's PA announcer directed the crowd's attention to the opposite side of the field, where the Senators were presenting a war bond to a lucky fan. While this was going on, the President was lifted out of his car by four burly Secret Service agents and carried up a special access ramp to his VIP box. Once he was settled in his chair, the Secret Service cued the announcer again, and that's when the President was officially acknowledged to the crowd. The stadium roared again.

The President waved to every part of the grandstand, posed for pictures with some young kids, then made a surprisingly good effort on the ceremonial first pitch. Then the game began. One o'clock, on the dot. Howley loosened his tie and let out his jacket.

He had nine long innings to go.

THE FIRST THREE INNINGS WENT BY VERY slowly as the Red Sox proceeded to thoroughly drub the Senators. It was getting hot, and Howley was regretting his decision to wear his winter duty trousers instead of his light spring pants. He'd been sweating even before the Senators took the field in the first inning. He was absolutely roasting now.

Not only did Howley have zero interest in the game, his very visible presence—just 150 feet away from FDR's box—had somehow turned him into a human information booth. What was it with some people? They see a cop and automatically they think he knows the directions to the nearest exit, the nearest rest rooms, the nearest snack bar. Howley did his best to direct everyone who asked to a nearby park attendant, and while never losing his scowl, he strived to keep his responses civil.

But this did not stem the tide of people asking him questions or inquiring about directions. A lost kid with a melting ice-cream cone, a mother with a baby whose diaper needed changing, a guy with dirty fingernails looking for the men's room.

By the fifth inning, Howley could take it no more. The score was 12–0 and the Senators were throwing the ball around like a bunch of Little Leaguers. He walked over to his colleague Jeep Mann and asked if Mann could cover his post while Howley went down to splash some water on his face. His partner agreed.

Howley walked down the ramp and ducked into the nearest men's room. But no sooner had he taken a pee than the walls of the lavatory began shaking. The commotion was so sudden and so loud, Howley's hand went right to his gun, purely on instinct. It took a few moments for him to realize that it was the roar of the crowd shaking the foundation.

The Senators were making a comeback . . .

Howley zipped up and stepped out of the rest room. Hundreds of fans who had been at the refreshment stands were now stampeding up the ramps to get back to their seats. Even Howley knew that a comeback for the Senators was as rare as the coming of Christ and that no true Washington fan would want to miss such a historic event.

Which was fine with Howley. If everyone's attention was on the game, then the chances he'd be missed became ever less.

A long black curtain had been set up to cordon off the ramp by which FDR would exit the stadium once the game was over. This curtain stretched from the street all the way up to the men's room exit, near where Howley was standing. He soon realized he was the only person in sight; everyone else was up watching the suddenly exciting game. This was a golden opportunity, and Howley knew it. He pulled out his cigarette pack and ducked under the curtain. Here he lit a cigarette and dragged on it greedily. His hat off and fanning himself, his intention was to make this smoke last as long as possible.

Then he saw the first Secret Service man.

The agent walked down the ramp and approached him.

"Are you part of the special presidential detail?"

Howley wasn't sure how to reply. He was here to protect the President. Is that what the agent meant?

"Yes, I am," Howley finally answered.

"OK, then," the Secret Service man said. "Straighten up—and put that butt out."

Howley did as ordered. He turned to see that a presidential limousine had been backed up to the ramp. However, it was not the same car that had deposited the President on the field about an hour before. Another Secret Service agent was standing next to it. Howley turned back to his left to see a third agent casually pushing a wheelchair down the closed-off ramp. In the chair was a man wearing a white suit and two-tone shoes. They went by him so fast, the man in the wheelchair barely looked up at Howley.

But there was no doubt in the policeman's mind who this was: It was FDR. No more than two feet away from him.

Wait till I tell the wife, Howley thought.

He watched now as the Secret Service agents helped the man out of the wheelchair. Indeed, the man seemed perfectly capable of standing on his own.

Maybe his legs just get tired a lot, Howley thought. *Maybe he just needs the wheelchair to make it easier to get around.*

Suddenly there was a commotion at the other end of the curtain, just down from the men's room door. *Crack! Crack! Crack!* A trio of sharp reports nearly shattered Howley's eardrums. What had happened? Just as the man in the wheelchair was climbing into the back of the limo, the shots had rung out behind him. Now Howley turned back to see all three of the Secret Service men were down on their knees on the sidewalk, a woman holding a smoking gun standing over them. The woman calmly fired the gun again—three times. The three agents slumped to the pavement, each with a chest wound gurgling blood. Another man emerged from behind the curtain, no more than twenty feet from Howley's position. He walked over to the limo and, leaning over the dying Secret Service agents, calmly slit the throat of each one, even as they weakly begged him to stop. The agents thus dispatched, the assailant turned to the man sitting in the back of the presidential limousine. Without a moment's hesitation he set upon him, stabbing him viciously. Howley could not only hear the victim's screams, he could also hear the ripping and slashing of the knife as it hit both skin and bone.

At this point, Howley finally got himself moving. He still couldn't believe this was happening in front of him. But he pulled his pistol out nevertheless and in the loudest voice he could muster, shouted: "You there! *Halt!*"

The man with the knife stopped stabbing the lifeless body in the back of the car. He turned slowly toward Howley. That's when Howley realized this guy looked familiar. He had asked him for directions earlier in the afternoon.

The man smiled at him so queerly Howley froze again. This all seemed like a nightmare, something that defied explanation.

FDR stabbed? FDR dead? Right before his eyes?

Those would be Howley's last real thoughts. For the man with the knife threw it at him with such unbelievable quickness, the next thing Howley knew, the blade was sticking halfway into his chest.

He felt no pain, just surprise. The gun in his hand suddenly felt very heavy. His knees buckled and he fell to the sidewalk right next to one of the dead Secret Service men. Howley hit his head on the pavement and felt life start to ooze out of him.

Above him the man and woman appeared. They stared

down at him for a long moment, then the man took the knife from Howley's chest with the finesse of surgeon.

"I'll be needing this," the killer said to him calmly.

A moment later, Howley felt the cold steel against his own throat. He let out a cry but nothing came out. He heard the woman laughing, and then footsteps running away.

After that, everything just went black.

19

LATER THAT NIGHT

SIRENS . . .

Willy Skass loved the sound of them.

As a child in Johannesburg, he would get so excited whenever he heard a siren, he would pee his pants. He knew that a siren usually meant a fire, an auto accident, or some other small catastrophe. If he was able, he would rush to the scene to see if any blood had been spilled. Much bodily excitement usually followed. In those early years, the sound of a siren worked as deeply on him as it had on young Ulysses.

And it never failed to make him happy.

But where were they now?

The President of the United States had been murdered. Skass still had the man's blood on his clothes, on his hands, on his face. Yet where was the commotion over in D.C.? Where was the panic? Where were the radio reports, the church bells pealing mournfully, the people weeping in the streets?

Where were the sirens?

Nearly seven hours had passed since he felt his knife sink deep into his target; seven hours since they'd rushed back here, to Maxie's house to watch the Free World start to collapse. And yet it seemed like nothing had happened at all.

There had been no mention of anything on the radio. No calls from Maxie's connected friends, seeing if she'd heard the startling news. The night was calm. Peaceful. Quiet . . .

Don't worry. That's what Maxie had told him, before she passed out from the champagne, that is. This was normal, she'd said. It made sense that the U.S. government would keep news of the President's death a secret for as long as possible. After all, this was still wartime and safeguards for the transfer of power had to be installed. The vice president had to be located. The deceased's family had to be notified. This was a historic moment, she'd insisted, and the ramifications would be felt around the world. These days, such things of great import usually took a while to show their face.

That said, she assured him that by the seven o'clock news broadcast, funeral music would be playing for the dead president.

But it was now past nine o'clock, and the only thing Skass heard playing on the radio was the Artie Shaw Orchestra.

He was drinking champagne now too, and fairly into his cups. He knew this was not a good thing, he should be alert during this time of uncertainty. He drank heartily anyway.

He hated this feeling. This not knowing. Not being able to figure out what had happened exactly. God, after all the time he'd spent on this, and after all that was at stake, he would have thought he'd be so happy by this time that he'd be walking on the moon.

But no . . .

Instead he was twitching very nervously in a chair by the huge bay window in Maxie's bedroom. It was a clear night. The wash of stars twinkling above seemed to mock him. On the bed nearby, Maxie was splayed out, naked, her head propped up by a pillow, sleeping off the gruesome intoxication of the last twenty-four hours.

Skass just looked at her now. Who would have guessed this? Who would have thought that the last person in this world that he could have reached out to would share a little bit of the sickness that had weighed down on him since he was a kid?

Skass thought back to that last day in his jail cell at the prison on Wecht Street. The psychiatrist that had been sent to see him. What was his name again? He couldn't remember. But he wondered what that learned doctor would have thought about this? It never occurred to Skass that there were more people in the world like him. All these years, he'd thought of himself as being quite unique. So what were the chances that he would find a kindred spirit so to speak? And in the form of such a beautiful woman yet?

He shook his head, guzzled some more champagne and turned back to the stars.

Where were the sirens?

HIS LAST HOPE WAS WITH THE NEWSPAPERS.

He'd sent out one of Maxie's housemaids with orders to scour every newsstand between Georgetown and the White House and buy one copy of every different newspaper she could find. He now began nervously tapping out the seconds awaiting her return.

He sucked on some giblets left over from their killings the night before and washed them down with more champagne. Outside the window a bird was chirping fitfully. What kind of bird sings at night? Skass wondered.

Finally he heard the front door open and then slam shut. Next came the sound of a coat being thrown across a chair. Then he heard the maid coming up the stairs.

He immediately put his hand to his chest. Did anything feel warm inside there? He wasn't sure. He was too drunk to tell. How he hoped though that when he opened the door and saw the maid, that he would feel that warm pang of hope rise up from inside him again—and see a headline banner blaring the death of FDR.

He covered Maxie with a sheet and reached the door just as a soft rapping came. He opened it to find the maid, frozen in fear, her arms full of newspapers. No lightning bolt hit Skass. His chest remained cold and barren. He stared at the maid for a long moment though. She seemed younger than when he'd sent her off on this mission just two hours ago. Younger—and more attractive, in a petite dark beauty sort of way. Maxie had told him about her unique arrangement with her help. They were all in the country illegally, and they had all seen enough during her tenure to be tried and shot as spies. Therefore they knew not to speak of anything—*anything*—that they'd seen transpire inside the town house. What a masterful way, Skass thought, to keep the servants under thumb.

Still he momentarily contemplated killing the maid. A slice to her neck and chest just might be interesting. She might not even resist too much. But just as quickly, he decided against it—at least for now. He wasn't sure how Maxie would take to such an action; good help *was* hard to find. Besides, he had some much bigger issues to resolve.

So he took the papers and dismissed the servant, shutting the door in her face. He threw the papers on the couch and began flipping through the front pages in a blur. *Damn!* Not one of them said anything about the President being assassinated. In fact the headlines were about a different topic entirely: their murder of the two young girls the night before.

Skass angrily swept all the newspapers off the couch, then slumped to the floor as well.

How could this be? He'd killed the President—as well as three Secret Service men and a police officer. Why was none of that screaming off these front pages?

Now came a thought that froze Skass to the bone. Had he gone insane? Could he have dreamed it all? Had it all been some kind of vivid hallucination? He felt a deep panic rising up inside him. *What was going on here?* His hands began to shake. He looked over at Maxie. Who was she . . . really? Why had he chosen to take her into his confidence? To take her on his mission? To show her how easily he could kill?

He was petrified with anxiety now, so much so, he thought he was going to faint. There was only one cure when he got like this. He stood up, took his knife from Maxie's bed stand . . . and pricked the tip of his right index finger. A trickle of blood appeared and he started sucking on it nosily. Calm down, he told himself. Take it easy. Be still and breathe deep. He sucked some more blood and could taste the two young sisters in his veins. The panic in his chest began to subside. His throat began to clear. He lowered his head and took another long deep breath,

Yes, he felt better now. . . .

And he found himself staring down at one newspaper; a small story in its upper right-hand corner caught his eye. It was surrounded with white stars and dollar signs and was announcing a massive war-bond rally to be held in Potomac Park the next day. And who would the main speaker be?

FDR himself.

Skass smiled for the first time in what seemed to be an eternity. He reached over and took another handful of giblets and stuffed them in his mouth. The cosmos had thrown him a few curve balls in his lifetime and he'd always managed to hit them back through the wickets before. It shouldn't be any different now.

At Potomac Park tomorrow then, he thought.

That's where this mystery would be solved.

20

THE CROWD BEGAN ARRIVING EARLY AT POTO-
mac Park.

The day had dawned hot and sunny, but with a light breeze. By ten A.M., five thousand people had already gathered in the field across from the reflecting pool. A huge wooden stage had been built here during the night. A large banner floating above it read: BUY WAR BONDS NOW! The entertainment was set to go from eleven o'clock to six that evening, kicking off with an appearance by Bob Hope's USO show band. The President was scheduled to speak sometime before noon.

Skass and Maxie arrived around eleven. She was able to park her car in an area designated for diplomats and low-level VIPs. The crowd was swelling mightily by now. People were making their way toward the park entrance from every direction. Fathers, mothers, grandparents, kids, soldiers, sailors, veterans . . . A quick scan told Skass the crowd would soon top ten thousand or more.

There were many hobos hanging around as well. A few were eating food out of nearby trash barrels as Skass and Maxie pulled up. Two approached Skass as he emerged from Maxie's sedan. Hats out, they asked him for money. Skass would have assumed that a space sealed off for diplomatic automobiles would be free of beggars—but no. One came up to Maxie's window and pounded on it, frightening the daylights out of her. Skass told her to keep the windows rolled up and the doors locked while she was waiting for him. She needed no further prompting to take that piece of advice.

Skass crossed the street and waded into the crowd. As always, it appeared to him that everyone was dressed in the same way. All the men were in white shirts, loose-fitting trousers and brown shoes; all the women were wearing some variation of blue, be it skirts or blouses. It was funny, Skass thought. Before coming here he'd assumed America was a much more colorful place to be than Europe. But he was wrong.

He bought a bag of popcorn, another American obsession, and wound up throwing it away after just two mouthfuls. It was much too salty for him. He bought a cup of lemonade, but with one sip he thought his throat was going to constrict. The tartness was overwhelming; he immediately threw this away too. This was an odd place, this world of American dullness and crappy food. He wiped his hands on his pants and went about his business.

He wasn't nervous, not exactly. True, his left hand was trembling a bit, but that was only because he was gripping Maxie's pistol with it, and that was making him feel a little unbalanced. Skass really hated the gun. Hated the way it felt, hated the way it smelled. But after the strange events of the day before, his instincts told him that if he had to strike again this hot morning, he might need more than a knife to get the job done.

He was carrying a small purple piece of paper in his shirt pocket. This was called a D-Card; Maxie had given it to him. It was a free pass of sorts distributed by the U.S. State Department to low-level diplomats and foreign embassy personnel. It didn't carry much authority, just enough to avoid a parking fine or a speeding ticket, or possibly a charge of drunkeness. Skass was carrying it for another reason: He hoped it might help him get closer access for what he was about to do.

He eventually reached an area just to the right of the big stage. Here a rope barrier marked off the slight grassy knoll over which FDR's car would enter the park. The temporary roadway went around the front of the stage and ended on its opposite side, where the President's access ramp had been built. There was slight bend in this path about twenty feet from the near side of the stage; a temporary light pole had been installed here. Wouldn't the presidential limo have to slow down when it reached this curve? If Skass could get right up to the rope barrier and station himself near the bend, he would be standing no more than ten feet away when the presidential car went by.

Growing excited, he checked his surroundings once again. There were many policemen about, and many soldiers too. But none of the cops were watching this particular stretch of the rope barrier, and most of the soldiers were in dress uniform and bearing only ceremonial arms, which Skass knew were unloaded. So he bought an ice-cream cone, only because he believed it would allow him to blend into the crowd better, then walked over to the rope barrier near the curve and simply stood next to it. No one stopped him. No one tried to shoo him away. In fact, once he'd set the precedent, a small part of the crowd swarmed up to the temporary barrier and staked out their own positions as well. Much to Skass's delight he was now perfectly hidden—in plain view. Even using the D-card couldn't have got him a better vantage point.

The sun grew warmer, and the breeze died away. High above the park, an airplane was skywriting a huge V for Victory sign amongst the clouds. Two children wandered up beside Skass and peered out under the rope. Balloons in hand and completely unattended, he could have easily led both of them away. On the stage about thirty feet from him the USO band was tuning up for its first song. The noise of the trumpets would mask the sound of gunfire, Skass thought now—that is, if the president even made an appearance.

He was ready then, and feeling confident, and only a bit unsettled. He was here and either one of two things was going to happen: The President would not appear, and he would be that much more confident that he had indeed fulfilled his mission yesterday at the ballpark. Or, if by some miracle, the President *did* appear, Skass would use the huge pistol and kill him for good. Finally, he had a plan!

He licked his lips at a fleeting thought from the night before, when he and Maxie had taken the two young girls, so easy to do in the rough-and-tumble slums. And yet they had tasted so sweet! Skass unconsciously sampled his melting ice-cream cone, and suddenly longed for a cup of fine sorbet. The frozen sugary stuff that passed for ice cream over here was just awful. Perhaps some day he and Maxie would stroll Paris, sampling sorbets of all textures and flavors all over town.

Time passed and he found the people around him happy and friendly. He kept his ears open, trying to hear any mention of the President being hurt or sick or wounded and thus not being able to attend the rally. But he picked up nothing of the sort. Indeed these people were brimming with anticipation that their hero would soon arrive. Was someone fooling them? Or had Skass been fooled instead?

What could have happened the day before? he wondered again for what seemed like the millionth time.

He had no rational idea.

But at least he would soon find out.

ELEVEN-THIRTY ARRIVED AND NOW CAME THE sounds of commotion from the roadway next to the stage.

A number of policemen appeared; some walking, some on motorcycles. Then the sounds of cars arriving could be heard. Skass fingered the gun again. The two children were still standing beside him, still unattended, waving small flags. Two policemen on motorcycles roared by. The crowd became energized. More people rushed up to the rope barrier. A line of soldiers marched around the bend, each one carrying an American flag. The USO band began a rousing rendition of "The Star-Spangled Banner." The kids beside Skass began to scream. Skass reached for the trigger of the gun . . .

That's when he felt someone nudge up against his back. He turned to see it was another hobo. Dirty face, overgrown beard, ragged clothes and a ratty hat pulled low over his eyes.

"Go away," Skass ordered him.

But the man did not move.

"I said leave me alone," Skass repeated harshly.

Again, the hobo stood his ground.

Skass began to lose his temper—he didn't need this. Not now. He raised his hand as if to swat the man away.

But the hobo said: "I wouldn't do that, pal . . ."

Suddenly Skass felt something touch him between the legs. He looked down to see the barrel of a tommy gun sticking out from beneath the man's coat. It was aimed right at Skass's genitals.

Skass looked up and just stared at the hobo. He pushed his hat back and now Skass could see his eyes. He was shocked. He recognized this man! Rough face. Broken nose. Back in Kansas. The chase out on the highway.

"You?"

"Me . . ."

It was Joe Copp.

"Make one move and I'll blow your nuts off," Copp whispered to him.

Skass dared not breathe. He had no doubt Copp would do it. But how could he have found him here?

"I have a pair of handcuffs in my coat pocket," Copp was telling him now. "I'm going to take them out and put them on you. Then we are walking away from here, very slowly. Do you understand?"

Skass could barely nod his head.

Copp reached into his coat pocket—but suddenly felt a very tight squeeze around his own wrist. He turned to find five D.C. policemen had come up behind him—and one had put a pair of handcuffs on him!

"What the hell are . . . !" Joe yelled—but one of the cops lunged forward and put his hand over his mouth.

"Shaddup you wise guy," the cop yelled.

Joe immediately swung at the cop and connected fiercely with his jaw. The cop went over on his ass. But just as quickly the four other policemen tackled Joe and they all went down in a heap.

A woman nearby started screaming. And kids went scattering in every direction. More police arrived and began beating Joe with their fists. Meanwhile the USO band just kept on playing, as if nothing was happening at all.

"You fools!" Joe was screaming at the cops. "I'm FBI! *FBI!*"

"We *know* who you are, G-man," one of them growled back at him. "We've been looking all over town for you."

Joe was finally forced to the ground for good. His machine gun was ripped from his coat, and both his hands and feet were locked into shackles. Then he was picked up and carried away.

The last he saw of Skass, he was walking away through the crowd, calmly eating his ice-cream cone.

21

THE JAIL CELL WAS TWELVE BY TWELVE WITH crumbling walls, rusty bars and a smell that combined vomit and urine.

Joe Copp had spent the last twelve hours sitting at the end of the same rickety bench in the far corner of the cell, wondering what he needed more, a bath or a smoke. He hadn't washed properly in nearly two weeks, and had gone just as long without a shave. On the other hand, his last cigarette had been less than a week ago, the tail end of a Pall Mall butt he'd found still burning in a rail yard outside Skokie. He couldn't imagine anything tasting so good and yet so repulsive at the same time.

Actually a change of clothes should have been his first priority. His once-prized jacket was now ripped at the seams, his pants were splitting in the crotch and worn at the knees. He'd lost his tie a long time ago, and his hat . . . well, it was no surprise that people had mistook him for a hobo.

The D.C. lockup was more appalling than he could have ever imagined. There were eighteen other people in the cell with him; the place was designed to hold no more than five or six. Most of them had been arrested as he was, during the war-bond rally.

Drunk and disorderly, fighting, vagrancy seemed to be the most likely charges. But there was a difference between him and his fellow inmates: They knew why they were here. Joe did not. No one had told him why he'd been picked up, what D.C. laws he'd broken. And there was another thing: He seemed to have pissed off the D.C.

cops so much, they had pummeled him all the way to the station house. Two black eyes and at least one cracked rib was the result.

He was a marked man for some reason, so much so, the other bums in the cell refused to even look at him, never mind lend him a smoke.

In some ways, he couldn't blame them.

IT WAS NO MIRACLE THAT COPP WAS IN WASH-ington. No divine wind had brought him here, nor any employment of his finely honed fugitive-tracking techniques.

Joe had come by train. Or more accurately, by hopping trains, freight cars mostly. After the debacle in Kansas, he'd been left with no money, no car, nothing but the clothes on his back, stuck out in the middle of nowhere. It had taken twenty miles of walking through the bare cornfields to find the railroad tracks, then another day of waiting by a curve in the rail bed for a freight train moving slow enough for him to jump on. Somewhere along the way he'd figured out the obvious: that the killer he was tracking was actually trying to assassinate the President, and the string of bodies he'd left in his wake were done more for his amusement than anything else.

And so his destination was purely academic: Where would a presidential assassin go having missed his mark the first time?

Washington, D.C., of course.

The only problem for Joe, aside from his suddenly indigent state, was that there was no exact science to hopping freights. One just selected a train heading east and hoped for the best. It took him several days to reach his goal, sleeping in hay cars and eating stolen tomatoes and raw corn. At one point of his journey he'd found himself in Canada; at another just outside Louisville, Kentucky. He'd slept with cattle, in coal dust and once in a car full of broken eyeglasses.

Through it all he fought back the temptation to walk into the nearest law enforcement office, identify himself, and then call the bureau in New York. But what would that have accomplished really? He was still AWOL from his job, he still had a slew of infractions, if not outright felonies, hanging over his head. And from that shaky foundation, he was going to call his bosses at SWS and tell them, what? That he was tracking a bloodthirsty cannibal who was also trying to kill FDR in his spare time?

To Joe's mind, the response to that statement would have been for him to sit quietly and wait for the men in the white coats to arrive. No, he knew how the Bureau worked. On the cut and dried stuff—bank robbers, kidnappers, those who manufactured illegal whiskey—the G-men were there in a flash. But on things that came at them from out of left field—psychotic presidential assassins, for instance—well, their wheels moved a little slower.

In his fractured state, Joe convinced himself that it was up to him. Only he could find this nutcase and stop him cold. Asking for any help, or even telling anyone of his theories, would serve no good purpose and only slow things down. So he set his sights on getting to Washington, D.C., and then seeking out the most likely place where the potential assassin might strike again.

And he'd made it, arriving just that morning, and immediately heading over to the well-publicized war-bond rally, hoping to sniff out the psycho in the early spring breeze—only to wind up in jail instead.

He would have laughed if it wasn't so pathetic. He felt like absolutely nothing made sense anymore—except one thing:

He'd fucked up again.

HIS JAIL CELL WAS ACTUALLY A TROUBLE TANK, the place found in any big city police station where the really bad sorts were parked indefinitely. Joe knew this because he'd been here for almost thirteen hours and in that time not one of his cell mates had been bailed out. No angry wives, no blank-faced lawyers. Nothing.

This told Joe one thing: There was a chance that he could be in here for a while.

That's why he was so surprised when the two cops ventured down into the dungeon shortly before one in the morning and called out his name.

Copp was at the bars in an instant.

"Yeah, present!" he yelled out.

The cops were unimpressed by his enthusiasm.

"This is your lucky day, hobo," one said. "You've got a guardian angel upstairs."

They opened the cell door and Copp squeezed out. Suddenly he didn't smell so much like urine anymore.

He followed the cops up three flights of stairs. Reaching the top floor he found himself in the main justice hall. The cops pointed him toward the desk sergeant and gave him a push. The old Irish mug looked down at him.

"At least we didn't have to feed you," he said, tossing a few papers at Copp, which he signed without any pretense of reading them.

"And to whom do I owe this pleasure?" he asked the sergeant.

The cop didn't answer. He just pointed behind him. Joe turned to find a very familiar face looking back at him.

It was Big Jim Tolley.

IT WAS NOW ONE A.M.

The streets of Washington were wet, dark, empty. Copp was in the backseat of a huge Ford; Big Jim was squeezed in beside him. A man he believed to be a Secret Service agent was behind the wheel, pressing the gas pedal so heavily, even his Saint Christopher medal was afraid to look.

Thankfully Big Jim had given Copp a bag of new clothes; before leaving the police station Joe had retreated to the men's room, gave himself a quick paper-towel bath and then climbed into the pants, jacket, shirt and tie. The new suit fit him better than his old one. The pair of new shoes did too.

Now, speeding along in the car, Copp wanted to ask his boss a million and a half questions. But Big Jim had given him the high sign just before they'd climbed into the waiting Secret Service car, the meaning of which was crystal clear: Don't open your mouth until we are truly alone.

They drove past the White House. It was dark both within and without. Even the porch lights were extinguished. If the intent was to lead people to think that no one was home, it was a successful one.

They drove past the Washington Monument; a police car was parked next to its main entrance, lights flashing, casting weird shadows everywhere. They went further downtown, past Memorial Hospital, the Capitol Building and hundreds of government office buildings. Finally the car pulled up to the rear of an all-white windowless structure close by the Union Station railroad yards.

What is this? Joe thought. *Are they going to put me back on the freights?*

The Secret Service man climbed out of the front seat, opened Joe's door, and dragged him out. Big Jim followed close behind. They went through a red entranceway lit by a very dim bulb above its frame. This led into a long dark corridor that seemed to gradually fall into the earth. As they began walking down this hallway, Copp tried to read some of the titles on its recessed doorways, but they gave him no clue as to where he was.

They finally reached another door at the far end of the sloping hallway; here, two soldiers were standing guard. Rock-jawed and tough, they looked like they'd just got off the boat from Iwo Jima. The Secret Service guy nodded to Big Jim, who flashed his ID for the soldiers. Then he made an indication that Copp was OK too. The soldiers stood aside and allowed the Secret Service agent to open

the door. The odor that rushed out of the room hit Joe
harder than a punch in the nose.

Formaldehyde . . .

This place was a morgue.

They walked in—and even Copp's weary brain pro-
cessed something resembling shock. Standing in the room
were two more soldiers, both waiting near a set of drawers. Next to them was a man wearing an all-black suit,
with a huge red mustache and an unlit cigar firmly
clenched between his teeth. Beside him was a guy Joe
recognized as one of the FBI's top dogs, Ed Beedy. Next
to him were three men in German SS uniforms. Copp felt
his jaw fall open. He began to say something, but Big Jim
grabbed his shoulder and squeezed it so hard, Joe thought
his collarbone would snap. Again the message was clear:
Keep your eyes open and your mouth shut.

The door was closed behind them and Beedy nodded
toward the soldiers. One of them pulled a drawer out.

There was a body on it. Covered by a white sheet.

Copp looked at Big Jim. They really didn't know each
other very well, which was not good because Joe had no
idea what his boss was up to at the moment.

Copp turned back to the covered body. "Anyone we
know?" he asked.

Beedy ignored his question and grabbed the end of the
white sheet.

"You ready for this?" he asked.

Copp gulped and nodded. Beedy pulled the sheet back.

Lying on the table, cold, white and quite dead, was
Franklin D. Roosevelt.

Or . . . at least it looked like him.

The hair was unmistakable. The nose, the chin, the eyebrows were too. Beedy pulled the sheet down further;
Copp felt a pang in his chest. The body was covered with
stab wounds—dozens of them. Most were located on the
lower torso, but the neck had been slashed deeply as well.
Copp knew these were signs of anger in the hands of the
killer.

But he also sensed something was wrong here.

"That's not really him, is it?" he asked Beedy.

The FBI man shook his head. "No, it isn't . . ."

"Who is it then?" Joe asked.

"A presidential double," Beedy said. "Every president since Harding has used them in some capacity. FDR has employed several over the years. This poor bastard was killed at the baseball game yesterday. Someone shot three of his bodyguards, then stabbed him and then a cop—this while FDR was leaving by another entrance."

The soldier covered up the body again.

"This guy was in wrong place at the wrong time," Beedy said. "But of course, that was his job . . ."

The body was pushed back into the wall.

"So, you're probably wondering what all this has to do with you," Beedy said to him.

Joe just shook his head.

"Nope," he said. "I *know* what it's all about. This psycho I've been tracking. He did this, just like he did about a dozen more people from here to Kansas and back. And you guys want to catch him, and ice him . . . as much as I do. Right?"

Beedy was immediately uncomfortable. He eyed the man with the huge red mustache, who just shrugged and readjusted his unlit cigar.

"Well, that's it, of course," Beedy finally said. "Partially anyway . . ."

Joe looked at Beedy queerly. "Partially . . . ?"

Beedy rubbed his hand over his balding dome. He looked like he needed a stiff drink.

"Look, Joe," he began again. "We wanted to show you all this just to emphasize what this man—his name is Skass—is capable of . . ."

Joe laughed in his face. "Believe me, I don't need an education on that."

"And we were able to hush up this killing," Beedy went on without stopping, "as well as the others at the ballpark, but probably not for long. This Skass is, well, quite *un-*

balanced, and judging from the audacity of this attack, obviously he'll stop at nothing to fulfill his mission."

With this, Joe gave everyone in the room the once-over. He knew what Big Jim was doing here, and Beedy as well. The guy in the black suit—who knew what his story was? But why the guys in German uniforms? And why did Beedy just refer to Skass's antics as "a mission?"

"This guy, Skass . . ." Joe started to ask. "Are you telling me that he's a—"

Beedy cut him off. "He's a Gestapo agent, yes . . ."

Joe just shook his head. That was another thing he should have figured out.

"And the Three Stooges here," he said, pointing to the Germans. "They're authentic?"

Beedy's face went red. "Look, Agent Copp, it's not necessary that you know *every* aspect of what is transpiring here. In fact we simply want to know just one thing from you: Do you have any idea where this man Skass is? If you do, you must tell us immediately."

Somehow Joe managed to keep his cool. "Well, I knew where he was earlier today," he replied snidely. "In fact I had the barrel of my gun pointed at his dick. Yet that was the moment you people decided to arrest me. Was that part of the plan too?"

Beedy was becoming infuriated.

"Because of your recent nonadherence of Bureau policy," he began saying through gritted teeth, "that was the only way we knew of to make contact with you. Every cop on the East Coast has had your picture in his pocket for the past three days."

Joe unconsciously rubbed his sore cheekbone. "Well, the D.C. contingent is certainly an enthusiastic bunch," he said. "But why was I kept in the clink for twelve hours?"

That's when one of the German officers piped up. "Because if you had been left to your own devices, this man Skass would be dead by now . . ."

Copp turned slowly toward the German. "Well, ain't that the whole idea?"

Silence. From Beedy. From the Germans.

"Well, ain't it?" Joe repeated. "This guy slaughters children and *eats them* for Christ's sake. You do want to see him rubbed out, if that's what it takes to stop him? Right?"

More silence. Ten long seconds of it.

"You are on the low end of the order here," the second German officer finally said. "Why can't you just do what your superiors tell you?"

That's when Joe lost it. He took two giant steps and was quickly nose to nose with the SS man.

"Mister Beedy," Joe said between clenched teeth, "may I ask why three enemy officers are here, in our capital city, apparently moving about of their own accord? What is their function exactly?"

Beedy cleared his throat uncomfortably. "They are here to help us find Skass. That's all you have to know."

"Help us *find* him—or help us *stop* him? Those are two different things."

Now the German exploded. "For God's sakes man," he screamed at Joe. "Just follow orders!"

Copp hit him—square in the jaw. The German went down like a sack of bricks.

The next thing Joe knew, he was slammed up against the wall by the two MPs. Their burp guns were suddenly one inch from his face.

"What's the matter with you guys?" Copp roared at them. "You're holding a gun on me, so I won't brain this Nazi?"

He could tell he made an impact on the two MPs, but they stood firm. Joe tried to get away from them, tried to get at the other two Germans, but the soldiers slammed him even harder against the wall. The situation went very tense. One wrong move, one slip of the trigger, and Joe's chest would be perforated with bullets. Yet it was his instinct to fight back. Suddenly Joe felt a huge presence come between him and the soldiers. It was Big Jim. He pushed both MPs aside as if they were rag dolls, then pulled Copp out between them.

"I'm taking him outside so he can cool off," Big Jim announced to everyone in the room. "Anyone have any objections?"

The German officers didn't say a word. Beedy just shook his head. The man with the red mustache didn't move a muscle.

Big Jim steered Copp toward the door, saying over his shoulder: "Let me talk to him . . . I think I still speak his language."

THEY WALKED FOR TEN BLOCKS WITHOUT SAY-ing a word.

The streets in this part of D.C. were deserted and filthy. Warehouses, loading docks and nondescript buildings prevailed, and the only noise they could hear was coming from the nearby railroad yards. Even that was fairly muted.

They finally turned a corner to find a diner just opening up. Joe was too furious to eat, but Big Jim directed him toward the eatery's door and Joe reluctantly went in. They sat down in a corner booth, the only two customers in the place. A sleepy waitress appeared and dropped two menus in front of them. Joe just ordered a coffee, black; Big Jim ordered the full steak breakfast, double the meat, double the toast. Their food arrived in incredibly short order. Copp took one look at Big Jim's plate and felt his stomach do a somersault. He couldn't bear to even look at food.

Not so Big Jim.

"So, tell me," Big Jim began with his first bite. "*Do* you have any idea where this monkey Skass is?"

Joe took one sip of his coffee, then pushed it away from him.

"What's the amendment in the Constitution that prevents you from ratting on yourself?" he replied instead. "The one the wise guys always use?"

"That's the Fifth Amendment, Joe . . ."

"Yeah, that's the one," he said. "Well, I want to plead the Fifth Amendment. That is, if there's still a Constitution in force around here."

Big Jim dumped a half bottle of ketchup onto his first steer-sized piece of steak. "In the theater, Joe, they call that being melodramatic . . ."

"I'm being dramatic, am I?" Joe shot back. "There are Nazi officers in Washington, D.C., not a mile from the White House for Christ's sake. Living here. Free. Doing God knows what—and you're saying *I'm* being too dramatic? How the hell should I be?"

"They're trying to help us, Joe," Big Jim said. "They're providing assistance in finding this guy."

"Again—they want to *find* him," Joe growled. "Whatever happened to shooting him on sight? The guy's a frigging monster."

"That's not part of the plan apparently . . ."

"No, it sure isn't. I mean, if it was, then it would have been Skass's picture in every cop's pocket east of the Mississippi, and not mine. Right?"

Big Jim paused in his chewing—this approximated deep thought for him. Copp saw his face change a little.

"You know, don't you," Joe said to him. "You know what those assholes are up to. They don't want him dead, they just *want* him. But why? Why do they want to take this guy alive so badly?"

Big Jim tore into a piece of toast.

"Let's just say he's part of a bigger mission for the Germans," he mumbled.

"A bigger mission?" Joe repeated, stealing one of Big Jim's Chesterfields. "What could be a bigger mission for them than trying to kill our President?"

Big Jim burped once, then began working on his second piece of steak. "Let's just say this guy Skass speaks very good Russian," he said.

"*Russian?*" Joe said. "You mean, they want to pull this guy back . . . so he can go . . . to Russia? To do what?"

Big Jim looked Joe straight in the eyes.

"What do you think?" he asked.

Joe pondered this for a few seconds. "To kill Stalin?"

Big Jim raised his coffee cup, took a noisy sip and set it down again. That was his way of confirming Joe's theory.

"Uncle Joe is the new enemy," Big Jim said. "Or at least everyone around here seems to think so. Their belief is, if he's out of the picture, well, the world will be a different place once the war is over. Very different."

Joe just shook his head. He felt like the world he knew was collapsing all around him.

"So, that's the way it is? No wonder those three goose-stepping assholes weren't adding anything constructive to the conversation. They're not really here to help us, we're the ones *helping them* . . ."

Big Jim shrugged uncomfortably. "That might be one way to look at it, I guess."

Joe became so enraged he threw his lit cigarette down onto the table, where it bounced in a blaze of sparks and landed squarely in Big Jim's coffee. Unfazed, Big Jim simply fished it out of his cup and took a sip.

"But why are we in league with them?" Copp continued angrily. "They're not doing this as a favor to us. They're just doing it so they can save their own asses. For God's sake Jim, the Russians are *our allies*. What right do we have to help our enemies dump a madman like that into their laps? To bump off one of our friends? And God knows how many innocent Russian women and kids? Different world or not, doesn't that seem crazy to you?"

Big Jim just kept on chewing, but he was doing so a bit slower.

Joe raged on: "Are you telling me that when they find this guy Skass, no matter what he's doing, they're just going to ship him out—let him go? Scot-free? And allow him to get away with the crimes he's committed over here?"

Big Jim shrugged again as he devoured the last of his

second steak. He didn't have a reply. They were quiet for a long time.

"Let me ask you something," Joe finally said, his voice lowered a notch. "What the hell have we been doing all these years? You, me, the entire Bureau? I'll tell you what *I've* been doing. I've been having pieces of me shot away to protect this country . . . from assholes like the Dentons and Stringy, and counterfeiters and drug pins, you name it. I did it because I thought that's what we were *supposed* to be doing. Protecting America and everything it stands for. So kids can sleep good at night, and parents believe that no matter what happens, a brighter future always lays ahead. Well, frankly helping the frigging Nazis doesn't seem like part of that plan. No matter what screwy reason there is. These guys are still killing hundreds of our guys a day—and now we're *helping them*?"

Big Jim could no longer look him in the eye.

"Am I wrong here, Chief?" Joe went on, though he was getting weary, like a car running out of gas. "Is it me? Am I the problem? Am I the guy who just isn't getting it? Because, if I am, well, then you better give me your gun so I blow my brains out right here and now—because . . . because . . . I always believed that . . . that . . ."

He was suddenly all out of words.

So Big Jim said for him instead, "That this country is better than that . . ."

Joe was stunned.

"Exactly," he whispered.

They sat in absolute silence now for more than a minute. Big Jim never looked up at him. He just contemplated his empty plate for a long, long time. Then he drained his coffee cup, stood up and threw a fifty-dollar bill on the table.

"I'm off to the man's loo," he said. "Be back in a moment."

With that, Big Jim left Joe alone in the booth and walked slowly to the rest room. He didn't really have to go. He simply spent the next five minutes combing his hair, washing his hands and picking stray pieces of steak from his teeth. He checked his watch, then washed his hands again. Another check of his watch—he bought a drop of Wildroot from a dispenser and did his hair again. He checked his watch once more, and then satisfied, walked out of the rest room.

When he got back to the booth, Joe Copp was long gone.

22

THE FIRST SMALL MIRACLE OF THE DAY CAME
when Joe found a bar that was actually open before seven
in the morning.

He didn't need coffee or a steak or toast and eggs. He
needed a drink. A drink and some place real quiet where
he could think.

He figured he had twenty-four hours tops to find Skass
before the D.C. police found *him* again. The problem was,
how could he accomplish in one day what the U.S.-
German shadow team had failed to do in many?

One thing was for sure though: Neither the Germans
nor Army Intelligence had a clue as to where Skass was.
If they had, why would Joe have been dragged in and
asked if *he* knew the whereabouts of the madman? In
other words, if they had to ask him, then they really were
at square one.

But this was a good thing for Joe. This meant they had
no advantage over him in finding Skass first. And at that
moment, that was all Joe wanted. To find the monster
first . . .

The question was, how? He didn't have an ace in the
hole and he sure didn't have much time.

But he did have a jack, maybe.

Or, more accurately, a queen.

He found the bar of his dreams at the opposite end of
Washington, D.C., after a long bumpy bus ride from the
blocks of white buildings over near the railroad yards.

Were they all morgues? Joe had thought once he'd
cleared the area. Top secret government repositories

where all the famous dead, or their doubles, were kept on ice? It was a strange thought.

Luckily it dimmed the further he got away from the neighborhood.

The bus was just one stop away from its terminus when Joe spotted the tiny dive at the far end of Connecticut Avenue. As he was the only one on the bus, the driver let him out right on the corner.

Joe walked into the saloon to find it was darker than he could have imagined. It had a small bar and about a dozen tables. One was located deep in the far corner. Beside it was a cigarette machine.

The grumpy bartender poured him a shot of Old Museum whiskey and then a glass of Knickerbocker beer. Joe tipped him a dollar, which all but said he wanted to be left alone. Then he bought a pack of Pall Malls and retreated with his breakfast to the far corner of the barroom.

It was now just seven A.M.

Joe had seen many things the day before at the warbond rally—and it was these memories now that he would have to mine if he was to come up with some kind of lead on Skass.

Before spotting the assassin inside, Joe had scouted out the main entrance to Potomac Park. He'd tried to study every face that seemed out of place to him—a throwback to the days when he would dress in civilian clothes and sit on a bench outside a bank the FBI suspected was marked for robbery, taking mental notes on any strange people or strange cars that happened to pass by. Joe was an expert at this type of countersurveillance. Whether it be a crowd of ten thousand or a small-town population of two hundred and change, someone up to no good usually acted differently than everyone else. Sometimes a bit too nervous, sometimes a bit too casual. If you knew what to look for, it was usually easy to spot.

Joe's nasty attire the prior morning had helped him in this regard. Everyone who took notice of him assumed he was just another hobo and gave him a wide berth. It was a great cover; he found he could go just about anywhere and do just about anything, and everyone just kind of let him be. An odd power, for someone who was supposedly down on his luck.

After about a half hour of watching for any unusual behavior, he'd spotted not a man, but a woman acting oddly near the park's main entrance. She was sitting in a huge stretch-style sedan, with all the windows rolled up and the engine running, this even though it was a very warm spring day.

Joe had cautiously approached the car, walking about fifteen feet in front of it, head down, but eyes looking right. As soon as the woman spotted him, she immediately checked to make sure all her doors were locked, then revved the motor as if she was contemplating driving away.

Joe just kept on walking, but her actions had called attention to herself. That was usually the first clue that something was rotten in Denmark. Another strange thing: Her's was the only car parked in the cordoned-off area set aside for diplomats. What foreign diplomat would come to a U.S. war-bond rally, early in the morning, in such high heat? A war-bond rally had to be the most common gathering of American citizens. A foreign diplomat would seem out of place. Why then was this big car parked here, in this special diplomats' section, engine running, with a beautiful but frightened-looking woman sitting behind the wheel?

As he walked away, Joe took note that although the car had Washington, D.C., tags, there was a flag decal stuck on the rear window. He had no idea what country the flag represented and he wasn't about to stop and ask.

He simply filed all this away in his head and moved on.

*   *   *

JOE HAD HOPED TO SPOT SKASS EVEN BEFORE the assassin entered the park, but that had not worked out. As soon as he became aware that the President was close by, he'd changed tactics. He moved to the area near the stage and started scanning the faces up close. If Skass was already there, it made sense he'd be trying to get as close as possible to his target. And sure enough, that's where Joe found him. Right in the front row. Whether he knew it or not, the potential assassin stuck out like a sore thumb. Although he was dressed just like everyone else, and was holding an ice-cream cone, and was surrounded by families and kids and flags and balloons—he just didn't look *American*.

Joe had quickly swept in and in their brief confrontation before he was hauled away, he'd noticed something sticking out of Skass's shirt pocket. It was a small purple card with two black stars on it along with the letter *D*.

From what he'd seen in that moment, the style, print face and the design of the card had reminded Joe of one thing: a gas rationing coupon. Stark, yet official looking. Almost like a dollar bill. Something the U.S. government had a hand in creating. Why would Skass be carrying such a thing?

Joe pondered all this for a long time now. Two strange things: the purple card in Skass's pocket and the woman parked in the VIP section who was frightened of hobos.

Could there be a connection?

HE DRAINED HIS SHOT OF WHISKEY AND OR-dered another. At the same time he bummed a pencil and some paper from the morose bartender.

Joe tried to draw from memory the flag he'd seen attached to the sedan's rear window. He was sure it consisted of three parts: two blocks made up most of the flag, but they were not of equal size. Either the one on the right or the one on the left was bigger than the other. There was also a symbol in the middle of it. If Joe recalled correctly, the main colors were either green and red or red and blue. The design in the middle contained a cross—or so he thought.

He drew several different variations of the flag, none of which struck him as being totally right. Still, it was a start.

He still had no idea what country this flag was from, but he thought he knew a way to find out. He wanted to keep as low a profile as possible and that meant avoiding very public places, so going to a library or one of the universities seeking an atlas of the world's flags was out. Besides, he knew there was a certain section of Washington that held the vast majority of the district's foreign embassies. If he could get there, undetected, and scour the neighborhood, he might find not only what country this flag represented, he might find that sedan as well.

With nothing else to go on, he decided to give it a shot.

He collected his smokes and notes and headed out of the bar. He waved casually to the bartender, who had his nose stuck in a racing form.

"Yeah, see you in church, buddy," the bartender called after him.

Joe turned. "What do you mean?"

The man barely looked up from his racing sheet. "It's Good Friday, mac," he said. "You know? Two days before Easter? Why do you think I'm open so goddamn early? All these government workers take the day off—and half of them wind up here."

"Easter, huh?" Joe mumbled. He had no idea the holy day was upon them. "It must have come early this year . . ."

IT WAS NOW JUST A FEW MINUTES PAST EIGHT A.M.

Joe climbed onto yet another empty bus and headed back toward central D.C. again. Several times police cars went roaring by them, their lights flashing, sirens wailing. Joe would have bet a sawbuck they were all out looking for him.

With the bus driver's help he located the section of D.C. unofficially called embassy row. Now began a grueling three hour hike up and down its streets, sun beating down, Joe looking over his shoulder every five seconds expecting to be brained by the exuberant D.C. cops again. What he found though was that many of the embassies were closed. Naturally those belonging to the Axis powers were locked up tight, but also those of their allies and countries conquered by them, like Rumania and Hungary. Even worse, while many of these places had flagpoles either implanted on their tiny lawns or hanging out of a second-story window, lots of these staffs were bare. Apparently in wartime, it was considered unwise for some countries to advertise exactly where their Washington address could be found.

Joe even stopped several nannies on the street and, pretending to be a foreigner, asked if they could tell him where the embassy belonging to this flag was located. The problem was the nannies were foreigners too, and they had no idea what he wanted or what he was talking about. One woman suggested, though, the flag was actually that of Liechtenstein. But Joe found that country's consulate and the flags looked nothing alike. A man selling papers thought it was the flag of Malta. Once again, Joe found a building belonging to that country, but the flags did not match.

IT WAS JUST PAST ONE IN THE AFTERNOON when, weary and hungover from his earlier spree, Joe literally stumbled upon the place he'd been seeking.

He'd just turned yet another corner when up ahead he saw his flag flowing in the hot breeze. Red, green and a symbol in the middle. It seemed like it was a mile away, but he practically ran to it. He found the pole was standing outside the Portuguese embassy.

But of course there was a catch. The embassy was torn apart and in the process of a major renovation. Even worse, there was no one around. It was, after all, Good Friday, and so no work was being done on the building that day. He did enjoy a second minor miracle though when he noticed that many of the cars parked near the building had small purple cards displayed on their windshields. Joe inspected one and learned that these were D-Cards, basically a free permit for diplomatic types to park anywhere they wanted. Though none of them were on the vehicle he was looking for—it had been almost limousine in length—he *did* have something that could connect Skass back to the nervous woman waiting in the VIP parking area the previous morning.

His intuition had scored again.

SO NOW HE HAD HIS LINK. BUT HOW COULD HE find out where the temporary Portuguese embassy was located?

He found a small drugstore about five blocks away. It was empty, its owner fairly sleepy. Joe commandeered the phone booth and began making calls: to the State Department, to the Commerce Department, to the Portuguese embassy itself. There was no answer at any of them. Because of the holy day no one was working.

Finally, in desperation, he called the Spanish embassy, thinking as it was the country right next to Portugal, perhaps they knew where their neighboring countrymen were holed up these days. And someone actually answered the phone. But as soon as Joe mentioned Portugal, they abruptly hung up on him. He called the British embassy, the Irish and the Free French. No one knew what he was talking about. He walked past the construction site again— no one was working, no one was around.

It was getting to be mid-afternoon now. Joe returned to

the phone booth and called the State Department again and this time asked the operator not for the political affairs department, but the protocol section. A woman got on and Joe told her he had to deliver flowers for an Easter party at the Portuguese embassy—did she know the new address? The woman put him on hold for ten long minutes—which cost him more than three dollars in change. His hand cramped up from throwing so many coins into the phone. But she finally came back on and gave him an address.

He asked her: "And exactly what part of Washington is that in?"

There was a long pause. Finally she replied: "You must be some kind of great deliveryman. That address is not in Washington—it's in Georgetown."

Thus, tiny miracle number three.

HE BOUGHT A COKE AT THE DRUGSTORE'S fountain and regrouped his thoughts.

It was now past two p.m. Nearly seven hours had been spent tracking down a piece of information that, had he been an agent in good standing, might have taken all of five minutes. Still after two more bus rides and another thirty minutes of pounding the pavement, Joe finally found the town house, its flag flying right above the front door.

He stood on a corner nearby and lit a cigarette in triumph. In many ways, it had been easier to pick up the scent of the Denton Gang over an area of four huge states than it had been to find where the hell the Portuguese had moved their embassy.

But that was OK with Joe. It would have scared him if the information had come to him *too* easily. And though some precious time had been lost, it was still good to know he had followed the right track.

*   *   *

A VERY DARK RAINSTORM HAD MOVED IN BY this time.

Within seconds, the sky was so black, it was as if evening were already upon them. Joe looked at the threatening dark clouds and had to smile a bit.

Appropriate weather, he thought. *For Good Friday . . .*

He moved down the street to find the car he sought was parked out front of the swanky residence. A colored chauffeur was pacing nervously next to it. He didn't look too happy. When Joe began strolling across the street toward him, the man froze, then tried to light a cigarette. But his hands were shaking too much.

Joe knew a lookout when he saw one. This man had seen things, heard things inside the house—and at that moment, he wasn't quite sure what to do about it.

Joe walked right up to him, lit a match and raised it to the chauffeur's cigarette.

"You an American, pal?" Joe asked him.

The man shook his head no. *"Cubano,"* he replied.

"You want to be an American someday?"

The man numbly nodded yes.

"Si . . . more than anything, sir . . ."

"Do you want to help out the war effort then?"

The man nodded again. "I sure do, boss . . ."

Joe finally showed him his FBI badge. "Then tell me, how many people are in that house right now?"

The man took a long drag of his cigarette.

"Alive or dead?" he finally asked Joe nervously.

"Let's start with those that are still alive . . ."

The man thought a moment. "One that I know about, one that might soon be dead . . ."

"Just two people in all?" Joe asked. He'd expected the place to be crawling with diplomats and staff.

But the chauffeur just shook his head. "No one comes here except to party—and just on Thursday nights. Everyone else is either back home or living in Brazil."

Joe contemplated the town house again. It seemed eerily quiet.

"You pull any triggers in there today, pal?" Joe asked the chauffeur. "You been throwing any knives around?"

The man shook his head vigorously. "No sir, boss," he said emphatically. "Not me. It's just those crazy rich people."

Joe believed him. He reached inside his pocket and came out with a five-dollar bill—a leftover from Big Jim's stake of fifty.

He gave the man the five-spot and said: "Take a cab home, and stay there. Don't talk to anybody. If no one comes looking for you in a week's time, you never think about any of this again. Got it?"

The man began to cry.

"I got it, boss . . ."

He shook Joe's hand, took the bill and threw his chauffeur cap and coat into the gutter.

Then he quickly walked away.

THE SKY WAS GETTING EVEN DARKER NOW, AND a stiff breeze had blown up. Joe sniffed the wind and it reminded him of the worst hours at Carson Bend. It had grown dark in the daytime there too.

He leaned against the sedan, lit a cigarette, and appraised the situation. Every window on the bottom floor of the house had been drawn and shuttered. Up on the second floor, a faint orange glow could be seen from one window. No lights were on anywhere else in the house.

Which way this time? Joe thought. Front door or back?

He wasn't armed—and that was not good. Prevailing on someone to let him in by threat of force wasn't going to work here.

A bluff maybe?

It was as good an idea as any.

He stubbed out the butt, then walked up the stairs and boldly knocked on the door. A very frightened maid answered right away.

She looked at Joe with the same terrified eyes as the chauffeur he'd just dismissed.

"I was told someone here needed a doctor," Joe said to her.

Her face lit up. Suddenly she was very animated. She practically yanked him through the door, not noticing, or not caring to, that he carried no medical bag, nor had he shown her any credentials.

"Where?" he asked her. "Where is the patient?"

She just pointed nervously upstairs. Joe gave her five bucks too, and she was out the door like a shot.

Joe quickly closed the door behind her, then reconnoitered the darkened first floor. Big rooms, lots of paintings, lots of antiques. No lights on anywhere. He detected a strange odor in the air. Like something had been burnt on the stove. Upstairs he thought he heard someone crying.

He still didn't have a weapon, and he knew that it would be foolhardy to proceed to the second floor without one. Again he stumbled around the first floor in the dark. This place didn't seem likely to have a baseball bat lying around. He went in the kitchen and looked through all the drawers and cupboards and countertops.

There wasn't a knife to be found.

Not a good sign . . .

HE FINALLY LOCATED AN OLD CHAMPAGNE BOT-tle. He wrapped a towel around the bottle and broke it as quietly as possible in the sink. The jagged stem was now his weapon. He returned to the hallway and started up the front stairs.

He felt like he was an expert at this sort of thing now. He knew some kind of horror was waiting for him up the stairs. Lots of blood? Guts? Pieces of bodies? He was sure of that and more. Yet whether it was for good or bad, his stomach was not flip-flopping as much as it had that dark day not so long ago when he'd searched Harry Strum's house and stumbled upon the most unspeakable horror.

This time, he felt ready. Steeled for anything. But what kind of person did that make him?

What exactly had he become when things like this seemed almost routine?

He ascended the grand staircase one step at a time and eventually reached the second floor.

There was a dim cascade of light coming from the master bedroom just down the hall. Somewhere close by, a phonograph record was skipping. Joe crept forward, wishing he had his trusty machine gun with him. He stopped every few steps and listened. But aside from the same, out-of-tune opera note playing over and over, he heard nothing more but the wind.

He finally reached the bedroom door. Bottle knife up and ready, he peeked in. The room was filled with lit candles. Dozens of them. The only electric light he could see was in the bathroom. What remained of a person wearing a maid's uniform was lying in the tub, bloody and dismembered.

He took two more steps into the room and found Maxie. She was lying on the bed, surrounded by candles. A twelve-inch butcher knife was sticking out of her chest.

A pistol lay on the dresser nearby. Joe quickly dropped his broken bottle and scooped up the weapon. It held five bullets. The malfunctioning record player was off to his left. He turned it off. Finally he approached the bed.

Incredibly, Maxie was still alive. Somehow, some way, she was conscious and breathing, though she made a ghastly gurgling sound every time she exhaled. She looked up at him queerly, as if nothing was wrong with her, as if there *were* no knife sticking out of her chest. That's when Joe realized something. He saw no sign of any struggle, no swatches of blood on the floor or bedclothes. Nothing at all seemed disturbed.

Maxie hadn't been stabbed. Rather, she was pushing the knife into herself.

"Since when can hobos afford a new set of clothes?" she asked him, her voice weak, yet defiant. Joe couldn't believe it. She remembered him from outside the park the day before.

"Since when do gorgeous women take up with child murderers?" he asked her.

She laughed—a glob of blood came out of her mouth.

"What a provincialist!" she gasped. "Read a history book, copper. How do you think the great leaders of ancient Greece and Rome entertained themselves?"

"By eating kids?"

"Yes, some of them . . ."

More blood from her mouth.

"Greece and Rome, eh?" Joe replied. "Well, *they're* certainly riding high on the hog these days."

She was dresssed in an elegant nightgown. Attached to its plunging neckline was a bauble Skass had apparently given her. It was the deputy's badge the killer had taken from Sammy Silk. Joe reached down and took it off her. It didn't belong here.

Maxie's smile disappeared now. She pushed the knife in a little deeper. She was like an amateur vampire, trying to drive a stake through her own heart.

"He told you why he came here to do all this?" Copp asked her.

She pushed further down on the knife and arched her back in what must have been excruciating pain.

"Yes, he told me," she gasped. "I told him. What difference does it make? He won't stop until he fulfills his mission. That much you can be sure of . . ."

"So he thinks the President is still alive?"

She laughed. More blood. "Thinks it?" she said, voice failing yet still defiant. "He *knows* it . . . we saw the crippled bastard himself, twenty minutes after they dragged your ass away."

"So who does your boyfriend think he killed at the ballpark?"

She smiled. Bloody teeth now. "*A doppelganger?* That means a double . . . A twin. I'm sure you don't speak the language of the *Reich*."

Joe almost laughed. "Honey, in a few weeks *no one* is going to be speaking the language of the *Reich* . . ."

She smiled awkwardly again and pushed the knife another inch deeper into her chest. Joe looked at her; she was a stunning woman, even in her present state.

"Is this his idea of the easy way out? Do it yourself instead of him doing it to you?"

She laughed again; it hurt her mightily. "This is how the proud Skiki tribe of Chad do it, you uneducated bluecoat. It's a ritual that guarantees if you die the most painful death possible, then all your misdeeds will be forgiven."

Joe just shook his head. This was a weird way to get into heaven. "If you wanted someone to absolve you of yours sins, well, personally I would have called a priest . . ."

She jammed the knife in deeper. It was meeting with less resistance now. Joe heard a slight pop; she'd hit an artery. Blood came gushing out of her.

"You're way too beautiful to die like this," Joe told her.

She gasped again. "So you think this is all a waste? You think that I'll go straight to hell?"

"Help me out and maybe not," Joe replied, speaking faster now. It was already like talking to a corpse, something from a horrible dream. "We can end this thing right now."

"How?"

"You said he knows the President is still alive. So just tell me . . . where did Skass go? Where is he now?"

She laughed again. More blood gushed out of her wound. In her last dying moment, she looked up at Joe like he was the dimmest bulb in the bunch

"Where is he now?" she asked. *"Where do you think?"*

23

JOE TOOK A TAXI TO THE WHITE HOUSE.

It had been a calculated risk: He knew that in big cities, many of the cabdrivers were actually off-duty cops making some extra money. If the taxi he hailed turned out to be driven by one of D.C.'s finest, and the moonlighting cop recognized him, well, it would be a quick ride back to the trouble tank for Joe.

But when he finally grabbed a cab a few blocks away from the macabre town house, the driver seemed to be anything but a cop. A boxer or a bank robber, maybe. But not a cop. Joe threw him five bucks and got to say: "Take me to the White House . . . and step on it!"

The driver obeyed, but with a bit more reckless abandon than Joe would have liked. They were soon careening through the busy streets at speeds higher than some car chases he'd been in. Joe hoped there wasn't some kind of cosmic justice at work here, some kind of destiny fulfillment that would get him killed in a car crash just as he was about to corner his fugitive for what he hoped would be the last time.

But then a smashup would probably just confirm Joe's weary belief that he had screwed up once again. Sure, he'd used his top-notch deductive abilities to find the wayward Portuguese embassy. But it took just a few words with a dying woman for him to realize that the White House was the place to be. *Where else* would Skass go once he realized his prey was still alive?

In any case, they reached Pennsylvania Avenue in record time. Joe had assumed the area around the White

House would be dark and deserted, just like when he drove by the night before with Big Jim. But as it turned out, just the opposite was true. One half of the presidential block was lit up like a summer's day with police lights. Joe felt his heart sink once again. This couldn't be a good thing.

The reason for the hubbub? Well, even though the war in Europe was just weeks away from conclusion, an "America First" rally had brought out about two hundred protesters for a Good Friday march in front of the White House. The holy day seemed to indicate to the protesters that the urgency of their cause had been multiplied somehow. They were chanting protest songs and carrying picket signs, urging the President to get the U.S. out of Europe now before it was "too late." Even worse, watching the protest from across the street were about a hundred onlookers—and a small army of cops.

Exactly what Joe didn't need.

BUT THEN CAME YET ANOTHER TINY MIRACLE.

The cab was crawling along Pennsylvania Avenue now, passing the protesters and the gawking bystanders. Suddenly, Joe took a deep sniff of the air—and yelled for the driver to stop. The hack obeyed with a screech of brakes and Joe jumped out. And at that exact spot, he found Skass. Holding a purloined America First protest sign, the killer was leaning on the White House fence, gazing in toward the Executive Mansion.

Maybe I still got it, Joe thought instantly.

But he didn't spend more than that one moment celebrating this latest piece of good fortune. He didn't have to remind himself that he'd been this close before. He had to play it very very carefully this time. After the legion of miscues over the past few weeks, he *had* to get this one right.

So he reached into his pocket and slowly brought the pistol up to his left side, out of sight of the cops. There were five bullets in its chamber. Joe was intending to put all five right into Skass's head.

But it was almost as if Skass had heard him thinking. For as Joe took two steps toward him, the killer turned around very slowly and was suddenly face-to-face with him. Those eyes. They hit Joe like twin knives in the gut. And that terrifying little smile. Every piece of the killer's sickness was on display between those very dirty teeth. And Skass stayed cool. He didn't seem a bit perturbed that Joe was standing no more than ten feet away from him, a gun in his left hand. He even gave Joe a little wave, as if they were old friends. Joe stared right back at him, trying not to be mesmerized by the cool and collected cannibal. That smile *was* disarming though—and finally Joe had to blink.

And when he did, Skass took off.

It was amazing. One moment the killer was standing there, the next he was weaving in and out of the crowd of protesters with the greatest of ease. Joe meanwhile set off in quick pursuit, but found himself crashing into these same people, knocking down at least two elderly ladies and maybe tripping over a kid or two as well. Yet a quick look over his shoulder told Joe that none of the cops had joined the chase or even noticed what was going on.

Once again, it was just he and Skass.

The killer had lit out toward the northeast corner of Pennsylvania Avenue. Joe was astonished by the man's foot speed. He could run at least three times faster than a normal human being, this while wearing dress shoes, floppy trousers, a suit coat and a hat. Joe nearly lost sight of him when he turned the corner and went south toward the most desolate end of the presidential block. There were many weeping willow trees on this side of the street and they made darker what was already a very dark afternoon.

And it was in these deep shadows that Joe saw Skass leap the White House fence, going over it as if he'd suddenly sprouted wings.

* * *

JOHN CAHOON HAD WORKED THE BACK GATE
at the White House for almost twenty years.

He'd served in the post since before the Hoover Administration. In fact, the running joke was that Cahoon
knew more people at the White House than the President
himself.

He'd arrived early for his afternoon shift in the somewhat-isolated guard station. There was a message waiting
for him. The President would be leaving town in less than
an hour. This meant a convoy of moving trucks would be
arriving at Cahoon's gate at any moment. It would be his
job to check them in to the Executive Mansion's loading
portal. This was where the President and his staff sent
their luggage so it could be taken to Union Station and
placed on the presidential train.

The man who worked the day shift was driving out just
as Cahoon was coming in. Cahoon asked his colleague
why the President was leaving Washington on such short
notice. After all, he'd just returned from a long trip out
west—and everyone knew the Boss was not in the best
of health these days.

"Didn't you clean out your ears before coming to work
today?" his colleague replied. "Can't you hear all that
commotion out there?"

Cahoon perked up his ears, and yes, it sounded like the
afternoon was filled with the wail of sirens.

"The D.C. cops have a dragnet out," the day man told
him. "They got roadblocks on every major street, at the
airport and down at the train station too. I hear the army
has all the bridges blocked off; they're checking every car
leaving D.C. Now, I'm not the smartest guy in the world,
but I gotta think the cops are looking for someone they
want to catch real bad . . ."

"So this is a security thing?" Cahoon asked the day
man. "The Boss bugging out and all?"

The man nodded and lowered his voice to a whisper.

"Yeah, real top level," he said. "I heard Hopkins himself ordered this one, and that he's all worked up because he's been going back and forth about it for days. Something about an Axis agent here in Washington, planning to attack the Boss. That's got to be who the cops are looking for, right?"

"Sure sounds it," Cahoon agreed, watching a police car streak by them, lights flashing, siren screaming.

"In any case," the day man said before departing. "They had us on our toes all day. You'll be up on 'em too."

THE PRESIDENTIAL MOVING VANS ARRIVED LESS than a minute later. It had started to pour; thunder could be heard off in the distance.

They were army deuce-and-a-half trucks that had been painted all black and had their rear canvas coverings removed in favor of sheet-metal housings, also painted black. As usual an army staff car led the trucks up to the White House gate. A jeep full of army reservists brought up the rear.

Cahoon put his hand up to halt the army staff car; this was just a formality. The small convoy had to stop at the back gate and wait until it got the official word to proceed to the loading zone. Usually this took no longer than Cahoon dialing the guard house phone and hearing the White House Secret Service station chief growl: "Let 'em in . . ."

But something odd happened this time: When Cahoon dialed the three digit number that connected directly to the Secret Service station, no one answered the phone. Cahoon let it ring, six, eight—ten times. No one picked up. He hung up, thinking that maybe he'd dialed the wrong three numbers for the first time in twenty years.

But again, the phone just rang and rang.

"What's up, pops?" the driver of the army staff car asked him.

"They're not answering," Cahoon replied.

The officer riding in the passenger seat leaned over and

yelled up to him: "You mean you're getting a busy signal? That means the line is dead . . ."

But Cahoon just shook his head and put the receiver as close as he could to the driver's ear. They could clearly hear the phone ringing and ringing . . . and ringing.

"Why don't you run up there and tell them that we're here?" the army officer barked across the seat at him.

But Cahoon stayed glued to his spot. This was now a problem of White House procedure. Cahoon was under strict orders not to leave his post unless told so by one person and one person only: the Secret Service station chief. And indeed, he had never left the guardhouse once in his twenty years—not even to go to his car parked twenty-five feet away—without first clearing it with the chief.

So he wasn't about to start now.

"I can't do that," Cahoon told the army officer. "I can't leave my post without an OK from—"

"I'm giving you permission to leave your post," the officer shouted back. "We're in a hurry here, Clyde. The President is waiting for us and you're holding up the show."

As if to emphasize that point, the pair of gussied-up army trucks began racing their engines.

But Cahoon stood his ground. "Sorry Major," he said. "No can do."

While all this was going on, Cahoon was holding the phone in one hand and the receiver in the other. Just as the officer was about to level another verbal salvo at him, someone suddenly answered the phone.

"Who the hell is this?" an unfamiliar voice roared through the earpiece; even the guys in the loading trucks could hear it.

It was strange because the crackling voice startled Cahoon so much, he took the question literally and replied: "If you don't know who you are, why the hell are you asking me?"

Now came a string of expletives and the sound of the

phone being dropped—or slammed—onto the station chief's desk.

"Listen whoever the hell you are—you've just got yourself fired . . ."

Though these were words that could strike fear into Cahoon's heart, he stayed calm. He simply took a deep breath and said: "Back Gate . . . can I help you?"

There was a moment's hesitation on the other end, and then someone else came on the phone.

Cahoon did not recognize this voice either.

"Who am I talking to?" the voice asked urgently.

"John Cahoon, Back Gate," he replied crisply.

"OK, Cahoon, we have a grade two emergency in progress here," the voice said. "Do you understand what I'm talking about?"

Cahoon felt his chest immediately turn to ice. He knew what a grade two emergency meant. Someone unauthorized had gained entry to the White House grounds, had failed to stop when ordered to do so and was currently being pursued.

"I understand, sir," he quickly replied.

"We might even have two people inside the wire," the person then told him. "What is the status at your position?"

"I'm clear except I have the moving trucks here—they're waiting to get buzzed into the loading area . . ."

There was another long silence at the other end. Finally the voice said: "Hold on . . ."

Yet no sooner were these words spoken than Cahoon saw someone running across the lawn, no more than fifty feet away from the guardhouse. He stared at this figure for a moment. He was dressed in a dark suit, a white shirt, a dark tie and a gray fedora. He was running extremely fast. Was this the intruder? Or was it one of the Secret Service agents in pursuit? Something told Cahoon this was *not* a Secret Service guy, only because he'd never seen any White House agent move so dang fast.

But just as Cahoon was about to report this to the people on the other end of the phone, another man appeared out of the murk—he too was running full out, but was nowhere as fast as the first man.

Cahoon began speaking loud and clear into the phone.

"I think I have the two intruders in sight!"

"Jessuz! Where are you?"

"The Back Gate!" Cahoon yelled as the two men dashed right by the guardhouse and around the waiting army vehicles. "Should I pursue?"

"Damn yes . . . pursue!"

That was all Cahoon needed. He dropped the phone, picked up his billy club and was off.

"Jessuz! Hey!" the officer in the staff car yelled after him. *"What about us?"*

But Cahoon was already out of earshot.

He hadn't run this fast in two decades. He'd gone only about two hundred feet and already his ankles and thighs were searing with pain. But he did not give up. He was gaining on the second man even as the second man was gaining on the first.

Cahoon had done time as an army military policeman before coming to work at the White House. As an MP, he knew a bit about foot pursuits. That's why he'd brought his billy club. As soon as he was about ten feet behind the second man, he let the nightstick go, flinging it at the man's feet. It hit the guy high in the ankles and he went down like a ton of bricks.

Cahoon stumbled himself and landed right on top of the sprawling figure. A brief fistfight broke out, then Cahoon retrieved his nightstick and begin pummeling the man.

"Stop!" the man was bellowing. *"Jesus stop!"*

Somehow, the struggling man was able to reach inside his pocket and come out not with a gun or a knife, but with an ID badge. Even as Cahoon was beating him about the head and shoulders, the man was able to force the

card up into his face. Cahoon stopped swinging his billy
club long enough to look at the ID.

It read: SPECIAL AGENT JOSEPH COPP. FBI . . .

"Oh my God," Cahoon gasped. "I've just beaten up a
G-man!"

"You don't have to sound so proud about it," Joe fired
back at him.

Cahoon picked him up and tried to brush him off.

"I'm sorry, pal," he apologized profusely. "But we got
a report of an intruder. Two intruders, in fact . . . and it
just seemed like . . . I mean, was that the intruder you
were chasing?"

Joe didn't reply. The less he said here, the better.

"Is there anything I can do?" Cahoon asked him.

Joe put his ID back into this jacket and said: "Yes—
go tell your bosses to forget it, it was all a big mistake.
The FBI has the situation under control . . ."

Then he disappeared again into the storm.

Cahoon returned to the guardhouse, scratching his head.
His phone was still off the hook and the four army vehicles were still waiting for the OK to drive through.

Cahoon picked up the receiver and said: "Hello? Sorry
false alarm . . ."

The voice on the other end asked; "What do you
mean?"

"I mean I just tackled an FBI agent and not the intruder.
He said the FBI was on the job and not to worry about
it . . ."

There was a short pause then the voice said: *"FBI?*
That's impossible. There are no FBI agents on the
grounds. What did you say the name of this guy you
stopped was?"

Cahoon froze again. *Oh God, what had he done?*

"His name?" he said trying to dredge up what he'd just
seen printed on the ID badge in the downpour. But it was
useless.

"I'm sorry, Chief," he finally said. "I just can't remember . . ."

* * *

THE WHITE HOUSE LOADING PORTAL WAS BA-
sically one large room with two heavy doors that swung
outward.

It was full of steamer trunks, suitcases and duffel bags
at the moment, all sent here in anticipation of the President's departure. The biggest steamers belonged to the
President himself—sixteen in all.

The smaller suitcases belonged to lower staff people
and Secret Service agents. The duffel bags belonged to
six navy seamen who would serve as railway butlers for
the journey. In all, two dozen people would be traveling
with the President.

The destination was Warm Springs, Georgia, a place
also known as the Little White House. It was FDR's favorite retreat. The weather was predictably warm, and he
enjoyed the countryside, the locals, and the therapy pool
located nearby.

That the President was leaving town—again—was still
a closely held secret. It would not be known by the press
or the general public for some time. Nor did the President's movements have to be announced officially. Under
the Wartime Powers Act, he was allowed to move freely
without having to inform anyone, including Congress, not
even after he'd reached his destination. This had come in
handy the past five years, when he met in secret with
Churchill, for instance. But it was also a very convenient
device to employ when he just wanted to get away, or
when the Secret Service thought it was a good idea to get
him out of town.

The reason for this trip was a little bit of both.

JOE COPP WAS BARELY ABLE TO CLIMB UP TO
the loading dock of the south portal.

His already gimpy legs had been so severely battered

in his tussle with the guard, he was wondering if his knee-caps might be broken. His left shoulder was aching badly too where the man's billy club had come down especially hard on him. He was also suffering from a nosebleed.

He'd gone over the fence right after Skass but there had been no wings, real or imagined, involved with him. He'd lost sight of the killer soon after hitting the ground, but caught up with him about a half minute later, just as Skass was trying to dislodge a window leading into the White House basement, using the downpour and some thick bushes as cover. Joe chased him around to the back of the executive mansion, only to lose Skass again after he was tackled by the enthusiastic guard. Only Joe's quick display of his badge prevented the game from being over right then and there.

But now he was in the portal, the same place he'd seen Skass climbing into before losing sight of him. The room was empty, though, except for the stacks of luggage. Where could Skass have gone from here? Joe thought. Deeper into the White House? He didn't doubt it. Skass was just crazy enough to go wandering around the Executive Mansion, knives out and ready to cut. Damn, he was *so* smooth, if he was able to find a butler's uniform, he'd be serving a drink to the President if someone didn't stop him first.

But Skass was no fool either. He never acted like a caged animal because he never got himself into a situation to be cornered.

Joe on the other hand was not so talented.

He knew he had to find Skass fast—if he was caught in here, there was little chance that flashing an FBI badge would save him, even from a bullet. And in the back of his mind was that one throbbing fact: He was just as much a wanted man as Skass. Maybe even more so. What would happen if someone found him here, inside the White House, with a gun? Well, they just might shoot first and save the questions for later.

Still he pulled the pistol from his pocket and began

walking among the small forest of steamer trunks. He even tried sniffing the air, hoping to magically pick up some kind of useful scent. But it was not to be. Skass had vanished again.

Then suddenly, Joe heard something echoing from a hallway nearby.

Voices. . . . Coming closer. . . .

He ran to the adjoining door and peeked around the corner. Heading toward him was a small army of cops being led by the gatehouse guard who'd just tackled him. Joe then heard a noise behind him. He turned back to the portal to see the two army trucks pulling up to the loading dock, armed soldiers walking on either side of them.

He was stuck. . . .

Damn, he cursed under his breath. What to do now?

He had no idea. Tracking bad guys down to their last change of underwear—that was easy for him.

But disappearing into thin air?

He wasn't so good at that.

PART FIVE

PART FIVE

24

WASHINGTON, D.C.

THE ARMY MOVING VANS WERE LOADED AND ready to go by four o'clock that afternoon.

Leaving the reservists behind to help search for the two phantom intruders, the trucks exited the White House grounds through the back gate. Here they were met by a police escort and, with sirens wailing, were led at high speed through the streets of Washington.

Many of the major intersections had already been blocked off for the President's limousine, which had left the White House just minutes before the moving vans. The army drivers quickly caught up with the President's car and together traveled to Union Station Annex. The *Lulabelle* was already in place when they arrived, engines warmed up, ready to go.

The President was put on board, the luggage went in right after him. Then in a huge cloud of steam and smoke, the train quickly pulled out of the station and headed south.

They were out of D.C. within minutes, passing over into Virginia only to collide with an even bigger rainstorm that had been waiting there. Though the precipitation became heavy at times, and the visibility fell to zero, the train crew did not reduce its high speed one iota. Their orders were to get to Warm Springs as quickly as possible, and they were doing just that.

The tracks for hundreds of miles ahead of them had been cleared in advance. No traffic was allowed to move on the rails while the *Lulabelle* was en route. Only after the presidential carriage had roared by could regular trains resume their journeys. This would result in a plethora of scheduling foul-ups up and down the eastern seaboard throughout the night.

National Guard units in Virginia, North and South Carolina had been turned out to watch every railroad crossing the presidential train would pass. Every bridge had been checked for explosives, every switching station taken over by the army. These were normal procedures whenever the President was traveling by rail. But on this stormy night, they'd been ordered with a sense of added urgency. As if something very bad was blowing in the wind.

The tracks became bumpier once the train crossed over into North Carolina. The rain increased and the storm front seemed to defy atmospheric common sense and followed the *Lulabelle* southward. Those soldiers lined up at the guarded crossings were soaked to the bone by midnight; many would endure several more hours of misery for what would turn out to be no more than a few seconds of presidential guard duty.

It went on like this all night—rain, wind, bumpy tracks. By the time the train finally crossed over into Georgia early the next morning, the rainstorm had grown even worse.

GEORGIE STENSON NEVER DID GET TO SLEEP.

He was the ranking presidential aide for this trip, once more against his will, and his stomach was not agreeing with his enforced travel plans.

He hated trains even more now after his experience during the cockeyed trip back from Denver. He'd spent this night, sometimes tossing and turning, sometimes sitting up and consuming two kinds of liquid: stomach medicine and whiskey. They did not make for a good cocktail, but Stenson didn't care. He needed the whiskey to keep the medicine down and the medicine to keep the whiskey down.

And he knew the worst was yet to come. When they finally arrived at Warm Springs, simple things such as unloading the passengers and moving the luggage always evolved into major headaches. Stenson was not a good traveling secretary, his forte was politics. He didn't have the magic touch that made all things run smoothly or at least make them appear that way. If anything, his presence seemed to make things worse.

So lying in his berth now, lights out, Stenson could tell by the train's decreased speed that they were about an hour away from arriving in Warm Springs. This only depressed him further. He reached over and felt his traveling bag; six unopened bottles of rye were hidden within a wrap of towels. The Boss was due to stay at the Georgia White House indefinitely.

Stenson wondered if six bottles would be enough.

IT WAS IRONIC THAT STENSON HAD JUST BEGUN to drift off to sleep when he was awakened by a rapping on his berthing door.

He rolled off his bunk and stumbled around looking for his robe. He finally found it, wrapped it around him, then opened the door just a crack. On the other side was one of the navy stewards.

He was holding an envelope which Stenson knew contained an MRM—mobile radio message.

"We just received this from the White House, sir," the steward said, trying not to sniff the booze on Stenson's breath. "The Secret Service chief said it's only about two hours old."

Stenson took the note and closed the door in the man's face. No thank-you. No good-bye.

He sat down on the edge of his bunk and wearily tore open the envelope. What lay within was a type of electronic telegram, it had sprung from a secret mobile radio that had just been installed on the *Lulabelle.*

Stenson read the note, then pushed his fingers through his messy hair and read it again. *Why the hell are they bothering me with this?* he wondered.

The gist of the message was that one of the White House porters was missing. The man had last been seen near the back gate loading portal, this shortly before the President left for Georgia. No one had any idea where he was now, or what might have happened to him. The note ended with the suggestion that its contents be brought to the attention of Harry Hopkins immediately.

But Stenson just crumpled up the paper and threw it across his stateroom.

"Harry Hopkins?" he grumbled. "I haven't seen that man in more than a week!"

25

THE *LULABELLE* ARRIVED IN WARM SPRINGS just after dawn.

The rain never stopped, and the presidential train was covered with mud and soot.

The President was carried off with the luggage and transported up to the so-called Little White House.

It wasn't a long ride from the railroad station to the presidential retreat. The road went through a wooded section and past some fields, a huge swimming pool, a place called Georgia Hall, and finally a small chapel. From here it was a winding clay path through some giant pine trees up to the presidential cottage.

The estate was fairly grand. The main house boasted three fluted columns, a circular garden, and a sterling flagpole out front. On the other side of a portico was a white fence with gates for a presidential car and two sentry boxes. A small guest house was located nearby.

The presidential house was filled with sailing-ship models, framed naval prints and lots of shiny hardwood furniture. The President's bedroom was modest, just a single bed with a thin mattress located off to the left of the living room. A more formal bedroom for him could be found upstairs. Various members of his staff stayed in rooms throughout the house and in the guest residence down the hill.

The kitchen was one of the biggest rooms in the house.

*   *   *

ONE OF ITS SMALLEST WAS THE ROOM GEORGIE
Stenson would use for the duration of the visit.

It was attached in back to the main house, accessed by
a small hallway that ran off the kitchen. It was known as
the rumble room for the vibrations it suffered on those
infrequent occasions when the house's furnace was turned
on. Modifications had been made to the basement of the
house to cut down on the noise the creaky old heater
made. Nothing though had been done about its vibrations.

Stenson dragged himself into his room now, his stomach feeling like it would rupture at any moment. On the
desk next to his bed was long telegram that had been sent
down from Washington several hours before. It was ad-
dressed to his attention. He took off his suit coat, his tie,
and his shoes, eased himself up onto the bed, and began
scanning the message.

It was soon clear that the information contained in the
telegram had been intended for Hopkins and not himself.
Hopkins was in a hospital somewhere, getting his own
stomach ulcer operated on—or at least that was what
Stenson had been told. Several things made him disbe-
lieve this, though, most of all Hopkins's strange behavior
of the past few weeks, and his failure to mention to anyone that he was going anywhere. Stenson suspected his
boss was off on a drunken bat—or recovering from one.
It would not be the first time.

But if that was the truth, oh how Stenson envied him!

The telegram was marked secret and started off positively
enough: Allied troops were pouring over the Rhine and were
striking deeper into the heart of Germany. The Russians
were approaching the outskirts of Berlin. In the Pacific,
things were proceeding smoothly with the invasion of Oki-
nawa, an island just a stone's throw from Japan itself.

Stenson shifted his weight on the bed and felt the resulting pain in his stomach. He reached into his travel bag,
retrieved his medicine and took two huge gulps. The result
was only mild relief.

He continued reading the communiqué. All was in readiness for the Boss to address the opening of the United Nations Conference in San Francisco in a few weeks— another trip Stenson was absolutely dreading. A confidential message passed on from a friendly source in Poland stated that Stalin's inner circle was convinced that (a) the Germans and the OSS had brokered a deal in which the Germans would make a stand on the Oder River, and thus allow the majority of German troops to surrender to the British and American forces in the west, and (b) that the SS and U.S. Army Intelligence were hatching a plot to assassinate Stalin. Stenson took two more gulps upon reading this part of the message; he would be hesitant to bring this last section to the Boss's notice. He already had too much to worry about.

The final part of the telegram reiterated the radio message he'd received on the train shortly before arriving in Warm Springs—that one of the White House porters was missing. In a rather desperate attempt to locate the man, the communiqué suggested the presidential train be searched, "from one end to the other."

Stenson nearly threw up on reading this. No one had seen the man anywhere near the train; he'd gone missing in the vicinity of the White House, not Union Station. To search the train made no sense. . . .

But it had to be done and Stenson knew he was the guy who had to oversee it. He took another gulp of medicine, then unwrapped his first bottle of rye and took a healthy belt of that too. Outside, the storm clouds were getting darker.

In less than an hour, it would begin to rain even harder.

STENSON WAS FIFTY-FIVE YEARS OLD.

He was divorced, nearly broke from alimony payments, and had an ulcer in his stomach the size of a half dollar. Cold damp weather affected his arthritic knees and tended to fill his lungs with mucus. If he caught a cold, it could last for weeks.

So the conditions couldn't have been worse for him as

he rode back down to the railroad station. With him were two Secret Service agents and two of the navy stewards. Stenson felt no need to brief them on what the messages from Washington had contained. Instead, he simply told them to search the train from the engines to the caboose and back again.

This took two hours, during which Stenson waited in one of the staff cars, heater blowing oily warm air, gulping down his medicine. One of the Secret Service agents finally ran through the rain to tell him that all seemed kosher on the presidential carriage.

Stenson told them to search it again. Two more hours went by. Again came the report that the train was clean. Finally satisfied, Stenson thanked the men and then returned to the presidential mansion.

He could barely walk to his room. His knees were creaking badly, and his stomach felt like it was on fire. Even worse, he began coughing and wheezing.

He reached his room and immediately collapsed on the bed, too sick to even pour himself a drink.

Thus began a long, private ordeal for Stenson. His stomach ulcer began bleeding sometime during the night, releasing a stream of septic fluids into his intestines and his bloodstream. These were not enough to kill him—not just yet—but plenty enough to lay him up and give him fever dreams whenever he managed to fall asleep.

Though he'd told the rest of the staff that he was just tired, he forbade them from informing the Boss that he was not feeling well. Passing off the majority of his duties to the handful of lower aides, Stenson took to his bed and, bolstered by rye and stomach medicine, didn't move for what seemed like a month.

THE BOSS HIMSELF WAS NOT WELL—THIS WAS no secret to anyone. In the last six months, his pattern had become disturbingly familiar. He would rise with back and neck pain, warm up by breakfast, be chipper by midmorning—only to faint almost every day around noon. He was here for rest; they all were. His staff hoped that once the war was concluded, and that huge burden was lifted from his shoulders, the President's health would improve. But all agreed that had he not been the leader of the Free World, the man would have been put in the hospital a long time ago and probably have stayed there for quite a while.

Stenson knew how he felt. But unlike the Boss, he was unable to avoid many of the mundane details of life on the road with the President. It was part of his unofficial duties to deal with the domestics working in the Little White House. That's why his room was located right down the hall from the kitchen.

On the fourth afternoon of his illness, Stenson received a note under his door. Had Berlin fallen? Were the Japanese suing for peace? Had Russia finally attacked Japan?

No—the note was not from anyone in the President's inner circle. It had been written by one of the kitchen staff.

The dumbwaiter was broken.

THE NEXT EVENING, STENSON THOUGHT HE FELT well enough to join the others for dinner.

But when he appeared unannounced in the dining room at eight o'clock, he found only three members of the kitchen staff and Gertrude Baulis, the President's alternate stenographer. The President had long ago gone to bed— his labored breathing could be heard now throughout the first floor of the house. The rest of the senior staff had disappeared for the night, most of them to their rooms.

Stenson gloomily took his seat and had no choice but to listen in on a conversation among the four girls. The President had requested that the cooks prepare his favorite meal sometime soon. The dish was Brunswick stew and Stenson's bad stomach turned over at the mere mention of the name. The main component of Brunswick stew was pigs' heads. Usually three of them swam in a sea of broth and vegetables, and its preparation was as revolting as it sounded.

A middle-aged colored woman named Selly was the head cook at the Little White House; it would be up to her to make the stew. She had already located the pigs' heads. Three of them could be had on a moment's notice from a nearby farm. The problem was, Selly needed new knives with which to perform the necessary butchering. Her old set of carving knives had somehow been misplaced. She planned to travel to town the next day and purchase a new, sharper set and joked that she'd send the bill to the War Department because, "It will look like a war in there after I'm through with those porkers."

Stenson took his meal to his room.

HE SKIPPED ALL FOOD THE NEXT DAY, BUT FELT well enough the following morning to report for breakfast.

Once again, he found that of the senior staff, he was the solitary member at the morning table. In fact, he was the *only* one there. Anyone else in the house had already taken breakfast or was still asleep. The President was part of the latter group. His irregular breathing—his doctors called it "asymmetric snoring"—could be heard above almost everything else.

Stenson ordered a tomato omelet, but when Selly put the plate in front of him, he discovered it contained an omelet plain.

"Someone stole my tomatoes," Selly told him before he could say a word. "I just picked them last night, washed 'em up and put them near the cellar door to dry. They was gone this morning . . . If those Secret Service boys want some tomatoes, all they got to do is ask . . ."

With that, she disappeared through the swinging door, only to reappear on its next cycle.

"But I do have some good news, Mr. Stenson," she said, as Stenson began to pick at his dull meal.

"What's that?"

She smiled, showing a mouthful of gold teeth.

"The dumbwaiter is back working again," she said.

STENSON STAYED DRUNK FOR THE NEXT TWO days.

He remained in his room. He made no noise. He did not sing loudly or rant during the day. He simply drank and read and drank and slept, and then drank some more. No one bothered him, not out of respect of his privacy, but simply because there was nothing for him to do. The President himself spent his days puttering around or napping; most of the senior staff was out playing golf.

However, in that time, two notes did get slipped under his door. Both of them were from Selly. She was complaining of a foul odor in her room at night.

The other said the Secret Service was stealing her tomatoes again.

IT WAS ON THE SEVENTH OR EIGHTH MORNING that Stenson was awakened by a scream.

It was Selly. She was in the kitchen next door. She sounded hysterical.

"Please! Help!"

Dressed in his robe and slippers, Stenson came through the kitchen door ten seconds later. The first thing he saw was blood everywhere—on the sink, on the table, all over the floor. Something was propped up against the back door. It was a head—a pig's head. It was staring up at him, blood running from its mouth and nose.

Stenson took another step into the kitchen. Two more pigs' heads were lying on the floor in front of the sink; they too were bloody and staring up at him.

Then he heard Selly yelp again. The maid came running into the kitchen from the huge pantry, a broom over her head. A large white bird came through the door with her. She was swinging wildly at it, but with her eyes closed.

Stenson took charge of the broom and downed the bird with a single swipe. It crashed into a corner, stunned, its wings flapping madly. Stenson just kept hitting it with the straw end of the broom until it didn't move anymore. Selly began crying. It had been a dove.

Out of breath, heart pounding, Stenson retrieved the dead bird, deposited it in a bag, and then dropped it into the garbage pail. Then he took a dish towel from the sink and gingerly picked up the three pigs' heads, one at a time. He knew they were being prepared for the Boss's Brunswick stew. He wondered how much their brief trip to the kitchen floor would affect the taste.

Selly got a mop and began cleaning up the pig's blood. She was still softly crying; there were more than a few tiny white feathers in the little pools of blood. Exhausted from his battle with the bird, Stenson began to retreat to his room.

But no sooner had he gone through the door than he heard Selly say: "Where did they go now?"

Stenson knew he was just saving time if he turned on his heel and went back in the kitchen. He found Selly on her hands and knees, looking under the table, the cabinets, and the hutch cupboard.

"What are you looking for?" he asked her.

"My new set of knives . . ."

Stenson began scanning on top of the cabinets, through the clutter on the table, and pig gore in the sink. "Did we knock them over, swinging at the bird?"

"I don't know . . ." Selly said, getting back to her feet. "They were right here before that poor thing flew in the house. Now? Where can they be?"

"You're sure you had them in here with you?"

She put her hands on her hips and stared at Stenson. She was a large woman and was known not to take any nonsense. "Now how do you think I got those pigs' heads off those pigs' bodies?" she asked him. "Think they fell off themselves?"

Stenson had no reply.

And even though he and the maid searched the kitchen extensively for the next twenty minutes, they never found the missing cutlery.

A FEW MORE DAYS PASSED.

The weather improved and the scent of honeysuckle flowers now filled the air. The entire estate was invaded by squadrons of blue jays, chirping and cackling and generally making a racket. Selly's Brunswick stew had been so good, the Boss asked her to whip up another batch extra soon. She agreed, but only if she could buy a new set of carving knives.

This day found Stenson's stomach almost agreeable. It settled down long enough for him to take his dinner with the staff and afterward play some cards with the night-shift Secret Service agents.

It would have been his best day yet at Warm Springs, had it not been for the maid, who approached him just as he was leaving the card table for bed.

She caught him in the small hallway that separated his room from the kitchen. She was Selly's niece, Carmel, a beautiful girl, not yet twenty years old. This was her first time working at the Little White House when the Boss was in residence.

She was weeping softly, obviously upset and nervous for having to speak to Stenson, who she regarded as her superior. At that moment, he would have bet that she was going to confess the theft of not one, but two sets of kitchen knives. But her story was a bit odder than that. She revealed that she had encountered a stranger on the estate grounds very early in the morning two days before and had not told anybody.

"I was walking down to the chapel—I wanted to pick some of the lilies down there for my room. I was doing just that when a man came around the corner. He just stood there—very surprised to see me. But not as surprised as I was to see him."

Stenson felt his stomach start gurgling again.

"What did he look like?" he asked her.

"He looked like an agent of some kind but he was dirty as well," she replied. "I mean, he was wearing a suit and a tie, but it was mussed. He needed a bath, but his shirt seemed clean. His shoes were wet with dew—the sun wasn't even up yet—as if he'd been walking on the lawn all night."

"Did he speak? Did you have words?"

"No, sir. He just looked at me for a moment and walked away up toward the house. By the time I gathered my flowers and came back up here, there was no sign of him."

Stenson was at once upset that he was hearing this two days too late, but at the same time relieved by the description of the man. It was not uncommon for vagrants to approach the Presidential retreat, knowing that the Secret Service men on guard at the gates were likely to give them some money just so they'd go away. That's what sounded to be the case here. But why hadn't the maid told anyone before?

"Because I didn't think I was allowed to pick lilies down by the chapel," was her weepy reply.

Stenson grabbed his stomach but at the same time patted her kindly enough on the shoulder.

"It's all right," he told her. "But if anything like this happens again, you tell me right away. Deal?"

She shook his hand, then kissed his cheek and flitted away, obviously in great relief.

Not so Stenson. He returned to his bed and, having run out of stomach medicine, drank from his rye bottle instead. It was the stupidest thing he could have done, for that night he had the most awful fever dreams of his life.

In the worst, he imagined that a pair of eyes was watching him through his room's heater grate.

26

THE CELLAR WAS WRAPPED IN SOUND-proofing.

The President didn't like bumpy train rides and he didn't like noisy houses. He especially didn't like the racket made by the Little White House's heating system on those rare occasions it was turned on.

So, back in January of 1941, a team of army engineers layered the entire basement as well as all of the heating ducts with the best soundproofing material of the day: asbestos. The President himself supervised the job, pronouncing it the perfect solution to the noisy furnace, with the extra benefit of fireproofing the basement too.

There wasn't really much to the basement, though, except its size. Stone walls all around, the furnace, the terminus of the dumbwaiter and a modest workbench holding two dozen dusty, rarely used tools. The only ornaments were two cracked mirrors, which were hanging on either side of the single wall lamp. Just by routine, this dim lamp was left turned on both day and night.

There were also sixteen steamer trunks in the basement; this is where they'd been placed upon arriving from Washington. Typically, the President had overpacked. Just about everyone who had made the trip to Warm Springs already had clothes and personal items here, stored away for trips such as this most recent one. The Boss was no exception.

This was why the steamer trunks had sat here, unopened, for nearly two weeks.

*   *   *

THE FIRST SCREW CAME UNDONE AND FELL TO the floor, making no sound.

The second screw soon followed it, then a third, and a fourth. One hinge was now loose. More screws were reversed over the next ten minutes, each hitting the floor, bouncing once on the thick carpet before coming to rest nearby. Soon the third and fourth hinges were loose from the trunk lid. There was silence for another few seconds, then the lid slowly opened—and a battered bloody body slid out.

It was Eustiss McKray, the missing White House porter. Half his neck and one of his lungs was missing; his heart and liver were gone too. He'd been dead for almost two weeks. His congealed blood had already turned to black. He'd ceased to smell a long time ago.

Willy Skass now pushed the body completely out of the trunk, then more or less flopped out himself. This was the same steamer trunk he'd utilized to make his escape from Washington and, by happy accident, it had deposited him here, in the Little White House, right where he wanted to be. He'd unwrapped himself from a position that would have made a yogi cringe, a necessity if he wanted the dead porter's body in here with him. Skass felt like he really knew the man by now. Had they not met when they did, Skass would have been apprehended in the White House almost immediately after gaining entrance through the loading dock. But things had gone another way.

And the porter had also served another purpose. Though black skin was not to Skass's liking, he'd managed to stay well fed since his serendipitous arrival in Georgia.

Lucky for him, Eustiss had been a sweet old guy.

It was late morning now. Skass put Eustiss back into the trunk, retrieved the hinge screws, and put the fasteners back together again, his first ritual of the morning. Then he moved along the carpeted floor, each step routinely heel to toe, stopping and listening for any noises coming from above, but hearing none.

The cellar of the mansion was damp and musty. Except for the one dim bulb, it was very dark as well. There was only one entrance to the place from upstairs, a long metal staircase running down from the kitchen. There was an old bulkhead nearby as well. But other than that, it was like a small dungeon. No windows, no coal chutes, no natural light of any kind.

No surprise no one ever came down here from up above.

He now made his way over to the gigantic furnace. The heating contraption looked like an enormous and filthy octopus. It smelled of burnt coal dust and oily sheet metal. It had twenty hollow metal trunks which extended to the floors above. These were the heating ducts, and they traveled up to every room in the house, almost like a network of arteries and veins in a body.

After living inside them for nearly two weeks, Skass now knew almost every inch of the duct system. Most of the shafts were eighteen inches around, though some were much bigger. Most were square, though some extensions on the third floor were circular. The inside of all of them had been coated with a two-inch layer of asbestos. This had come in very handy for Skass's purposes. Because of the overall mustiness of the house, the asbestos coating was still moist in some places, which made it tremendously easy for him to contort his body and slither through with the greatest of ease.

The heating vents had been like his ears and eyes to the entire house. By positioning himself just a few inches from the inside of the grating, he could hear any conversation going on in any room, and usually see everyone in the room as well.

Thus, he'd witnessed all of the small dramas that had occurred since the presidential party arrived, from the President's incessant, irregular snoring, to the dove caught in the kitchen, to the chronic drunken illness of the man he knew as G. Stenson—the same guy he'd met briefly on the train back in Carson Bend. Skass had an uncommon dislike for this man and enjoyed watching him suffer. Had it not been for Stenson's sudden appearance back on the train that day, the real Roosevelt would have been dead a long time ago.

As it was, this latest attempt was taking longer than Skass had ever imagined. The problem—what had prevented Skass from striking already—was the blind doggedness of the Secret Service agents protecting the President. Awake or asleep, there was always at least one agent no more than ten feet away from him, always armed, always alert. Skass needed no education on the spunk of the presidential bodyguards. They reminded him of robots. Yet, he was certain that if he tried to attack the President under less than ideal conditions, the attending agent would shoot him down like a dog long before he was able to deliver the first blow.

The trick would be to locate the President when he was alone somewhere in the house—or at least when he was not in the company of the Secret Service agents.

So Skass had been doing what he did best, biding his time and waiting for the precise moment to strike.

In that time, he'd gotten to know his new environment fairly well.

There were more than two thousand feet of heating ducts running through the Little White House. This was at least three times too many, but there was an explanation for it. The mansion was extremely old by Skass's reckoning and had gone through so many renovations, some of these tunnels had been bled off into dead ends, others were missing sections, still others ran back on themselves. Even after so many days of slithering through them, Skass wasn't sure he knew them *all*. With their labyrinthlike excesses, that might be impossible.

But he had come to learn the most important ones— these were the vents that ran past the main dining room, the living room, the kitchen and the small room on the first floor where the President slept. He'd also checked out some of the more obscure connections, those that ran up to rooms that no one ever seemed to use in the house. He felt he should be familiar with them too. He'd also tried his shimmying act up through the dumbwaiter shaft, but abandoned this just a few feet in. The narrow wooden tunnel was noisy, smelly, and it gave him splinters to move through it. The heating shafts were much more pleasant.

Though Skass had had no trouble at all moving through the asbestos-lined ductwork—he'd needed to employ only minor contortions when faced with the most extreme angular turns—after a while he believed that being inside the dark vents had started to affect his thinking a bit. It was a strange thing to admit to himself, but at times, either while crawling from one point to another, or while staying very still for hours on end, he'd felt a certain sensation rise up in his chest which he could only describe as mildly discomforting, a slight uneasiness. This had never happened to him before, and he wondered often why it was happening to him now. He'd once hid in the chimney of a victim's house for more than a week, waiting for her to come home so he could butcher her. Another time, he'd lived in the rafters of a synagogue's recreation room, again waiting for his victim to walk in alone. During both these times, he never felt the slightest bit claustrophobic, or anxious, or anything at all except excited by what was about to come.

But now, inside these sooty metal veins, there had been times when he felt his heart beating out of his chest; that his hands trembled and not from any sense of cold. He caught himself worrying whether the shaft might suddenly collapse from his weight or that he was making noise that only he could not hear.

He was, in a word, *nervous,* at times. And he wasn't quite sure why.

He began to worry that maybe the Secret Service men swept the vent works routinely, looking for potential assassins just like him. This thought had preyed on his mind since the beginning, and for that reason, he had kept moving whenever he was in the main ducts, never staying in one place long enough to be caught by some enterprising agent. He'd also been very careful where and when to urinate and defecate. He'd found a dead end of ductwork on his third day, one with a two-way dampener. It was here that he went to do his business whenever he had to, which, due to his superior control of most of his bodily functions was actually not very often at all. Sometimes though, when he felt himself really spooked, he would retreat there as well.

Another odd thing distracted him occasionally. It was very noisy *inside* the ductwork, this even though the asbestos layer was supposed to provide sound-proofing. Many times, while he was listening in on some conversation, trying to ascertain if the President was actually going to be left alone for a spell of time, Skass had thought he heard weird banging and clanging come from right behind him, causing him to slither away as fast as he could and retreat to one of the several hiding places he'd found, again, among the ductwork's many dead ends. It was these sounds that came to convince him that the Secret Service did in fact sweep some part of the heating system every day.

It was these sounds that kept him on the move for long periods of time, either that, or rolled up and hiding in the blackest end of the tubes.

This is also why he traveled the vents only during the latter part of the day and evenings and, on most occasions, chose to sleep back inside the trunk with the remains of Eustiss.

For some reason, he felt safer that way.

HE POSITIONED HIMSELF NEXT TO THE FURNACE now and took out the three knives he'd filched from the kitchen several days ago. This was the second set—the first had proven too old and dull to fascinate him. And if it was one thing Skass needed, it was a oneness with his weapons.

The second set excited him to the point of sexual arousal. They were pearl handled—of British manufacture, he was certain. The largest was nearly ten inches long, gleaming, and razor sharp. The middle knife, eight inches in length, was also finely sharpened. It had sliced Skass's forefinger when he first ran it across his cuticle. He'd sucked the blood from the cut and tasted the wife from St. Louis. What a surprise! His favorite though was the shortest knife. At five inches long, the blade was not only intensely sharp, it was also heavily serrated. And he just liked the look of it. When the time came, this was the one he would use first.

He stood up and contemplated the multiarmed metal monster. He followed each duct as it rose away from the burner on its destination to some far-flung part of the mansion. It was time to start listening in.

He picked one shaft and pressed his ear against it. He heard nothing. He selected another—it was reverberating with distant mechanical sounds. Again, this did him no good.

He checked six more ducts, none gave him the sound he was looking for. Finally, on the ninth try, he heard what he wanted.

Voices . . .

Two women and a man. The women were relatively young, the man old, wheezing, with a cold. Skass knew that voice by now. And he knew exactly where they were.

Suddenly the crotch of his pants began to bulge.

Something told him this would be his day.

SKASS CAREFULLY DISCONNECTED THE THREE quarter-inch metal screws which held the shaft together and shimmied in. Using his longish fingernails to dig into the soft asbestos coating, he pulled his body upward, silently, taking in deep breaths of the asbestos-laden air every few feet or so. It was an aroma that he liked.

Halfway up the shaft he stopped and listened. The voices were still above him, beyond the first floor. He became more excited. This was very unusual—to hear a voice beyond the first floor. He slithered up another few feet and stopped again. Someone was walking quickly down a set of stairs on the other side of the wall from him. Heavy footsteps, not a maid and definitely not heading toward the kitchen. The voices were still loud and clear just above him. Had that been a Secret Service man moving off his position?

Skass felt the excitement further well up inside him. He pulled himself up another foot or so. The footsteps had disappeared below; the voices, laughing now, were even stronger, even closer.

He could hear the words. . . .

"Do you know why I prefer photographs, my dear?"

"Why is that, sweetness? . . ."

"Because sitting for a portrait I can only stick this heroic jaw of mine out for so long before it becomes tiring . . ."

"Or embarrassing dearest . . ."

Laughter. Two females and a tired jovial old man.

Skass reached a junction and slithered up into the vertical shaft. He was now on the second floor, and so where they. He pulled himself up nearly his full length now, only his ankles remained in the bottom vent way. The voices were but a wall away.

"I'm afraid the only embarrassment here my friend is that of our guest," the man was saying. "These are state secrets we are discussing here."

More laughter.

"As an artist," the second woman said, "I know how to keep my mouth shut."

More laughter.

"If that's the case, would you consider being my vice president? My secretary of war? My valet?"

Even more laughter. Skass caught himself chuckling.

"But who then would paint your picture, sir?"

"Well, if you did all those jobs as well as I imagine, I'd have time to paint the damn thing myself."

More laughter. A cigarette was lit.

"Oh, a self-portrait, my dearest? How heroic would the jaw be then?"

"At least twice its present size!"

Gales of laughter. Skass was grinning ear to ear. Very close now.

He stared up the shaft and as his eyes were now adjusted to the near-complete darkness, he could see the outline of the heating grate. It was no more than an arm's reach away from him. Like every other vent in the house, it looked old and flimsy. Again, the excitement doubled from within his body.

He slowly pulled himself up even with the grate. Now he could actually see into the room. Moving through the narrow shafts of light bleeding in from the flimsy cover, he saw just two women facing him. No Secret Service agent in sight. Indeed, this was his lucky day.

His target was sitting just three feet from the large grate, his back to him, a naval cape thrown over his shoulder, obviously posing for a portrait. Three feet . . . Skass could easily throw his first knife that distance and still attain great accuracy. Pushing through the grate in a moment's time would be no problem. Then he could leap out, throw his first knife, then attack the other two victims with his second and third. He was confident he could stab and/or slash the throats of all three people in just a few seconds. The old man, of course, would have to go first. But the ladies' voices sounded so sweet, Skass felt a craving to see their insides as well, if just for a few seconds.

Nothing like an extra incentive, he smiled to himself, to guarantee a job well done.

He would have to work fast though. If that had been a Secret Service agent leaving the scene, he probably wouldn't be gone for long.

Skass positioned his second and third knives in his belt so they would be easy to reach. Then he put the shortest one between his teeth, not unlike a pirate. After a moment of thought though, he allowed his tongue to scrape against the razor-sharp serrated blade, slicing it. He sampled the resulting blood and, to his delight, tasted the Philadelphia schoolgirl. This further fueled his lust. Tasting his own blood was just like tasting the blood of many others. It was the next best thing to an orgasm. Whenever he needed that one last rush before falling on his prey, a taste of his own always did the trick.

He was becoming so excited now, tiny bubbles of bloody saliva were forming at the corners of his mouth. He wrapped his jacket sleeve around his right hand and balled it into a fist. He studied the flimsy grate again. It was even missing three of its six tiny screws. Skass could have sneezed and it would have probably fallen open.

He adjusted himself one more time, bringing one of his legs up and contorting it in back of him. This would act like a spring. He would lunge off of it, hit the grate with his protected fist and literally fly into the room. The bloodletting, and his climax, would then begin.

He reared back, ready to hit the grate, when suddenly . . . the banging in the vents began again. Skass froze. This sound that had come to grab him right in the throat was suddenly louder than he'd ever heard it.

Banging . . .

Clanging . . .

Banging . . .

Clanging . . .

Getting closer.

Skass began looking about him frantically, trying to figure out where the noise was coming from. Was it above him? To his right or left?

No . . .

It was right below him.

He looked down just in time to see a hand grab his right ankle and give it a mighty pull. It happened so fast,

Skass did not have time to cry out. He was violently yanked out of the vertical heating shaft, cracking his head with a bloody thud on the horizontal vent way. Then the hands grabbed both his legs and began dragging him further downward.

Skass began yelping—it was in a high voice, one he'd never heard come out of him before. It was like some unseen monster was dragging him right down into hell. He began desperately trying to grab on to the sides of the vent way, to dig his fingernails into the soft asbestos. But they would not hold. He was being pulled down the shaft with such intensity, his fingernails were actually breaking off, leaving tiny bloody stumps behind. He began yelping again. He'd been nervous in here for a reason.

His worst fears had come true.

Finally he was dragged right out of the last vertical vent and back into the basement. He landed on the floor in a heap, burning his forehead on the carpeted surface. Stunned, he rolled over on his back and found a shoe suddenly pressing on his throat.

Skass saw the face, dimly lit by the cellar's ten-watt bulb. It was dirtier than his. The eyes were wilder, more sunken in, madder than even his own. The mouth was stained red—but not from blood. No, Skass could see bits of tomato skins and seeds dried onto the rough, two-week growth.

Tomatoes?

Skass screamed—the face looking back at him was so horrible, it frightened even him. Even worse, he recognized it.

This was no monster from the underworld dragging him home. Nor was it a heat-shaft-sweeping Secret Service man.

It was Joe Copp.

He'd been living in the shafts too.

"You think you're the only one who knows how to shit like a snake?" Copp hissed at him.

Skass began crying—a first since his very early child-hood.

Joe had his pistol pushed right up against Skass's temple. His finger was just a millimeter away from pulling the trigger.

"Why?" he growled at Skass. "What were they going to give you that was so important, you'd go through all this . . ."

"If I tell you," Skass whispered back. "Do you promise not to kill me?"

Joe pushed the gun deeper into his skull. "Sure," he lied.

"They were going to give me a doctor's license," Skass said, his voice jittery. "No matter who won, they said they'd set me up in my own children's hospital."

Joe had to take pause with this; the sickness of the notion ran so deep, it couldn't be absorbed in just an instant.

But that was just the amount of the time Skass needed. . . .

His two carving knives had somehow survived his violent trip down the heating shafts. He quickly retrieved the ten-inch knife now, raised it up and slashed to his left. The blade went right through Copp's left ear, taking part of the lobe with it. Skass swung it again—this time it took the buttons right off Joe's jacket. Joe stumbled back, taking his shoe off Skass's throat, and kicked the knife from his hand.

But this was just what the killer wanted. For no sooner had the first knife flown away than he pulled out the second knife, the one with the eight-inch blade, and slashed mightily at Joe's right hand. But the blade of the knife suddenly snapped away—it had hit the barrel of Joe's pistol. The force of the blow caused the gun to go one way and the broken knife to go the other.

The busted-off blade became lodged in Joe's shoe; it went right through the leather and cut his big toe open. Joe flipped over and lunged for the pistol, leaving a trail of blood in his wake. He retrieved the gun and turned to find Skass crawling on the floor right behind him, licking up his blood.

Joe leveled the gun at him, but Skass was too quick. He threw a punch which caught Joe under his left eye. Joe fell backward, whacking his head against the only exposed wooden beam in the basement. He hit so hard, the crack of his skull echoed around the soundproofed room.

The gun went flying through the air again, hitting the far wall and landing right at Skass's feet. The killer contemplated it for a few frightening moments. Joe tried to shake himself out of his semiconscious state; he was seeing double, and his gimpy leg had gone numb. He tried to get up, but his knee would not support him. He crashed to the floor again.

Skass finally leaned over and calmly picked up the gun. It was the same one Maxie had given him so long ago. He stared at it, studying it all over, no doubt baffled how the pistol had made it all the way down here to Georgia with them.

He clumsily checked the cartridge chamber. Five bullets remained. He looked at Joe, still struggling to get to his feet. The sick smile returned to Skass's dirty face. He pointed the gun at Joe and fired off one shot. The bullet hit Joe right in the chest.

Skass immediately began choking on the smoke from the gun blast. It was the first time he'd ever fired a pistol and never did he think it would be so loud, so violent. The experience was revolting for him. He dropped the weapon to the floor and smelled his hand. It stunk of cordite and burnt gunpowder.

When he looked up, he saw Joe Copp's fist coming right at him.

Joe connected with the bridge of Skass's nose and dropped the killer to the floor. Blood was flowing down Joe's shirt, but he was not hurt. Instead of penetrating his chest, the bullet had hit something instead. He reached inside his coat and retrieved the object.

It was Sammy Silk's deputy badge.

It had saved Joe's life.

Skass took this moment to recover and retrieve the pistol yet again. He didn't hesitate this time. He pointed the barrel at Joe's unprotected stomach not three feet away and pulled the trigger. The gun clicked. He had tried to fire it on an empty chamber. Joe managed to kick the gun from Skass's hand once more, tearing several ligaments in his bad leg in the process. Joe collapsed again. He was within arm's reach of Skass; the murderer's hands were quickly around his throat. This was not good. Joe had fallen awkwardly, his bad leg twisted up underneath him. He had to use what was left of his strength to pull Skass's hands from his throat *and* get his leg out from under him. It seemed like an impossible task. Joe's heart was pounding like a jackhammer. Blood vessels began bursting on the tip of his nose.

With one last painful lunge, Joe's leg came flying out from under him—and hit Skass right in the groin. The killer's hands immediately loosened from his throat. Skass fell backward and involuntarily went in the fetal position. Joe's shoe had scored a direct hit. But just his luck, the killer had landed right next to the discarded gun. He picked it up and fired another blast in Joe's direction. The bullet whizzed by his head and imbedded itself in the foam column behind him. Joe launched himself across the room, diving for the gun and somehow getting his thumb lodged behind the trigger. Skass was trying to squeeze off another shot, and was slowly breaking Joe's thumb in the process. Joe managed to raise his right hand, and gun barrel and all, hit Skass once, twice, three times in the jaw. The killer let go of the gun and it went spiraling across the padded room again.

Skass immediately started crawling toward it; Joe tried to get to his feet but his knee gave out again. In desper-

ation he reached out and grabbed Skass's right foot and
began yanking him away from the gun. Skass's shoe came
off in his hand. Joe hurled it at him, beaning the killer in
the back of his head, opening up a small gash. It stunned
Skass long enough for Joe to grab hold of the killer's belt
and pull him even further away from the gun. Strangely,
Skass gave up his effort to retrieve the pistol and instead
grabbed on to his pants and held them up—as if the worse
thing that could happen at that moment was for him to
lose his trousers. Joe took this opportunity to pull off his
other shoe and begin hammering Skass on his back and
neck with the heavy rubber sole.

But Joe was using his battered left arm to deliver these
blows, and just as quickly, it became drained of all
strength. It suddenly fell limp at his side. He'd caused a
half dozen severe gashes along the base of Skass's skull
though. Blood was beginning to ooze out of them. But
then to Joe's disgust, he saw Skass reach around, take a
sampling of his blood and bring it to his mouth.

Old habits really die hard with this guy, Joe thought.

He was quickly running out of strength to deal with this
monster. He was in a weakened condition as it was. Both
his legs had gone bad, and his left arm was hanging so
loose he thought it was about to fall off. Skass on the other
hand was suffering from the swift kick in the balls and
seven nasty wounds on his head. He still had full use of his
arms and legs though. And he still had his pants on.

Joe's only chance was to get to the gun. He made one
last surge in its direction but did not get half as far as he
needed to. He landed square on Skass's back instead,
where he took a few seconds to beat on the man's half
dozen gashes before being thrown off like a cowboy riding a bronco.

Joe tried to roll with this blow, but his legs and his left
arm had other ideas. He went over on his right shoulder,
colliding hard with the workbench, sending a rain of sharp
tools—files, planing blades, jigsaws—down onto his

head. Next came the nails. Hundreds of them, perforating his skull, face, and neck. The combined weight of all this hard steel was the equivalent of getting an anvil dropped on him. Once again, Joe was slammed to the floor. Blood began flowing into his eyes.

It was strange, but at that moment, when the blood was cutting off his vision just as if he had his eyelids shut tight, he saw himself toddling into his first day of elementary school so long ago. His brother's face, laughing at him on Christmas day. The time he'd fallen through the ice at the skating pond. The first time he'd kissed his neighbor Molly. The first time he'd touched her breasts. The first time he'd . . .

Joe shook his head vigorously. He wanted no part of seeing his life flash before him.

Not yet . . .

He finally was able to wipe away enough blood only to see a very disheartening sight.

Skass was standing over him. He did not have the gun in his hand. Instead he was holding the butcher's knife. Even in the bare light of the cellar, Joe could see the gleam coming off its razor edge. And Skass's eyes—they looked truly maniacal now. His mouth was even watering, like a fat man contemplating his meal before devouring it.

Joe started seeing more life episodes flash before his eyes. His first car. His first drink. His first gun. He shook them away again . . . but then Skass came another step closer.

Joe tried one last time to move his legs, but it was no use. Skass knelt down and brought the knife blade to his throat. It felt both hot and cold at the same time.

Skass lowered his face so it was now not an inch from Joe's. Joe thought he was going to plant a kiss on his lips. Instead Skass whispered to him: "You have really ruined my trip here. You're such a pest! Your persistence has been too much of an interference for me—you and your dull clothes and terrible ice cream . . ."

Skass licked the blade of the knife. "In other words, you should have stayed in Kansas, *Dorothy* . . ."

Then he began to draw the blade across Joe's throat.

That's when the three good fingers remaining on Joe's right hand wrapped themselves around something solid, something that had come down upon him when he hit the tool table. He grabbed it just as the knife began to cut his skin and brought it down onto the back of Skass's head. It cracked the killer's skull as if it were an egg—and kept on going. Blood and brain fluid splattered everywhere.

Skass fell on top of Joe, his knife still digging into his throat. Joe frantically tried to push him off but Skass began laughing and wrestling with him, this even though his head was coming apart in pieces. Joe attempted to dislodge his weapon from Skass's skull but he could not pull it out—it was stuck. He wiggled it from side to side. But this just caused Skass to go into a spasm, pushing his knife even deeper into Joe's gullet. Joe fought back with all his strength, horrified at the thought that he was about to be killed by a man who was practically already dead.

Finally Joe managed to yank his weapon out of Skass's head by moving it sideways; this destroyed the left half of Skass's brain and caused such a violent reaction, he literally hopped off Joe, leaving the knife still imbedded in his neck, not a quarter inch away from his aorta.

Joe was able to shake the knife off him. It fell to the floor, and he collapsed on top of it, so exhausted he could barely breathe. He lay there for what seemed like hours, but in reality was only a few seconds. Finally he pulled his good arm over to him and at last saw what had delivered the crushing blow to the Skass's head. Even in his battered state, Joe had to laugh.

It was a ball-peen hammer.

Same size, same make as the one he'd used to cripple Stringy Hatfield.

* * *

AND HE MIGHT HAVE GONE A BIT MAD, LYING
there, in a pool of his own blood, Skass's body still shaking just a few feet away from him. The craziness of the
situation suddenly came flooding in on him. He too had
chosen to hide in one of the steamer trunks that day back
in Washington. He too had found himself here, in the
basement of the Little White House, after a long suffo-
cating trip to Georgia. And though he'd seen no evidence
at first, he just knew that when he arrived, Skass was in
the house as well. He could smell him. And Joe knew that
here had to be their final battleground—there didn't
seemed to be anyplace left on earth to do it. So Joe had
done what he did best. He had tracked the man through
the labyrinth of heating shafts. Sometimes getting very
close, most times not. His big mistake: Skass had been
sleeping in the steamer trunk all along; Joe had slept in
the tunnels.

But all this was a blur to him now. A crazy fever dream,
without the benefit of being sick. It took him five minutes
to gather enough strength to lift himself up to his savaged
knees. He seemed to be bleeding from more parts of his
body than not, but one thing was for certain: His tie and
thick shirt collar had saved him from a mortal slice of the
neck.

He dragged himself over the pile of scattered tools to
where the gun lay. He picked it up in his right hand, trying
to balance it between the broken and unbroken fingers. A
shovel was lying nearby. Joe believed it had hit him on
the head at some point in the fight. He grabbed it now
and, using it as a crutch, somehow managed to get himself
to his feet. His knees locked into position and he was able
to stand, though unsteadily. He rubbed his left shoulder
with the ball of his right hand and tried to get some blood
flowing through it. He was amazed he could even feel it
at all.

Before him was a mirror that had been cracked during
the fight. It was now still hanging in three jagged pieces,
distorting all that it reflected. Copp looked in it and was

astonished by the face looking back at him. It was covered with caked blood, gashes about its head and neck. Blood was even flowing from the eyes.

He did not recognize this face as his own . . . with good reason.

It wasn't his.

It was Skass's.

He was standing right behind him.

Joe twirled on his bad leg, put the pistol to Skass's forehead and squeezed off one shot. This relieved Skass of much of what remained of his skull. Still he remained frozen in place, looking straight at Copp, that same weird smile on his face. Then his tongue slithered out from between his lips and tasted one of many rivulets of blood running down from his massive head wound.

"Ahhh!" he whispered. "My Annie . . . so sweet!"

Then he fell over for good.

Copp leaned down, took his pulse, and felt nothing. The blood and gore didn't bother him a whit now. To him it was not much worse than looking in a butcher's meat case.

He put the pistol to Skass's heart and pulled the trigger, blowing it away.

Then he slumped back to the floor and watched Skass's body for the next ten minutes. It did not move again.

At last, Joe Copp had got it right.

Or so he thought.

JOE COULDN'T RECALL EXACTLY HOW HE wound up out on the back lawn of the mansion.

He must have crawled through the bulkhead and rolled down the hill at the back of the house, no doubt in an effort to be in a place where people would see him and prevent him from dying from his multitude of wounds. But those few minutes had been dreamlike—as if Joe was watching himself do it, his body no doubt flooding itself with adrenaline. He was still alive, but didn't even have enough strength left in him to celebrate that the monster Skass was at last, truly dead.

Instead, Joe lay facedown on the grass, surprised how wet and dewy it was. With this heat, he would have thought all the moisture had been sucked out of it by this time.

He was badly cut in several dozen places, badly bruised in several dozen more—but that was not why he was lying here like this, doing a great imitation of a corpse. He was just plain tired. Exhausted. Worn out. Maybe even close to dying. Still, in that strange moment, with blades of grass sticking into his bloody nose, it dawned on him that he had not had a good night's sleep since he'd read the Annie Whitemeyer file back in his apartment that night so long ago. Now he just wanted to sleep, right here, on this strangely wet lawn. His wounds might heal with time. Now, he just wanted some peace . . .

But peace was still far off for him.

HE HAD NO IDEA HOW LONG HE LAY THERE. Minutes? Hours? It was hard to tell.

It was the wail of an ambulance that brought him out of his semiconscious state. He was able to open his eyes, though just barely, to see the ambulance speeding up the dirt road to his right. He heard voices fraught with concern. A small dog ran by him, climbed a nearby hill, and started baying at the clouds. Joe's eyes had swelled up horribly, and blood from a cut across his brow was still blurring his sight. Still, he was able to see people running in and out of the house. He could see some of the staff, standing by the back door, weeping. The ambulance finally arrived. Suddenly there seemed to be people everywhere.

Was all this hubbub for him? The concern? The crying? The ambulance? If so, why weren't they looking for him down here? He tried to call out, but nothing would come from his throat. He tried to move, but he felt paralyzed.

Finally he just gave up. All he could do was lie there and watch an entirely different drama unfold just three hundred feet away.

SOME TIME PASSED AND THEN JOE HEARD footsteps.

He could tell somehow that these were dress shoes, not the boots of any policeman, not the white footwear of any ambulance driver. He felt two sets of hands grab him under his armpits and haul him to his feet. Suddenly a face was close to his. He opened his blackened eyes and found himself staring at Big Jim Tolley.

"Sorry, Joe—this has to be done," was all his boss said.

The next thing Joe knew, someone slapped handcuffs on his wrists. Then he was unceremoniously dragged across the lawn, down to the road, and shoved inside a police car. Big Jim had disappeared, but other FBI types were around him—Joe could smell them.

"What . . . what are you doing?" he bellowed through cracked and broken teeth. "I'm not the criminal here! I just saved the President's life!"

"You'd best shut up boy," he heard a crackling Southern voice tell him. "You was caught red-handed."

Then someone hit him so hard in the jaw, one of his back teeth popped out. He hit the back of the police car seat hard. When he tried to get up, someone hit him again. And again.

And again.

Finally he just lay there, confused, almost unconscious. He was able to sputter out just a handful of words.

"Why . . . why are you doing this to me?"

"You're under arrest, wise guy," the voice with the distinctly mean Southern accent told him. "You're going to jail—for a long time I'd say."

"Jail?" Joe managed to blubber, his mouth full of blood and pieces of tooth. "For what?"

The Southern voice laughed cruelly. "For trespassing on federal property," it said. "Last man who did that got seventeen years, right in our little old county jail-house ..."

27

TWO YEARS LATER

THERE WAS NO WAY JOE COULD HAVE KNOWN that it was exactly two years to the day he entered the La Grange county jail that he would have his first visitor.

In those twenty-four months, most of his hair had fallen out, some of his teeth as well. His bad leg had grown worse, and he had twenty-three scars measuring more than two inches each on various parts of his body.

In those two years he had not conversed with anyone but the same old guard, and even then Joe had spoken only when spoken to. Usually that was in reply to the guard's weekly question of how dirty his bedding had become. It could only be washed twice a month—it was up to Joe to decide when.

In those two years he had lost track of time, dates, faces, names. He'd lost track of Christmas, Easter. The Fourth of July. He'd not been permitted to write letters or make any phone calls—he'd lost track of his parents. He had no way of telling them what happened to him— and he had no idea if anyone else had. He barely remembered his trial. He suspected that someone had injected him with something while he was lying in the backseat of the police car that dark day in Warm Springs. In any case, it had all been a blur, except the strange smile on the judge's face as he pronounced his sentence: "Seventeen years . . . no chance of parole."

After all this time, the sound of his gavel coming down still echoed in Joe's ears.

*   *   *

BUT THIS DAY, WHEN THE GUARD WORDLESSLY brought his breakfast of toast and evaporated milk, he found a note on his tray.

Joe had a visitor waiting for him. He would be fetched at nine, given a shower—his first—and then be presented in the visitor's room.

It was odd how little this news affected Joe's breakfast. This was not his parents coming to visit him—the note indicated a singular visitor, and he couldn't imagine his father coming all the way down here alone. And there was no one else he really wanted to see. So he ate his breakfast, dunking the toast in the sour tasting milk so he wouldn't have to chew it, and then stretched back out on his bunk until the knock came on the cell door at 8:45.

He was brought to a very grungy lavatory that featured an open water faucet hanging in one corner. Joe was handed a towel and a foul-smelling piece of soap. The water was ice-cold; Joe stayed under it for ten long minutes anyway, allowing it to wash away two years of Georgia grime.

A new jail uniform was waiting for him when he emerged, shivering and blue, from the ice-cold cascade. He pulled the white and black striped clothes on and was led up to the first floor of the courthouse.

FOR ALL THE WORLD HE EXPECTED HIS VISITOR to be Big Jim Tolley; his voice still echoed in Joe's ears as well.

But when he was ushered into the room he saw a man sitting with his back to him that was barely one third Big Jim's size.

The man slowly turned and looked at him. It was Leo Spank, the number-two guy at the SWS office.

Joe was instantly furious. His worst fear had turned out

to be true. Spank's presence here told him that others within the Bureau *had* known he'd been here all along— and hadn't done anything about it.

Joe started to walk out of the room, but Spank caught him by the sleeve and pulled him into the chair across from him.

"Cool it, Joe," Spank ordered him, though his voice was not without some nervousness, "I'm just here to talk."

"Talk?" Joe spit back at him. "Talk about what? How you guys left me here to rot for two years?"

"We did it for your own good Joe!" Spank yelled back at him. "Big Jim was protecting you."

"By putting me in jail?" Joe roared back.

Spank looked like he wanted to pull his hair out.

"Look, Joe," he began again, trying to control his emotions. "Once you greased that guy Skass, there was a bunch of people roaming around who wanted to grease *you*. People even we could not control."

Joe didn't believe him.

"But why would anyone want to kill me?" Joe asked. "I should be a hero for God's sake. Or at least not treated like some kind of criminal . . ."

Spank just frowned. He was clearly not enjoying this.

"Let's just say there were certain elements inside the government that didn't like what you'd done," he said. "They thought this guy Skass was, well, *valuable*—and when you put the *kibosh* on him, you made yourself some enemies."

Joe laughed. It made his remaining teeth hurt.

"Didn't like what I was doing?" he scoffed. "I was trying to stop someone from killing the President for God's sake."

Spank lit a cigarette.

"Yeah, well God beat you to that one, didn't he?" he said.

Joe looked at him queerly. "What do you mean by that?"

"I mean we were able to hush up everything that happened that day," Spank said with some annoyance. "But only because, by some divine mistake, you chose to ice Skass at just about the same time that FDR was drawing his last breath."

Joe just looked back at Spank, stunned.

"What are you talking about?"

Spank just shook his head. "Joe, you must've known that. Someone must have told you. You didn't save the President's life that day—because the President was already dead. He collapsed from a cerebral hemorrhage and died a short time later. You must have heard the ambulance, seen the chaos. That was all for him."

Joe was frozen to his chair. Could this be true? As he was fighting for his life, trying to protect Roosevelt, Roosevelt was dying all on his own? The only reason Joe didn't laugh was because he knew it would hurt too much.

He didn't speak for five long minutes. He just stared out the barred window, appropriately enough at a small junkyard beyond, and ran the events of two years ago through his mind like a movie newsreel.

Finally he spoke again.

"Whether that happened or not," he told Spank slowly. "I was doing what I took an oath to do. I was protecting this country. I was protecting the President."

Spank just shook his head. "Joe . . . you really are a dodo bird. Things changed a while back, and I think you missed the boat."

He drew heavily on his cigarette; the smoke was driving Joe nuts, but he refused to beg one off of Spank.

Spank spoke again: "All I can say is, things like that don't have the high priority that they used to."

Joe just stared back at him in disbelief. "What could be more important for me—or for any citizen—than protecting the President?"

Spank stopped in middrag. He began to say something, but stopped himself, angrily crushed out his cigarette, and lit another.

"Some things you are much better off not knowing,"

he finally said, though he was speaking as much to himself as he was to Joe.

Joe got up to leave again. Spank reached over and pushed him back into the chair.

"Look, Joe," Spank hissed at him. "Will you just shut up a minute and let me give you the good news?"

Joe began to argue even this, but then bit his lip. "OK, lay it on me."

"You're getting out . . . today," Spank said. "You're being released at noon."

Joe's eyes must have went wider than half-dollars. A wave of disbelief went through him, but it lasted for only a few seconds.

"What happened to seventeen years in solitary confinement?" he asked Spank.

"Let's just say it's being commuted" was the FBI man's reply.

"Do I still have my job?" Joe asked.

Spank just shook his head. "No," he replied. "That would have been impossible."

Joe just leaned back in his chair. "Then what the hell good is it for me to get out?"

Spank's face turned red. He stood up, exasperated almost beyond words.

"You know, that's always been your problem, Joe," he said angrily. "You ask too many damn questions . . ."

Joe just shook his head again.

"I thought that was my job . . ." he said.

NOON CAME AND JOE WAS BROUGHT UP again.

This time he was wearing the same clothes he'd been arrested in. They'd been cleaned, but not pressed or mended. The suit had become frayed and sampled by moths over the two years. His shoes were scuffed and badly in need of a shine.

The guard opened the back door and without so much

as a grunt, allowed Joe to walk out. The sun hit him on the face like a pan of hot grease. He didn't mind it a bit.

He had no bag, no possessions. No money. He was standing in the back lot behind the jail, a place that doubled as the town's dumping ground. It was filled with junk, mostly rotting, rusting cars—once proud Pontiacs, Fords, and Chevys. Cars Joe had driven during his heyday as a G-man. Now, they too had lost their hair and their teeth. They too had lost track of the time.

This should be interesting, he thought.

He walked around the front of the jailhouse and was surprised to see a car waiting by the dirt curb. A man was sitting behind the steering wheel, watching Joe's every move. He was dressed in a black suit coat and tie, and was wearing a gray fedora—clothes more appropriate for up north, or maybe Dallas on a chilly November day, but not the middle of Georgia, not this time of year. He also had a huge red mustache and was chomping on a massive unlit cigar. Joe recognized him—but just barely.

He walked up to the car and peered in the passenger side window.

"Any chance you're a taxi?" Joe asked the man.

"Just get in," the man replied.

Joe did so, without hesitation. What else was there for him to do?

The man pulled out a pack of cigarettes and offered him one. It was a Raleigh but Joe took it anyway. The man lit him up and Joe dragged greedily, coughed hard, then dragged heavy again. He felt his rear end rise a few inches off the car seat. His first smoke in two years. It wasn't a Pall Mall—but it tasted as good as one.

"Heard you've had a rough time of it since we first met," the man with the mustache said to him.

"Who told you that?" Joe asked, letting out another long stream of beautiful blue smoke. He knew that he'd seen this guy before—in the morgue, that day in Washington. But at the moment, he wanted to concentrate all of his faculties on his cigarette.

"I have my sources," the man said. "I probably know more about you than you know about yourself."

"Educate me then . . ." Joe exhaled.

The man spent the next few minutes doing just that. Indeed he knew a lot about Joe and what he'd done—and not done—as a G-man, especially in the past three years. He ran down just about everything in Joe's performance file. His time as an upstart hot G-man; his troubles with Stringy Hatfield, his long pursuit and eventual killing of Skass, thus depriving the Germans of getting to Stalin before Stalin got to them.

It was true, the guy knew it all. Joe recalled Spank telling him that there were some people out there who didn't like what he had done. Was this guy one of them? He decided to be direct.

"So? What are you here to do? Kill me?" he asked the guy.

The man laughed, an odd cackle.

"Hardly, pal," he said. "In fact, I'm here because you've managed to impress a few people."

Now it was Joe's turn to laugh. "Really? And who would that be?"

The man reached inside his coat pocket and came out with an identification card. It was coated in plastic and had no picture, but it did have the man's name: It was Charles Fox.

And above it was the name of a government outfit Joe had never heard of before: CENTRAL INTELLIGENCE AGENCY.

Joe stared at the ID for a few moments, then looked up at the guy. He was smiling back at Joe, in a crooked sort of way.

"Want a job?" he asked.

C. A. MOBLEY

RITES OF WAR

The Yellow Sea. A German U-boat destroys a North Korean subma-
rine, then attacks a U.S. command ship. The plan works: America
and North Korea hold each other accountable. As warships con-
verge across the globe the command of the USS *Ramage* falls into
the hands of Jerusha Bailey, who senses a hidden strategy
behind the attacks.
__0-515-12225-4/$6.99

RULES OF COMMAND

Bailey is dispatched on a peacemaking mission that could either defuse
an international crisis...or add fuel to the fires of an all-out war.
__0-425-16746-1/$6.99

CODE OF CONFLICT

While patrolling off the coast of Bangladesh on a routine peace-keep-
ing mission, a U.S. Navy ship is hit by a barrage of missiles. No one
knows who instigated the attack. The world stands on the brink of war.
__0-425-17108-6/$6.99